HOW THEY WERE TAKEN

CAROLYN RIDDER ASPENSON

Copyright © 2025 Carolyn Ridder Aspenson.

All rights reserved.

No part of this book may be reproduced in any form or by any electronic or mechanical means, including information storage and retrieval systems, without written permission from the author, except for the use of brief quotations in a book review.

Severn River Publishing
www.SevernRiverBooks.com

This is a work of fiction. Names, characters, businesses, places, events and incidents are either the products of the author's imagination or used in a fictitious manner. Any resemblance to actual persons, living or dead, or actual events is purely coincidental.

ISBN: 978-1-64875-632-0 (Paperback)

ALSO BY CAROLYN RIDDER ASPENSON

Jenna Wyatt Series

How They Were Taken

Never Speak of It

Before the Next One Falls

The Rachel Ryder Thriller Series

Damaging Secrets

Hunted Girl

Overkill

Countdown

Body Count

Fatal Silence

Deadly Means

Final Fix

Dark Intent

Foul Play

Trusted Lies

To find out more about Carolyn Ridder Aspenson and her books, visit
severnriverbooks.com

To my brothers
I didn't kill you off in this one either.

PROLOGUE

"Sissy!" Her cries reverberated down the hallway, each plea striking Jenna's heart like a relentless drumbeat. Fear tightened its grip around her, but she fought to block out the haunting sounds, to silence the anguished echoes that threatened to engulf her.

A sudden, thunderous crash pierced Jenna's senses, and she instinctively squeezed her eyes shut under the blindfold, hoping to shield herself from the horrors she could only hear, not see.

"Molly," she whispered. She willed herself not to listen, desperate to shut out the reality of the nightmare paralyzing her.

"Sissy!" Molly's cries echoed through their small home.

The chilling sound of breaking glass shattered the air, sending a shiver down Jenna's spine. Was it a window? Her mother's precious china cabinet? Disoriented, Jenna couldn't tell where she was. She saw the floor through a small slit of the blindfold, breathed in the cold air and shivered, and pressed her body into the hard, unyielding floor beneath her, but beyond that, her night had become a nightmarish blur of darkness.

Someone dressed in black had kicked through their front door and snatched her off the floor, using her helplessness as a weapon to draw out her deepest fears. His strength had overwhelmed her, his force bordering on painful. She was only thirteen, nothing against the man.

"Please," she'd begged. "Don't hurt us."

He slapped her.

She swallowed the scream threatening to escape her mouth. Jenna's helplessness from the restraints infuriated her as the pain worsened from fighting them. The zip ties digging into her wrists and the rope constricting her ankles made it impossible to escape. The darkness engulfed her, leaving her with nothing but the haunting cries of her baby sister.

"Sissy!"

Jenna's heart ached. She couldn't bear to listen to her sister's cries, but they persisted, seeping into her very soul. Her captor's voice intermingled with Molly's desperate wails, a horrific choir of terror that imprisoned Jenna's senses.

Another loud, jarring bang pierced her ears, followed by Molly's high-pitched, heart-wrenching pleas. "Sissy! Please! He's hurting me!"

The man's voice grumbled, his words inaudible, but the menace they carried sent chills down Jenna's spine. She knew she had to be strong, to resist the fear gnawing at her insides. But Molly's softening cries and the sound of the creaking door, so familiar yet suddenly ominous, broke the fragile dam holding back her tears. The same door her father had attempted to fix after he had kicked it down, but it was beyond repair, and the next day he had left, leaving them as shattered and abandoned as the door.

The door slammed shut, sealing their fates, as an eerie silence descended upon the small home. Tears streamed down her cheeks, her heart aching for her helpless sister. "Molly," Jenna whispered, her voice choked with sorrow and regret. "I'm sorry. I'm so sorry."

1

The man pulled the woman into a passionate kiss, making the bagel I had eaten for breakfast threaten a return. I snapped several photos, making sure to keep the hotel entrance in the shot. They always wanted the hotel entrance.

It was the same with every affair. Older man tells younger woman his wife doesn't understand him. Woman sees her future in his eyes in the first hookup. Man works late more often. Wife finds a receipt in a shirt pocket or a hotel fee on their bank statement. Wife hires someone like me to catch them in the act, then bawls her eyes out when she sees the pictures.

The man pivoted to face me with his arm wrapped around the woman. "Bingo," I said, then snapped more photos. "The icing on the cake." I watched him walk her to a black Mercedes, push her inside, and then head back into the hotel.

I stuffed the camera in my bag, then headed to the coffee shop to send the photos to my client and meet the next one.

My hand shook as I clung to that old photo, its edges digging into my skin like it tried to make a break for it. I swiped my eyes with my other hand, betraying the no-tear promise I'd made to myself. "Get it together, Jenna," I scolded under my breath. The photo took a nose dive from my fingers and fluttered down to my lap like a leaf in fall. Squinting at it brought my blurry past into HD focus. As if I could have ever forgotten it.

That day my emotions hit harder, the memories playing tricks on my sanity—laughs and sobs all tangled together balled my breath into a lump in my throat, making it almost impossible to breathe. There was my five-year-old sister, Molly, a dynamo of energy packed into a three-foot frame, hugging me like she had hugged her new Barbie, the one my mother bought at a garage sale the weekend before. Her grin so wide, those missing teeth turning her smile into a map of uncharted territories. Her red locks defied gravity, caught in the act by our mom's old camera. And then there was me, little Miss Attitude, inconvenienced by the horror of a stupid photograph. For a teenager, smiling for a family pic was painful and never-ending.

My mouth twitched, a reminder of the few good times that had checked out years ago. If I had known the future, maybe I would have slapped on a happy face. But nope, at thirteen, I was too busy hearing the mall's call, luring me away with promises of fun and wonder, not the depressing, dark life I had at home. Yes, at thirteen, a quick pic with Molly was a jail sentence. I survived the ordeal, and once our mother had cut me loose, I tossed a "Later, Mol," over my shoulder and made a beeline for sweet freedom and Claire's.

Sweat broke out at my temples, taking me back in time, not only emotionally but visually as well. As the memories flooded in, I coached myself like the therapist the school had made me see after Molly's abduction. "Just breathe, Jenna." Three times in, three times out, trying to dodge the memory avalanche that picture triggered. It was just a simple photo, yet it carried the weight of a lead brick, which was why I kept it in my wallet. As if I needed that constant reminder that Molly had disappeared without a trace.

I should have given her a hug. Those girls I was so desperate to meet? I couldn't even remember their names. Talk about a waste. If only I had had a clue. If only I had fought harder. If only I had forced him to take me instead of her. If only my father hadn't walked out on us.

How They Were Taken

My sweat morphed into a full-on glisten. I flopped back in my chair, riding another wave of breaths to ground myself. I hesitated as my hand hovered over the whiskey on the coffee table. No. Then, yes. No.

Next thing I knew, I had clutched the bottle for dear life, letting a shot of liquid courage scorch its way down my throat, offering a brief hiatus from the guilt trip.

But that photo carried a fading window to what might have been, to the hope shining in Molly's eyes, and the storm clouds in mine knowing her tomorrows would become broken promises. Because Molly was gone. And a piece of me had vanished with her.

People-watching could have been my Olympic sport while sitting in a local coffee shop waiting for my potential client. I had sent my other client her photos with a brief note and my final invoice and then sipped my coffee and stared out the window. I glimpsed cars zoom by and flinched from the surprise of a pair of skateboarding teens making a break for it past the window. A woman dressed in a mink coat and yoga pants. A man adjusting his package as if he were the only one on the sidewalk. I would take people-watching over TV any day.

My days at the Georgia Bureau of Investigation had whipped me into a pro at reading a crowd, a skill I polished to a high shine in my new gig. A woman had a meltdown on her phone, a guy dug for buried treasure in his nose, thinking he was invisible, and the classic—two smartphone zombies headed for a collision. Boom!

Wham, bam, thank you, ma'am, for playing spot the wreck.

I could have penned a dissertation on people just by watching. How they moved through a crowd, their little quirks, the stress written all over their faces. I owned front-row VIP tickets to the human parade. I studied them, understanding if I observed long enough, watching told me their secrets because actions always spoke louder than words.

It amazed me how some folks wore their lives like an open book. Me? I kept my feelings locked up tighter than a pair of skinny jeans. Nick, my soon-to-be ex-husband, hated my inability to share my feelings and had finally thrown in the towel on our marriage. That, and what he dubbed my enthusiasm for cocktails, killed our future, he had said.

I drank to relax, and I could admit, sometimes more than I should. He ran a software company. I hunted down the scum of the earth and fought for justice for their victims on the daily. His software glitches didn't compare to telling a woman someone had murdered her husband. After my days, I deserved a drink or two to calm my nerves.

I caught a guy sitting in the opposite corner watching me. Long legs, dark hair poking out from his Atlanta Braves baseball hat, a scruffy beard in need of a trim. We stared at each other for a good thirty seconds before he got up, tossed what appeared to be a full cup of coffee into the garbage, and walked out. My eyes followed as he strolled down the street, his hands in his jean pockets, with a gait that leaned to the left. Was he someone I had arrested? That would explain the uneasy feeling creeping up my spine. I scanned my photographic memory for recognition but didn't find a match.

"Well, look at you, sitting here like the queen of lost causes."

I turned from the window and straight into a belly so expansive, Santa would look skinny. "Bobby Hanford. What bridge did you find change under to afford a cup of coffee in this palace? Oh, wait. You stole it from a homeless person, didn't you?"

I had nabbed Hanford more times than I cared to count, for everything from petty theft to possession—a regular in the revolving door of my once daily grind. None of it was enough to scare him straight, or even sideways, but he wasn't my problem anymore.

There was relief in that.

He lobbed a wad of chew into a paper cup through the makeshift goal-post where a tooth should have been. "Heard they kicked you off the force for playing dirty. Tsk, tsk, Agent—or is it Miss Wyatt? Naughty girls need to be punished, huh?"

The way he said *Miss* made my skin crawl. I sipped my coffee as if I didn't have a care in the world. "The kind of punishment you deserve wouldn't give you a hard-on even with the little blue pill."

He slid, uninvited, into the chair across from me.

"Scram, Hanford."

How They Were Taken 7

"Oh, come on, Miss Wyatt. Can't we just catch up a bit? For old times' sake?"

"It's Ms. Wyatt, and no."

Bobby Hanford was a stubby man, about as tall as he was round, and wasn't worth the trouble of a takedown. With a client due any minute, the last thing I needed was a scene. I grabbed my phone, and just for show, said, "Siri, dial Leland Seymour," but ended the call before it started.

He flapped his hands, panic fluttering in his pigeon eyes. "Easy, easy. Just wanted to say hi to an old buddy, that's all. I'll get out of your hair." He pointed from his eyes to mine. "I'll be seein' ya, Ms. Wyatt."

I raised an eyebrow. "That supposed to be a threat?"

"No, ma'am," he said, and then beat a hasty retreat.

I sighed. Hanford always left me feeling slimy. Even the air needed a shower after he left.

A voice interrupted my thoughts. I glanced up at the woman.

"Are you Jenna Wyatt?"

"Mrs. Henry?" I stood.

She nodded and sucked in a breath.

Dear God, don't lose it here, lady, or at least get the words out first. I managed a smile. "Yes, I'm Jenna Wyatt. Please, have a seat."

I had snagged the corner table for its primo view—straight shot to the door and the counter, but with enough space from the window to make a quick getaway if need be. I had been there enough times to know the community bulletin board was about as popular as a diet menu at a barbecue joint, so we had some privacy.

"Thanks for meeting me on such late notice," Mrs. Henry said. "But please, call me Toni."

"Okay, Toni. What can I do for you?"

Her chin trembled. I counted down to the waterworks in my mind. Three, two, one... Bingo.

"My husband is cheating on me." She dabbed the corners of her eyes with a tissue, then dug into her designer tote bag and pulled out a file. "Here. This is everything I've got."

I knew the drill, what I would see and what I would say, but I played along, flipping through screenshots of texts, photos of Mr. Henry doing the walk of shame, and photos of cozy dinners with a blond, much younger woman, and then leaving ahead of her, as well as more photos of them at a hotel I didn't recognize. "Have you met with an attorney?"

"Not yet. I want proof first."

She'd just handed me a file full of proof. "How long have you been married?"

A single tear did the solo slide. "Twenty-five years. We have a son who just finished getting his master's." She patted her eye with a tissue. "He's going to be a college professor. History. I'm so proud of him."

"Congratulations," I said. "How much does he make?"

She grimaced. "My son? He's not working just yet."

"No," I said. "I meant your husband."

"Oh, about half-a-million-a-year salary, but he gets bonuses, so it is somewhere around one-point-two million."

"Do you work?"

"Not since Reggie was born. I've focused on raising our son instead."

With Reggie old enough to run for office, the woman needed a hobby. "Mrs. Henry, it looks like you've already had a PI on this, and from what I can tell, what you've got is enough to make a case. Georgia splits property down the middle. It's a no-fault state, and the court doesn't always care about extracurricular activities. Most of the time, at least. My advice? Get a lawyer before you drop more cash on another gumshoe like me. If your lawyer thinks you need a PI, they'll make the call."

Most of my bread and butter came from attorney gigs, especially the ones representing the well-heeled, and thanks to my success with the GBI, I was tops on the list of every major law firm in the Atlanta area.

"But I want this done as soon as possible. Can't you move it along for me?"

"Maybe, but my rates are up there, and you're already looking at a hefty bill from a lawyer, which will include PI expenses." I fished out a list of attorneys from my bag, something I carried several copies of for women like her. "These are the good ones I've worked with, but do your homework. If you end up hiring one, they can bring me on board if necessary."

My cell blared my husband Nick's unique ring, a digital siren, which meant one of two things: the divorce or our daughter. My eyes flickered down to the glowing screen.

She's asking for you. I'll let you come by, but don't screw it up.

I texted I would be there in an hour. "Mrs. Henry, I'm sorry I can't help you further, but contact these lawyers. They'll help you."

"Are you sure? I can pay your fees."

"Listen," I said with as much empathy as I could muster. Given how my marriage ended, I wasn't a fan of cheating by any means, but I saw things far worse than it in my line of work. I wanted to tell her to suck it up and put it in perspective, but she might want me for another case someday. "You have everything you need except an attorney. The sooner you get one, the sooner your nightmare will be over." I offered her a semi-smile. "Unless, of course, you don't want a divorce?"

"Oh, I want a divorce, and I want the bastard to pay for what he's done," she said.

"You might want to not say that to anyone else, just in case."

"Oh, I mean pay with money. Not something else." She stood, and her perfectly painted-on eyebrows furrowed. "I just want what I deserve." She pivoted on her expensive heels and sashayed away.

"Don't they all," I mumbled, but I understood why she'd think so. I had spent ten years in law enforcement, and when I got canned after Nick filed for divorce, I opened my own PI business. The next day, twelve women just like her requested my services, all thinking I could bring down their husbands, some financially, some physically. To the Mrs. Henrys of the world, a woman doing what I did, packing heat and chasing shadows, wasn't in their skill set.

Me? I thrived on it. The thrill, the chase—it replaced the oxygen in my blood. According to Nick, I had chosen it over family, over everything else. He had said I would end up an old woman toasting to my glory days alone. Sometimes, in the darker corners of my mind, that sounded like the way to go. Especially when during those glory days I had nailed the kind of lowlifes who had taken my sister.

There was nothing quite like the hunt, the game of cat and mouse with the worst of humanity. Molly. Her abduction had shaped my life in ways I had never expected. After her abduction, I buried my head into my schoolbooks as my mother's mental health dwindled away. Then a full-ride scholarship to college and Harvard Law after that. I had done everything in my power to prepare for the day I would find Molly's abductor.

Then I realized I needed to be the one to find him, and I joined the Georgia Bureau of Investigation to make it happen.

My cell phone rang as I packed up to leave. "Jenna Wyatt."

"Ms. Wyatt, my name is Jessica Steadman."

I froze. "*Steadman*?" Everyone in Georgia knew that name. "Jessica Steadman?" I hadn't realized I had said her name out loud with the big question mark, anchoring it to my big mouth. "Yes, ma'am. What can I do for you?"

"I think it's obvious. I want you to find my daughter."

2

The name Jessica Steadman floated through the air like an annoying Georgia no-see-um bug. A year before, she had become the main character in a Lifetime movie, one about the tragic widow left behind with her billionaire husband's empire because of his untimely demise.

Her big-shot hubby Richard Steadman's power and influence had stretched across Atlanta well into the suburbs and made him a billionaire. Murdered in his home while with his daughter, Emma, who had been abducted and disappeared without a trace. All the money in the world couldn't bring them back. The interesting detail of Steadman's murder was that the killer used a silencer, suggesting he knew others were home and had planned his actions.

The abduction stuck in my head, the date a cruel reminder of the day the man kidnapped Molly, like fate played a sick joke. The cases turned cold, the cops clueless about Steadman's murder and Emma's disappearance, leaving the whole mess to gather dust regardless of the victim's wealth and power.

And the kicker—Emma and Molly were both five, the same age when their worlds turned upside down.

Clenching the phone turned my knuckles ghost white as Jessica Steadman's demand echoed in my skull. "I want you to find my daughter," she said, desperation laced with iron will in her voice.

The request sent a shiver down my spine, reviving memories I had just locked up for the day only a few hours before. "Uh, I—okay. I can come by first thing tomorrow morning."

"No, I need you to start now. Come to my house. Are you familiar with it?"

Everyone was familiar with the Steadman home and considered it prime real estate. The house sprawled like a cruise ship, dominating the landscape and dwarfing the ten-thousand-square-foot homes dotting the same road. It was so opulent even the King of Pop would have been envious.

"I can be there in three hours," I said.

"Ms. Wyatt, please understand that you come highly recommended. I will pay you well over your current rate, but I expect to be your only client. I will give you one hour to notify your other clients and arrive at my home. If you can't accommodate, I have a second choice."

My client roster wasn't bursting at the seams at that moment, but you wouldn't catch me spilling those beans over the phone to Jessica Steadman. No, sir. That kind of news deserved the personal touch over a cup of coffee or, in Steadman's case, something more upscale, like a bottle of wine created from water by Jesus himself. "I'll do my best," I assured her, trying to sound like I had a lineup of clients waiting.

Jessica Steadman, who commanded rooms and bent wills, just replied, "Be here in one hour, not three," and killed the call. Not even a goodbye.

Guess pleasantries were optional when you swam in dough.

I had half a mind to ring up Nick, tell him I would be running late because I had a life-changing client on the line. But I could already hear that conversation going south, Nick accusing me of being a worthless parent, me cussing him out for breaking up our family, and ending with me all wound up before meeting Atlanta's most enigmatic widow. So, I opted for a text. Quick, clean, and hopefully with no room for back-and-forth bickering. Just a simple update, praying it wouldn't spiral into a text war.

I can be there at seven.

Nick responded. *Don't bother. She's got ballet at six.*

I'll come to ballet. Is she still at Stella-Bella School?
No.
Where is she?
I waited for a reply, but it never came.

Tucked away in the lush green embrace of Milton, Georgia, the Steadman mansion loomed as if it were the queen of the prom and the rest of us were just hoping for a dance. The place defied the usual rich folks' pads, radiating an elegance that left one feeling slightly underdressed at a mere glance.

Its columns stretched toward the sky from verandas sprawled out as lazily as a Southern belle after one too many mint juleps. The *Milton Herald* nailed it when they had said it lived in the clouds.

Sure, I had seen the photos that made it look like something off a Hollywood set, but catching an actual glimpse of the place was another story. It played hard to get, tucked away nearly a mile off the main drag. I whistled as I rolled up to the wrought iron gates, then tossed my name to the beefy security guy. While he gave me the once-over, I admired the craftsmanship of the iron security gates.

"Park on the right side near the six garages, ma'am," the security guard said. He handed me a blue sheet of paper with the date, my name, and tag number on it. "Have a nice day."

"Thank you," I murmured as the gates parted like the Red Sea and revealed the grandeur of the Steadman estate in its full glory.

The driveway stretched out before me, paved in blacktop and marked with speed limit signs dictating a snail's pace of ten miles per hour. I couldn't remember the last time I drove that slowly on purpose, but there I was, toeing the line, keen on making a good first impression.

The driveway wound toward the front with magnolia trees lining the path like silent sentinels guarding the mansion's hidden past as the monstrosity towered before me. The gardens exploded with colors. Driving up, everything appeared so perfectly arranged, I half expected a tour guide to emerge and spill the secrets.

"I can't believe people actually live like this." My gaze landed on a sign that said *Vendor Entrance*. Was that supposed to be for me? I brushed off the thought. It didn't matter how I got in, as long as I did.

Standing there, gaping at the mansion, I felt like I was being smothered by a big fat pile of money. Depending on one's mood, the place either celebrated all things rich and powerful or thumbed its nose at us regular folk. I walked up, mixing a healthy dose of admiration with a bigger scoop of what-the-heck-was-I-doing-there, and fearing I was about to step into a life-sized dollhouse where I was the doll and Jessica Steadman controlled my every move.

Instead of a fancy doorbell serenade, a woman dressed for winter in Vermont, not spring in Georgia, greeted me at the door. "Mrs. Wyatt," she announced.

It's *Ms.*, but whatever. "Thanks," I managed to say as I slipped into a version of myself that felt about as comfortable as a pair of high heels on a marathon run.

Despite my efforts—decking out in pro private investigator digs and a pair of heels I hated, flashing a fancy Harvard degree—I couldn't shake the feeling that I was a fish out of water. Deep down, I was just a country girl, more at home in boots than in stilettos, in a house the size of half her garages. My mom did her best, God love her, but after my dad took off and Molly vanished, things went from bad to worse. Mom's struggle with her demons left me to fend for myself. She died right as I trekked to Harvard to blaze my own trail.

The mansion's interior struck me just as forcefully as the exterior. Gorgeous, yes, but as alien to me as a foreign language. Crystal chandeliers, pricier than my car, glittered above marble floors cold enough to store meat. I stood miles and worlds away from anything I had ever known.

"Mrs. Steadman will see you shortly," the woman informed me, leading me down a corridor to what was unmistakably Richard Steadman's office. The scent of polished wood and a hint of old money nearly knocked me over the moment I walked in. And the deer heads mounted on the walls? Yeah, they screamed a guy had hung his hat there.

"Please, take a seat," she directed, pointing to a table set for what I imagined were high-stakes discussions or stories about shooting deer, neither anything important to me.

Then she entered. Jessica Steadman, every bit the figure the media portrayed her to be.

Tall enough to stand out in a crowd and moving with a grace as natural to her as breathing. Her intense presence lit up the room. She clearly lived a life of discipline, probably hitting the gym daily and leaving me feeling guilty about my last donut, even though I hit the gym almost as often.

Sure, her figure might have been the envy of anyone who appreciated aesthetics, but what grabbed me was her vibe. It said total package, what many women hoped to be.

"Ms. Wyatt, thank you for coming," she began, her voice carrying the same confidence as her stride. She moved with purpose, picking up a legal pad before settling across from me, ready to dive into the heart of the matter. "I'm sure you are aware of my situation."

How could I not be? The saga of her family's heartbreak trumped the latest binge-worthy series because it was impossible to ignore. The murder of her husband and the abduction of her daughter blared from every news channel for almost a year. Things that hadn't happened in the days after Molly disappeared.

"Yes, ma'am, and I'm so sorry for the loss of your husband and the disappearance of your daughter."

Her swift reminder said she didn't want pity. "Thank you, but I didn't request your presence for your sympathy." She slid the pad of paper across the table toward me. "I won't sugarcoat this. The details are long, and I'll provide you with everything, but as of tomorrow, my daughter will have been missing for a year. The police have no leads, and their efforts, while genuine and appreciated, have been ineffective."

Was she suggesting she wanted me to find the killer? I found myself momentarily lost. "I'm sorry about that, but I don't understand why you think I can help you."

"Of course, you understand," she countered, a knowing smile touching her lips.

Jessica Steadman was the apple to my orange, the oil to my water. We shared nothing to understand.

"Someone murdered my husband and abducted my daughter while I was here. The same thing happened to your sister. We share a very similar story. You will have a vested interest in finding the person who murdered my husband and took my daughter."

I bristled at the comparison. Our circumstances were worlds apart in more ways than one. Yet, there she was, insisting on a connection, a shared thread of tragedy and loss. One I didn't see.

"Possibly similar, but very different. I'm not sure—"

She cut me off. "A mutual friend recommended you. Given that recommendation, I had my people vet you thoroughly before contacting you. Your reputation as a relentless investigator with ties to similar cases made you the clear choice. I'd like you to start today. Now."

The mention of a mutual friend caught me off guard because the circles we ran in couldn't have been more different. "Mrs. Steadman, I appreciate you contacting me, but I'm not sure I'm the right fit for this." It wasn't that it was an impossible ask, though it likely was. My qualifications and unique skills topped those of all agents with the GBI. I had proven that multiple times with my high closing rates. The problem seemed obvious to me. It struck too close to home, and I doubted my emotional stamina could handle it.

But she was undeterred, her faith in me seemingly bolstered by the very doubts I harbored. "Our friend said you'd feel that way, but he's assured me you're the best person for this assignment. Your knowledge of the law, and most importantly, how to get around it if need be, is exactly what is necessary to find my child."

"May I ask what the mutual friend's name is?"

"Your former Georgia Bureau of Investigation boss, Leland Seymour."

Damn, she had just dropped Leland's name between us like a bombshell, tying us together in a way I hadn't anticipated. My history with Leland was the very reason she had sought me out.

"But there are others," she said. "The chief of Hamby police. The Fulton County Assistant District Attorney Zach Christopher, a member of the DEA, and you come with commendations from your coworkers with the GBI. I believe you are more than qualified to find the person who destroyed my family."

How They Were Taken   17

I knew those names, had worked with many of them. It shouldn't have surprised me, yet it did. Her insistence didn't waver, the firmness in her voice compelling me to stay seated, to listen, to consider the impossible task she set before me. And then, with a laugh, she shattered my expectations, revealing a preparedness that took me by surprise. The binder she presented, filled with checks and receipts, was just the beginning.

"What is your hourly rate?" she asked, cutting through my disbelief with that big checkbook laid out in front of me.

"My rate is a hundred and eighty an hour, but I—"

She sat back down at the table and shook her head. "You are significantly undercharging for your services based on your public track record, not to mention the information our mutual friend has provided." She scribbled on a check and looked at me with a straight face. No emotion whatsoever. "I'll pay you a thirty-thousand-dollar retainer and five thousand dollars a day." She tore away the check and handed it to me. "Because this is urgent, I will not ask for the retainer back, and it will not be included in the daily rate. Consider it a gift to convince you. Is this acceptable?"

Acceptable? A thirty-thousand-dollar gift? What? And five thousand bucks a day? I almost asked her to repeat herself, thinking my ears had played a cruel joke on me. Up until that moment, crossing the thousand-buck mark for a single client was still on my to-do list, somewhere between winning the lottery and learning to cook something that didn't come from a box.

"Yes," I said after the shock had at least begun to wear off. "That would be fine."

It was August, not April, and Jessica Steadman didn't look like the kind of woman to pull an April Fools' prank. I was afraid to look at the check, worried it would appear I didn't trust the woman or, worse yet, that I was desperate. "Thank you, Mrs. Steadman, but I have to be frank. Your daughter could very likely—"

She didn't let me finish. "Yes, I understand that it's highly probable my daughter is deceased. I've dealt with the possibility of that, and I have accepted it, but, Ms. Wyatt, I want my daughter back, dead or alive. She deserves a proper burial, even if that consists of burying only remnants of the shirt she died in."

That was something we shared. Molly had been missing too long to still be alive, but I still wanted, no, needed to find her abductor. As the reality of her request settled in, the weight of what she was asking—to bring her daughter back, dead or alive—struck a chord deep within me. We might not have shared the same path, but our destinations were marked by the same feeling. Profound loss.

Stunned by the offer, I agreed before I fully comprehended the magnitude of it all. A thirty-thousand-dollar retainer, five thousand a day—it was beyond anything I had ever imagined. Even though I had repeated that multiple times in my head, it still sounded unbelievable.

She picked up the landline and hit a button. "Charles. Will you please put the files inside Ms. Wyatt's vehicle? Yes. Come and get her keys and bring the main file." She smiled at me. "There are twelve file boxes. I've also included a MacBook." She stared above my head. "Perhaps a MacBook Pro?" She waved her hand dismissively. "I'm not sure, but it's got every interview, every podcast, every news report regarding my daughter's disappearance and husband's murder. It also contains every witness interview, and every public statement made about the investigation by the FBI and other agencies investigating. There are twenty-two hours of informational videos on the laptop. You can begin here, but it is all yours to keep until you bring my daughter home."

The woman had everything, except what I could do to find her child, figured out. Richard Steadman had been murdered. Shot multiple times in their daughter's bedroom with a silenced 9mm. Video released on TV and the internet showed a heavy man dressed in all black approaching Mr. Steadman as he placed his daughter in her bed. When he turned around, the man opened fire, hitting him multiple times in the chest. He took the little girl, and the video was the last anyone had seen of her.

She stared straight into my eyes and read my mind. "Leland's exact words were that you walk a fine line with the law. That, along with the powerful recommendations I mentioned earlier, sealed the deal."

I swallowed hard. "That's not exactly true." Not entirely. I only walked that fine line when absolutely necessary.

Jessica Steadman interrupted me. "I hope it is, because it's exactly what

How They Were Taken 19

I need. Leland understood that. Whatever you need to do to find my daughter, I want you to do it."

I said, "Ma'am," laced with the weight of what was at stake. Standing before Jessica Steadman, I clung to the last shreds of integrity I had. My life might have spiraled in ways I couldn't have imagined, my self-respect taking hit after hit, but if there was one thing I hadn't destroyed, it was my honesty. "I need to be up front with you. I can't promise any outcomes, and I'm not in the business of breaking the law." Wiggling my way around it, sure, but flat-out breaking it? I hadn't done that. Yet.

Her response carried an assurance that saw right through me. "You come highly recommended for multiple reasons. Ms. Wyatt, I do not trust easily, but I have been assured I can place my trust in you. I am taking a big risk in doing so, but I believe there is a reason you'll see this through. We can agree on that."

Her statement hinted at more than just a professional arrangement. It was personal for me, deeply so.

At that moment, Charles entered. He waved the file in his hands. "Your keys, ma'am?" he asked, turning toward me with an expectant look.

Fumbling slightly, I retrieved my keys from the depths of my bag and handed them over, trying to maintain a facade of composure. "Just put them wherever they need to go."

"Yes, ma'am," he replied before leaving.

Then, the moment that changed everything. Jessica Steadman handed me the large file. The world tilted on its axis the moment I opened it. Among the papers, five black-and-white photos stared back at me, each representing a nightmare, a missing girl's face frozen in time.

One of them, Molly.

3

I stared at the photo. "How did you get a photo of Molly?"

"I wasn't prying into your life," she said. "I hired a private investigator, and he made the connections. As I said previously, your sister Molly's situation is quite similar to my daughter's." Her tone carried a firmness and an unexpected softness new to our conversation. Her gaze locked onto mine as though she could see through to the core of my soul.

I stared at the haunting photos and imagined how it must have been for the girls. How it had become a nightmare on repeat lived by those they left behind. Molly's photo stood out. Her kindergarten smile, so full of innocence and untouched by the darkness that would engulf her, twisted my heart.

Other than the date they were taken, and some physical similarities, the abductions shared nothing consequential. "I'm not sure a private investigator would gain access to this information," I said. "Unless he knew someone."

Jessica's posture relaxed. "Not him, me. A woman of my fortune and connections has access to things others simply don't, Ms. Wyatt, and I've done my homework. Not just through Leland or my investigator, obviously. These girls," she motioned toward the pictures, "all share similarities. They all vanished at age five, for example. There are other similarities too, of course."

The feeling of violation overwhelmed me, though I wasn't sure why. Anyone who knew me knew of Molly. They knew I had spent years searching in some way for her abductor.

"In what ways do you believe these girls' abductions are connected? I don't recall the various departments connecting them."

"They didn't, but they don't have the tools I have. Please, it's easy to see. Look closer. They are the same age. They share similar physical characteristics. They come from the same state. They were abducted and removed from their homes while family was present, and in one case, nearby. Each abduction centered around a key element, and whether it is clear to you or not, I am certain they are connected."

I let out a breath I didn't realize I had been holding.

"Please. Look closer. Wasn't the person who took your sister wearing black?"

"Yes, but most criminals do." My words sounded defensive, though the similarities she pointed out appeared too generic to draw any real conclusions.

"It was later at night. Your mother left when you returned home. Your sister was already in bed. The man had a gun."

And she was wearing her clothes from the day. I hadn't pushed her to change. I just wanted her out of my way. "With all due respect, ma'am, your husband was in a secured home putting your daughter to bed. It's highly likely a business partner or scorned associate, perhaps, killed him and kidnapped your daughter." I had to challenge her theory, even as I reopened the file, and my gaze fell once more on the girls' faces.

"Of course we have exhausted every possible lead, including former employees and women in his life before me. Money does things to people, and many will kill for it, but we have yet to understand why my daughter was abducted and my husband shot multiple times."

"It's not always about money, Mrs. Steadman."

"I am aware."

"As I said, there are significant differences in the abductions. Your husband's murder." I looked at the notes typed next to each photo. "And Zoe Bryant wasn't even home. She was at a festival."

"No. She had returned from the festival. The media reported it incorrectly because the investigation warranted it. Of all people, you should understand." Jessica crossed her arms as she leaned back. "Perhaps Leland and the others were wrong about you."

I wasn't about to return that check. "He's not wrong, and I hate to keep harping on this, but your connections are weak."

She raised her eyebrow. "I disagree."

"I haven't looked at the files, but I believe they all lived in different cities in and out of the perimeter. Based on my sister and your daughter, their families lived different lifestyles. There would need to be much more to show a connection. Access points. Scene similarities. Perhaps something left or taken by the abductor."

"I understand," she said. "You are upset for failing to see the connections as I have, but you aren't the first. I haven't shown you everything." She asked me to go to the last paper in the file, one filled with more photographs.

I had noticed it, but I didn't mention it before. "They're all redheads and have freckles."

Her smile showed confidence and pride. "I know you've spent years chasing answers for your sister. That determination is exactly why I chose you. Who better to solve this than someone who truly understands the stakes?"

After being escorted out of the Steadman mansion, I climbed into my old Camry and turned the key. The engine roared to life with its usual comforting rumble. Jessica Steadman had dumped a massive investigation onto my lap, and I desperately wanted to dive in, but I needed to get to Nick's and pick up Alyssa. I paused before leaving the estate, feeling like I had stepped out of a different reality and back into mine, one where grandeur and opulence were mere fantasies and I considered Chick-fil-A a gourmet meal.

I gunned it toward Nick's, my mind set on snagging Alyssa and getting her to ballet on time. But the metro Atlanta area, in its infinite chaos, had other plans. Traffic was a nightmare, with an accident causing a standstill that had me trapped just north of Old Milton Parkway on 400. I stared at my watch and counted the precious minutes ticking away. Thirty minutes lost to the void, each one a tiny dagger to my plans and a check mark on Nick's list of reasons I sucked at being a mother.

The retainer check in my purse pressed down like a brick on my lungs —welcome, yet a demanding reminder of the enormous responsibility gripping my shoulders. I replayed our conversation, working through the puzzle Jessica had tossed my way.

Some of the things Mrs. Steadman had said made sense. The person who took Molly sounded like Emma's abductor, but so much time had passed between the two events, the person would have changed some. Enough to look different, however, I wasn't sure. The abductions occurring on the same day of different months could have been a coincidence, but they still intrigued me, however small the thread. The red hair and freckles ranked high on the more-than-a-coincidence scale, and she had hooked me then.

Halfway to Nick's, a deafening explosion shattered my concentration. The car careened to the right, causing my heart to catapult into my throat as I wrestled the steering wheel for control. Traffic thinned and drivers pulled away, hoping to escape the accident I would no doubt cause.

The steering wheel twisted violently in my grasp. I slammed down on the brake pedal, yet the car skidded and edged perilously toward the guardrail. I swore loudly, but futilely. Gravel crunched under the tires while I steered the car onto the shoulder. "Come on!"

At last, the car halted. I stayed frozen in my seat, hands clamped on the wheel, heart hammering. "What the hell?" I gasped through ragged breaths. Five more feet and I would have toppled over the bridge and into traffic below.

I exited the vehicle and inspected the damage. The right front tire had been obliterated, leaving half of it in tattered remnants of rubber strewn across the asphalt. "Great," I groaned. I threaded my fingers through my dark hair. A blowout. Just my luck. I had to reach Alyssa, or Nick would never let me spend time with her again.

I popped the trunk, yanked out the spare tire and jack, and got to work. Sweat soaked my clothes as I hurried, the lug nuts defiant and rusted tight, yet I wrestled them free. Before long, I had replaced the shredded tire with the spare.

A pickup truck pulled over behind me just as I finished tightening the last lug nut. A man in overalls stained with oil climbed out. He walked over and eyed the damage. His face appeared weathered from years of working under the sun, but his eyes were sharp and observant.

"Need some help?" he asked, his voice gruff but kind.

"Actually, I think I've got it," I replied as I wiped my hands on a rag. "Just a blowout."

He nodded, then strolled over to the largest piece of the shredded tire lying on the side of the road. Cars raced past us, their engines loud and intimidating on the small shoulder. He picked up the tire scrap and inspected it closely. "Looks like you ran over a nail," he said, turning the piece of rubber to show me one smashed into the other side of the scrap.

I frowned, taking the piece from him. "A nail? I'm surprised it blew out from that."

"It happens," he said. "But look at this. It ain't one nail. It's three." He examined the scrap more. "You know, it's even odder, the way the nails were positioned."

A chill ran down my spine. "You can see that?"

"I can."

"What does it mean?"

"Well, look here," he said, pointing to spots on the tire. "This here's the sidewall. That part doesn't touch the ground, and the odds of a nail flying off the road and stabbing the sidewall are rare, but for three to do it? That's either an act of God or someone's got it in for you."

I looked closer and noticed the angle at which the nails embedded into the tire. "You're saying it's possible someone put them there on purpose?"

He nodded slowly. "Not only possible, but probable. Can't see how they didn't. See how they're driven straight in at a right angle to the tire surface?

How They Were Taken   25

That's not usually how nails end up in tires if you run over them. They'd be at a slanted angle and in the treads like I said."

I swallowed hard as the implications sunk in. "And there are three of them."

"Yeah," he said as he turned the piece over to show me the other nails. "Look at the depth and condition of the nails. They're stuck in deep with what looks like consistent pressure, like someone hammered them in. Plus, they're a bit too clean, not worn like you'd expect from nails on the road. I'm no forensic person, but I know a planted nail when I see it. Here, I see three." He looked in my eyes. "You piss off your guy or something?"

"Or something," I said.

"Looks like you got lucky. Someone wanted you to have a blowout, and you did. Could've been a lot worse if you were going faster or couldn't pull over in time."

I nodded. "Thanks for pointing it out. I'll have to get this checked out."

"No problem," he said, tipping his hat. "Just be careful. Whoever did this knew what they were doing."

I sat in my car for a minute after he left. I had arrested too many people to count during my career. Most of my busts spent a lot of time in jail because of me, and a good deal of them wanted revenge. I expected that, even prepared for it at times. The problem was figuring out which drug dealer or murderer wanted me dead. I whipped out my phone, hoping for some miracle on the traffic app. The accident had cleared, the app cheerfully informed me. A glimmer of hope, at least.

I hit Nick's shortcut number. The phone barely rang once before it dumped me into voicemail. Not one to give up, I hit redial immediately. Sure, I toed the line, risking Nick's ire, but my desire to see Alyssa, to hold her close and whisk her away to ballet, overshadowed any dread of confrontation. Just because I had all but sacrificed my family for work didn't mean I didn't love them. It meant I did a crappy job showing it.

I didn't care if he got mad. Alyssa was my world, and nothing, not even Atlanta's best impersonation of parking lot hell, was going to keep me from her.

"I told you not to bother," he said instead of hello.

"I'm fifteen minutes out. I can take her to ballet."

He sighed and then fell silent.

"Nick, come on. I haven't seen her in two weeks."

"That's not because of me."

Nick had the final say of when I saw my kid, a win in his column for temporary custody of our daughter. He played it like a gracious move, doling out visitation at what he liked to call his discretion. It sucked, monumentally. My court attendance—or the lack thereof—was a glaring sign in his favor. Three out of four of the required visits I was off playing savior to the state, a commitment that the judge wasted no time throwing in my face.

Not at all a double standard. The justice system expected people like me to drop everything at a moment's notice but punished us when we did.

The problem was my job had me. It consumed me, turning days into blurry streaks that blended one case into the next, pulling me under a dark cloud of endless nights, making me forget more visitation days than I cared to admit. The crown for the world's "best bad mom" could rest on my frazzled head. I knew it, and it clawed at me day and night. But I was fighting to claw my way back, one mile of traffic and one missed voicemail at a time. I was in it, trying to do better, trying to be present. For Alyssa. But sometimes, trying felt like the steepest hill to climb. "Do we need to go into this now? I just want to see my kid. Please."

"Was it another case? What was it this time? Insurance fraud or some vengeful wife who wants to take her husband for everything he's got?"

"Tell her to go to hell," Heather said in the background. Heather, the chick living in my house.

"Tell her I'll meet her there," I said.

He covered the phone with his hand. I knew he was talking to her, but I couldn't make out his words. Too bad. I would have loved to hear him scold her.

"Just come another time," he finally said. "Go work instead."

"I'm already on my way." Nick had issues with my career choice. He always had, though he married me anyway. "It was Jessica Steadman, by the way."

"Jessica Steadman?" He cleared his throat and repeated her name, then stayed silent for a moment after.

How They Were Taken

27

I kept quiet as well, hoping it would make the enormity of my meeting perfectly clear. Finally, he said, "Hurry up."

I clocked it in at fourteen minutes flat. Pulling into the familiar streets of what used to be our neighborhood, where Nick and I had crafted a life together for a decade out of our fifteen years of marriage. Knowing I had destroyed that oozed like a self-inflicted wound that refused to heal. An unavoidable lurch in my stomach caught me—as it always did—as I guided my car into the driveway. It had become a low blow to the psyche that hadn't dulled with time.

We had called it quits the year before, but rewind six months before that, the first bombshell dropped, and I'd uncovered his affair with Heather. The time frame of Nick's infidelity before I caught it remained a shadow, murky and unwilling to come into focus. He had eventually owned up to his betrayal, crackling even deeper the already fragile ghost of a trust we clung to.

We danced the tired march of trying to work through it for Alyssa's sake, but that didn't last. I focused more on work and drank more than he liked, and he had drifted back into Heather's orbit. Despite every fiber of my pride, I couldn't fault him. I had made my cases, my career, what was supposed to be only part of not just my life, but of our collective being—it had all become a rockslide that crashed down onto my family.

Except, according to Nick, Molly. He claimed Molly hogged the spot at the top of every personal chart. Nick had insisted a ghost ruined our marriage, and in retrospect, he was right.

But nothing, not an aspect of the comedy of malice, could summon my fire quite like laying eyes on Heather passing platitudes of maternal warmth to Alyssa. Observing my daughter as she leaned into the veneer of a reality where Heather wore the figure of a second mom sent a complex cascade of poison and distaste down my throat without a chaser.

I mashed down my internal churning hell as I killed the engine. Did I deserve to be upset? No. I screwed up, and I understood that, but that didn't make it any better.

I fortified myself with a soft smile as I emerged from the car. I had perfected my sacred armor of coverups. "Hey, baby!"

Alyssa raced to me. "Mama! I'm going to ballet."

I scooped her into my arms and showered her with kisses. God, I missed her.

She giggled. "Mama, you're getting cooties on me!"

I didn't care. "Oh, no! Cooties? Oh, well." I kissed her several more times. "Now you're full of them."

She giggled again as Nick and Heather walked over. Bile creeped up my throat at the sight of her.

"Are you planning to stay at ballet?" he asked.

I didn't bother looking at my replacement. "If I can."

He eyed my spare tire. "With that?"

"It's a spare tire, Nick. I'm not going on the highway. We'll be fine."

He nodded once, but his tight jawline told me he wasn't happy.

"She likes McDonald's after ballet. Chicken nuggets and fries, but not the Happy Meal," Heather said.

I refused to look at her. "I'm aware of what my kid likes."

"I'm the one who's here for her every day. Not you."

I bowed up like a snake ready to bite.

"Jenna," Nick said with more than a hint of annoyance. "Don't."

I settled Alyssa on my hip and said, "I'll have her back after dinner." Not able to help myself, I added, "Where's her GPS tracker so I don't lose it?"

"Go to hell," Heather said and stormed back into the house.

"Real nice," Nick said and followed my replacement.

I put Alyssa in the booster seat and shut the door. "For the woman who destroyed my marriage, she's sure intimidated by me."

Ballet class for a bunch of five-year-olds was an organized mess, one notch above a circus. But Jasmine, the ballet instructor, cast a spell with her whistle. The chatter dropped from one hundred to zero to silent in a heartbeat. The girls, Alyssa included, all froze mid-giggle, mid-twirl, their expressions respectful and sprinkled with a good dose of fear.

"Ladies." Jasmine's voice cut through the silence. She clapped once, sharp and commanding. "Spots, now. We begin with the basics, first position." She paused, scanning the room as if to make sure her words had

How They Were Taken 29

taken root. "Heels together, toes out. Make a *V*. Arms in front, gentle curve in the wrists." Watching them, she nodded, her eyes stopping on Alyssa. "Alyssa, toes out more. Yes, like that. Excellent."

Molly had dreamed of ballet classes, but those dreams had shattered right alongside everything else deemed extra after Dad bailed. Money was tight, and dreams were a luxury we couldn't afford. I swore back then that if I ever had a kid, she wouldn't miss out like Molly and I had. Yet, the one thing I couldn't make up for was a sibling, a sister for Alyssa, something I had hoped for.

But Nick, he could easily offer Alyssa that sister through Heather. The thought was a jagged pill, hard to swallow and leaving a bitter aftertaste.

"Mama? Did you see me do my portie bras?"

Ballet Master Jasmine chuckled. "*Port de bras*, Alyssa. Remember how I taught you to say it?"

"Yes, Master Jasmine. Pordy bras."

"Very good," she said, smiling at me. "Alyssa is very talented. She's going to be a wonderful ballerina one day."

"Thank you," I said as I wrapped my daughter in her loose sweatshirt. "So far, that's her life's dream."

Alyssa ran to the door. "Come on, Mama! It's McDonald's time!"

I thanked Jasmine. "See you soon."

"Chicken nuggets and fries, no Happy Meal," I said on the way to Mickey D's. "A perfect after-ballet meal. So, why no Happy Meal anymore, honey?"

"Heather says plastic is killing turtles and deer."

I focused on not rolling my eyes or saying something snarky. According to Nick, Heather was a climate-change enthusiast. I would have used another term, but not because I wasn't pro-environment. Because I wasn't pro-Heather. "We need to care for our environment. I'm proud of you for not getting the toy."

"I don't like them anyway," she said. "They're for kids. I'm almost six years old."

I pulled into the parking lot and parked a few cars away from an idling black SUV. My cell phone rang. I checked the caller ID. Leland. "Just a sec,"

I said to Alyssa. I accepted the call. "Hey, I'm with my daughter. Can I call you in an hour? We need to talk about Jessica Steadman."

"I wondered if she'd called you yet," he said. "Call me back."

Alyssa and I ate our McDonald's and chatted until Nick called to check on us. "We're fine," I said in a tone he had always hated. "I'll have her back in a half hour."

"It's getting late," he said. "She's got school tomorrow."

"I'm aware of that. See you in thirty." I ended the call and swore under my breath.

"Mama, God doesn't like bad words. Heather says we can go to Hades if we say them, because they make God so mad. Hades is hell in case you don't know."

Heather said a lot of things my daughter didn't understand. "Yes, it is, but God isn't going to send me to hell for saying a bad word, baby. I promise."

"But Heather said—"

"God is very forgiving. As long as we do our best to be good, he understands we make mistakes."

"And let Jesus in our hearts."

"Did Heather say that too?" I asked.

"No. Miss Avery, my Sunday school teacher."

"Miss Avery is right."

"She tells us that all the time," she said with a mouth full of fries. "I'm glad you're not going to Hades. It's very hot there."

"Let me guess. Heather told you that too."

She nodded and dropped a fry onto the table. "She said it's a pit of fire and when you go there you burn forever and ever, and it hurts a real lot." She took a sip of her milk. "I'm a good girl, so I won't go to Hades. Daddy said. But Mama, why is Heather always saying you should go there? That's not nice."

Because Heather was a home-wrecking ho. "Does that make you uncomfortable?"

She shook her head and said no while chewing a fry.

"Has she said other things about me?"

How They Were Taken 31

"Not really, but one time I heard Daddy tell her not to say anything about you to me. Daddy used his strong voice, so I bet she listened."

"He does have a strong voice sometimes," I said, smiling. "Mommy and Heather don't really get along that well, but it's okay. That happens. And Daddy's right about you, baby. You would never burn in a pit of fire forever and ever." I wiped off her milk mustache. "We need to go. You ready?"

"Yup." She climbed out of the booth and skipped to the door.

The drive back to Nick's should have been smooth, but smooth wasn't my thing. My stomach clenched as soon as I pulled out of the McDonald's. In the rearview mirror, a black SUV with California plates swerved aggressively to lock onto my tail. The same one idling in the parking lot earlier. My fingers gripped the steering wheel tighter as my pulse spiked. I forced myself to breathe deeply, to suppress the rising desire to play Jerry in a game of cat and mouse. I refused to let Alyssa, happily licking her ice cream cone in my back seat, catch my sense of dread. But the SUV stuck to me like a shadow, echoing every move I made as if tethered to my bumper.

"Son of a bitch."

"Mama, Heather says that's a naughty word! Remember burning in a pit of fire?"

I exhaled. "You're right, honey," I said with all the calm I could muster. "Mommy won't do it again." I veered left, then right to test whether I was truly being followed or it was just my paranoid imagination. The SUV mirrored my every turn with unnerving precision. My heart pounded harder as fury bubbled just beneath my skin.

But I had to stay composed—for Alyssa.

"Mama, why are we going this way?" Alyssa asked, her voice curious and calm. "Heather says it's the long way."

Screw Heather. "Just taking a different route, sweetie. Sometimes it's fun to mix things up," I replied, with a calmness I didn't feel.

My mind raced, strategizing my next move. Confronting the driver with Alyssa in the car was out of the question. I needed to get her to Nick's safely, no matter what. I turned onto a busier street, the crowd of cars and pedestrians offering a sliver of comfort. If the person in that SUV intended to strike, they'd have to do it in front of witnesses, if they could get close enough.

"Mama, why do you look mad?" Alyssa's reflection stared back at me from the rearview mirror, her innocent eyes full of concern.

"I'm not mad, honey. Just thinking about some work stuff," I said, keeping my voice light.

"Is it because of the bad guys?" she whispered, as if discussing monsters lurking under the bed.

I frowned. I never talked about my job around Alyssa. She knew I helped people, but nothing more. I had made every effort possible to conceal the risks I took. "Bad guys? What bad guys?"

"The ones Heather and Daddy say you're always trying to catch?"

A chill swept through me. "Daddy and Heather are silly. You don't need to worry about me, okay? Mommy's got everything under control," I said, wishing my words felt as reassuring as they sounded.

The SUV stayed two cars behind me. I needed to lose it fast. The light turned yellow, but I spotted a strip mall up ahead and slammed my foot down on the gas pedal and sped through the light, spare tire be damned. I jerked the wheel, swerving into the parking lot, threading through cars, dodging shopping carts and pedestrians. The SUV hesitated, but it sat stuck behind two stopped cars, with no median for it to drive over, waiting for the light to turn green.

"Mama, where are we going now?" Alyssa asked, confusion creeping into her voice.

"Just taking a little detour, sweetie. We'll be at Daddy's soon," I reassured her.

I pressed down on the accelerator, darting through the lot, checking my rearview mirror for the SUV the entire time. I cut a sharp corner and slipped behind a delivery truck parked near the entrance of a Walgreens. The SUV shot past, the driver clearly not anticipating my sudden maneuver. I held my breath, watching as it cruised through the parking lot, searching for me but finding nothing. Finally, it sped off, disappearing around the corner.

"What are we doing, Mama?"

"I dropped my phone on the floor. I just pulled over to pick it up."

I exhaled slowly, my body trembling with the aftershock of adrenaline. I had shaken them. For the time being. But the unease gnawed at me,

How They Were Taken   33

warning of something far more dangerous. And I needed to figure out what before it was too late.

"You should get a new car," she said.

I completed a U-turn and used a Southern accent to ask, "You don't like this little old thing?"

"Heather says it's a hunk of junk."

I bit my bottom lip, promising myself to be kind. "Heather has a lot to say, that's for sure."

"She's very smart. Daddy said she's brillbent."

"Brilliant?" I wouldn't go that far.

"Yeah. I don't want you talking on your phone when you're driving. Heather told Daddy one day you're going to crash the car into a brick wall."

"I'm too good of a driver to let that happen, honey, so don't worry about it, okay?"

"You promise?"

"I promise. I also promise to not hold my phone to my ear anymore." With her in the car.

"Daddy has a phone in our car. He just says hello and talks to people. He says it's magic. Why can't you do that with your car?"

Because Toyota made my Camry before Bluetooth. "Daddy's got a fancy car, but Mommy doesn't."

"If you save your money, you can get a new one! I'm saving for a TV for my room. Daddy says I can have one if I pay for it myself."

"That's great," I said. Nick placated her. He and I had agreed to no TV in Alyssa's room, but I gave her slim odds for saving enough cash.

I took a deep breath, trying to calm the storm inside me.

My mind swirled with thoughts the rest of the way. The Steadman case, Molly's disappearance, my blown tire, and the tail. I didn't believe in coincidence. If it was connected, I had to find the thread. I needed to keep Alyssa safe, even if that meant I didn't see her for a while.

Nick's front door swung open as Alyssa and I walked up the steps. "We thought you'd be back sooner," Heather said.

"My husband knew when we'd be back. Why don't you ask him why he didn't make that clear to you?"

Her double-D implants puffed up as she inhaled her strength for the battle I had just started. "We aren't like you. We communicate. That's half the reason he left you for me."

I shook my head and grimaced, then eyed her chest. "I don't think so." I smirked. "Nick's a boob guy." I glanced down at my sagging-from-having-a-child A cups. "Obviously, I can't compete with saline."

Nick appeared beside Heather. He cleared his throat. "Babe, can you take Alyssa inside?"

"Fine," Heather said. "Come, child."

"Daddy," Alyssa said. "Mama dropped her phone and pulled over to pick it up. She promised no more talking on the phone in the car."

He eyed me. "She did?"

"I don't have Bluetooth," I said.

"Come on, honey," Heather said to Alyssa.

Alyssa hugged me. "Bye, Mama. Love you, mean it."

"You, too, baby."

Nick peered at me after she scurried away. "Pulled over to pick up your phone?" he asked.

"I didn't want to crash into a brick wall," I said.

He blinked but didn't acknowledge scaring our child. "Why do you always have to start something when you come here?"

"Come to my home? The one I helped purchase?" I stuffed my hands into my pockets and shrugged. "Don't blame me. You're the one that moved her into my house."

He sighed and said, "I'm not having this conversation with you. Our attorneys can handle it," then slammed the door shut.

"Nice seeing you, too," I hollered.

4

Shifting gears in my life had felt like swapping my comfy, lived-in jeans for a pair of stiff, new slacks. I had uprooted from the warm embrace of my family home in Alpharetta to a no-frills apartment tucked away off Peachtree Parkway in Cumming. The place wouldn't win any beauty contests, but the gated community whispered hints of security, and the tiny room I had fixed up for Alyssa shimmered with the hope that maybe, just maybe, Nick would cave and let her spend the night. I stood on the edge of a cliff, toes peeking over into the unknown, wondering if I could rebuild from the rubble of my old life.

Caught in the snarl of evening traffic, I barely believed the words tumbling out of my mouth. "Let me get this straight, Leland. You show me the door, pink slip and all, then spin around and toss my name into the ring with Georgia's queen bee of wealth?" I pressed the phone harder against my ear, as if the added pressure might squeeze out a more sensible explanation. Yes, it was against the law to hold a phone while driving, but at least Alyssa wasn't with me. I switched to speaker and set it on the passenger seat.

His response, half-amused, half-serious, crackled through the speaker. "More like most of the country."

I visualized the shrug in his tone. The conversation twisted and turned like the roads I drove on, leading me through a myriad of emotions—from disbelief to a begrudging acceptance of the bizarre situation Leland put me in.

"And yes. You're good at what you do. Jessica needs someone with your special talents."

"I've got a photographic memory, yet you still fired me."

"I didn't fire you because you weren't a good agent. I fired you because you failed to uphold GBI values."

I repeated what he had told me the day he let me go, something straight from the GBI handbook. "My actions were inconsistent with the core values and principles of the Georgia Bureau of Investigation, leading to a loss of trust and confidence in my abilities. Blah, blah, blah."

"And frankly, Jenna, you needed to be fired. Your mind is focused on one thing, and only one thing—finding your sister's abductor. You might not see it that way, but to those of us on the outside, it's clear as day."

Arguing that did nothing. "Okay."

"You were an excellent special agent, but it was happening. We all saw it. Eventually, you would be no good to the GBI until you either found Molly or accepted that she's gone." He exhaled. "Did you take the case?"

"She gave me a big check. How could I say no?" I tapped my security card onto the gate pad at my apartment complex and waited for the gate to open.

"She deserves someone that will be dedicated to finding her daughter."

"Wasn't that Jack Parks guy working for her?"

"He was, but they had a disagreement."

My cat, Bob, named by Alyssa, greeted me at my door as I entered carrying a box from Jessica Steadman's home. He rubbed his face against my pant leg. I crouched down to pet him, but only after I set down my things.

"Did you know she has a picture of Molly? And pictures of her daughter and four other girls."

Leland sounded surprised. "She has a photo of Molly?" He cleared his throat. "I didn't know about that."

"Did she ask about me, or did you recommend me?"

"She asked about you."

How They Were Taken 37

I had gone back outside for another box and set it on my dining room table and headed out for another one. "Because she knows I'm looking for Molly."

We talked more while I grabbed the rest of the boxes and finally the laptop. My body ached from lugging it all up three flights of stairs in heels I hated. I set the laptop on my coffee table and walked to the kitchen.

I put the phone on speaker, washed my hands, then poured myself a glass of whiskey.

Leland's drawl filtered through the phone, laced with a teasing tone that made me roll my eyes. "Have you caught your breath yet? You stop exercising or something?"

His Georgia accent both laid-back and challenging all at once.

I sipped my drink. The liquid comforted me, almost sympathizing with my racing heart and the sweat still clinging to my back after completing my third-floor apartment marathon. "I just went up and down the stairs, what, twenty-four times? You try it. See if you can breathe." My tone turned sassy, daring him to walk a mile in my heels.

He chuckled, the gesture both warm and infuriating. "Let me know if I can help you with your case."

I laughed at his offer. "Thanks for the offer, but we both know it's BS." Leland was many things, but a cowboy riding to my rescue? Not in his job description. Never had been at the bureau, either. Our relationship teetered on a fine line between professional courtesy and the unspoken truths of our past.

"This is a big case. GBI could use a win." His voice was casual, but I sensed the undercurrent of sincerity.

"Right. Got it. You give me a report or something I need, and I tell the press GBI assisted with the investigation."

He laughed. "You bet." His tone dropped an octave. "Jenna?" He said my name as if he were standing right there, looking me in the eye.

"Yes, Leland?" I tensed, waiting for the caution, the reminder of boundaries not to cross.

"Find those girls."

His words cut through the pretense and clung to my sense of duty. That wasn't the Leland I was used to; that was a plea wrapped in the guise of an order. And totally unexpected.

"I'll do my best." I barely spoke, almost lost in the significance of his request.

He hung up. The silence of my kitchen wrapped around me like a thick, humid Georgia night. I stared at the shot glass, the amber liquid promising oblivion or maybe courage, I never knew. I inhaled deeply, the scent of whiskey sharp, filled with memories of cases won and lost, of roads traveled and paths yet to take.

Filled with memories of Molly and Alyssa, and how I had failed them.

Raising the glass, I whispered, "Cheers to a big case." I tipped it to my mouth and swallowed it. The whiskey burned all the way down, feeling like a fiery trail of determination and fear. I poured another because the ritual was familiar and necessary. Guilt came with the package, but it was a small price to pay for my wrongdoing.

I stacked the twelve files, some stuffed, some partially filled, against my back dining room wall, then poured myself another shot, downed it, and sat on my couch. I grabbed the laptop beside me and opened it. Jessica Steadman had given me all the necessary log-in information in a file taped to the bottom of it. I immediately logged on and updated all the passwords. God only knew who had them, but I would keep the information private.

Bob climbed onto the back of the couch and purred softly. His little noises relaxed me. I leaned forward and poured myself another shot, kicked it back, then got to work.

The shrill ring of my cell phone yanked me from sleep, which was exactly the reason I picked it. I groaned as I buried my face deeper into the throw pillow I slept on. It was late—or early, depending on how you looked at it—and only a special kind of jerk would have the nerve to call at such an ungodly hour.

My head throbbed. My hand brushed over the cold, cluttered surface of my coffee table, sending a precarious stack of files tumbling to the floor. "Aw, come on," I muttered, the taste of the night's whiskey and regret thick

How They Were Taken

in my mouth. My head pounded a wicked beat, a bold reminder of my less-than-stellar decision-making skills. I squinted against the dim light, spotting the culprit of my early morning misery perched atop a mountain of paperwork.

I snatched the phone and closed my eyes, the bright screen blinding me for a second. "What time is it even?" I grumbled, swiping to accept the call. "Yeah?"

A man's voice, quiet but laced with a determination that had me straightening up despite the throbbing in my head, came through. "Jenna Wyatt."

It sounded more like a confirmation than a question.

I rubbed the sleep from my eyes. "Who's asking?"

"Jack Parks. You've got my case."

"Jack Parks, huh?" Laughter bubbled up my throat, though it quickly died as reality set in. "Who told you I have the case?"

"Jessica Steadman. Give me your address. We need to talk."

I licked my dry lips while glancing at the empty whiskey bottle judging me from across the room. "My address? I don't even know you. And what time is it?"

"Leland will vouch for me. Where do you live?"

I checked the phone's display. "It's three a.m. Can't this wait until this afternoon?"

"No. Come on. Don't make me wake up your former boss too."

The audacity of the guy. "Call me when the world gets up," I retorted, ending the call with a tap. I tossed the phone beside me, then leaned back into the couch, groaning again. The whiskey had overstayed its welcome, leaving my head smack in the path of a Mack truck.

No sooner had I closed my eyes than the thing rang again. "You've got to be kidding me," I muttered, picking it up with a resigned, "Seriously?"

"I'll be there in fifteen. I like my coffee black."

"You have no idea where I live."

"I do now."

And just like that, he killed the call. I stared at the phone with my jaw hanging open. Fifteen minutes to transform from whiskey-soaked couch potato to private investigator. The room spun slightly as I attempted to stand. I made a mental note: black coffee for pain in the ass with no regard for normal human hours. "Great," I sighed, wondering if the case—and Mr. Pain in the Ass—would be the end of me or the start of a beautiful relationship. I would put my money on the end of me.

And so, with Leland's unexpected command echoing in my head, I braced myself for Jack Parks. No more cheating husbands or car accident scams. It was time I dove back into the fray of chasing ghosts and justice in equal measure.

I peeled myself off the couch with all the grace of a zombie. The bathroom mirror didn't do me any favors. Even *The Walking Dead* zombies looked better than me. My dark hair, which I had optimistically tied in a ponytail the day before, had revolted. Half of it clung to the elastic band for dear life while the other half made a break for freedom, strands splayed out in a desperate bid for escape. I tugged the band free, then twisted the rebellious locks atop my head and secured them with a clip and attacked my face with cold water. The shock welcomed me to a new day—or rather, the tail end of a long night.

I swirled some mouthwash, trying to erase the remnants of whiskey and bad decisions, then gave my teeth a once-over with a toothbrush made from sandpaper. The twisted bun wouldn't fly for proving credibility, so my hair got a similar half-hearted attempt at grooming before I wriggled into a pair of jeans clean enough and an Atlanta Braves T-shirt—a souvenir from Nick before he decided to trade me in for a family-wrecking ho.

Dawn tried its hardest to infiltrate my apartment, sneaking rays of light through the blinds. I had stacked the boxes against my dining room wall, then as my blood alcohol increased, proceeded to dig through them and scatter their contents everywhere. They taunted me, each box a reminder of puzzles I hoped I could solve but feared were doomed to end up a lifelong regret.

The door buzzer cut through my contemplation, its shrill sound a jarring intrusion into my repetitive thoughts. I confirmed it was him at the gate, then poured myself a cup of coffee. The aroma comforted my pounding head. I had decided Jack Parks's request for a cup would be answered and handed it to him as I let him in. "I like it strong," I informed him, a bit too late.

How They Were Taken 41

He accepted the mug with a nod as he stepped into my cluttered reality. "Come on in," I drawled as I closed the door behind him. I dragged myself back to the couch.

"You smell like whiskey." His statement bordered on ridiculous, it was so obvious.

I gestured toward the incriminating bottle on my coffee table. "There's a reason for that." I sank back onto the couch and pulled my legs up beneath me, seeking some semblance of comfort in the soft cushions to combat the pounding in my head. "Why exactly are you here?" I pressed, not in the mood for small talk.

His gaze swept the room. "She give you all this?"

I nodded as I watched him closely. "Is it yours too, or does just the case itself belong to you?"

"I have copies of it all." He made himself at home on the other end of the couch with an ease in his posture that irked me—strike one—like he'd been there before and would be back again. "We need to work this together."

I raised an eyebrow. "Thanks, but I'm flying solo now." I clutched my coffee a bit tighter, the warmth from it soothing my racing heart. "Besides, Jessica Steadman fired you." A smirk played on my lips. "Why did she, anyway?"

"We had a disagreement. She's flighty, like most women." His casual dismissal annoyed me.

Flighty like most women? Strike two. "Nice stereotyping," I shot back. My voice dripped with disdain.

He shrugged, unfazed by my curt tone. "The truth's painful sometimes."

I sighed, the fatigue of the hour wearing on me. "Normally, I'd appreciate the casual conversation, but it's the middle of the night still, and I'm tired. Can we move this along?"

"You really should shower."

My patience waned. "You've mentioned that, but I'm hoping to get you out of here in five minutes so I can crash again. So, tell me what you want, Parks."

"I told you. I want to work the case with you."

His determination was clear, but I needed more. There had to be a reason. People like us fought for cases for a reason, usually something personal. "Why?" I probed, setting my coffee down with a clatter.

"Because these girls are dead, Wyatt. You know that as well as I do. With the abductions as similar as they are, there's a serial killer out there looking for his next victim."

His words cut through the haze of my irritation, sobering me faster than any cold shower could. Did I think the murders were connected? Steadman had provided a circumstantial argument, but I still needed convincing. I wouldn't think serial killer until I had concrete evidence or a much stronger argument to convince me. "What makes you think that?"

He glanced at the bottle of whiskey, then back at me with an unspoken judgment in his gaze. "You didn't review anything yet, did you?"

"I was with my daughter." My defensive tone came automatically, protective of my time with Alyssa, the one pure thing in my life. "But I did flip through some of it."

He nodded. "And Jessica Steadman didn't tell you anything?"

"She tossed some circumstantial evidence at me, but not enough to drive down your dark alley." I exhaled. "Listen, I've got a long day tomorrow. Just shoot straight, all right?"

"I had the case for nine months. Steadman's daughter is dead, and in case she didn't tell you, I believe the man that took Emma Steadman also took your sister."

I agreed with him about Emma Steadman, but I kept going. "How do you know she's dead?"

"The same way I know it's the same person who abducted and murdered your sister."

5

His abrupt, confident response sliced through the fog of my half-awake brain. I didn't know the guy, but his stark tone and flat lips said he believed his own words. Anyone in law enforcement, whether for a department or on their own, didn't make things up when it came to death and children.

He hoisted the laptop from the table and eased it down beside me. The cushion dipped under his weight. "What's the password?"

My brows pinched together. "What makes you think I changed it?"

He lowered his head and offered a look that included incredulity with a hint of respect. "You're ex-GBI. It'd be a poor show if you hadn't." His words hinted at a challenge wrapped in an unspoken compliment. Maybe he was tolerable after all?

I angled the laptop toward me, letting my fingers dance across the keys to unlock it before spinning it back in his direction.

He dove into the digital maze with swift keystrokes, eventually pushing the screen toward me. "Read."

His report from two months prior filled the screen. I skimmed it once, then with a deeper focus. "My sister vanished in a break-in. Emma Steadman was taken when her dad was killed. Not the same scenario." My hand automatically reached for my coffee, though my taste buds yearned for the burn of whiskey.

"Or her father was killed because he was at the wrong place at the wrong time. Did it ever occur to you the abductor killed Steadman because he had to in order to take Emma?"

"No, but I just got the case yesterday. I told you I flipped through it. Remember?"

"Good point." He leaned back with a smirk playing on his lips. "I've heard you're tough to crack, so I'll give you a little more." He flicked through file folders with purpose, then stopped, tapped on the laptop keyboard, then turned it my way again. "Look at these girls. Notice anything?"

I glanced at the photos on the laptop, my initial scan superficial. "Other than the red hair and freckles? Not much. But Molly's case is decades old, worlds apart from most of them. FYI, I already danced this dance with Steadman."

"Keep looking."

I met his stare, frustration bubbling inside me. "You're not here for a detective masterclass. Just point it out."

"The photos on the laptop are the same, but some are older and didn't scan well." He held up the printed copy of the one pulled up on the computer and traced the photo with his finger, highlighting features as if sketching them. "Square jaw. Blue eyes. Widow's peak. It's the widow's peak that caught my attention." He handed me the photos, each a snapshot of loss. "I'm sure Steadman already mentioned the girls were abducted on the same day of the month."

"She did."

"That and their similar appearances create a pattern, a profile of the victims."

I caught the pattern. The hair color and freckles could have been wishful thinking, but the rest of their similarities weren't chilling coincidences.

"These are the only cases on that specific date, starting with your sister," he said, his voice determined and somber. "And the only girls with the same appearance who went missing around those dates."

"And none of the girls were found." The statement sat like a lump in my throat.

How They Were Taken 45

"None. Each case turned cold after a few months, if that."

"If you had the case for nine months, how come you couldn't solve it?"

"Sometimes cases are too big for one investigator."

"And that's why you're here? You think I need you?"

"You do," he said. "Most of this information is in my head. I can give you the *Reader's Digest* version when necessary. I've met most of the parents. They've met me, and they understand I'm trying to help."

"Who made these connections initially? You or Steadman?"

"I did. Listen, I'm good at my job."

"Steadman might not agree."

"Then she doesn't need to know."

"I can't afford—"

He stood, cutting me off with a wave. "Forget the money. I'm after justice."

I rose too, resolve stiffening my spine. "Besides spending nine months without catching whoever's taken these girls, be it one person or five, what qualifies you to chase this phantom? Your private investigator card come with a magic wand?"

He paused, then sat back down, his eyes locking with mine. "Steadman didn't tell you?"

I shook my head.

"Leland either?"

"Nope. Guess he thought it was on you to show me your résumé."

"I'm former NCIS. Navy in case you're not familiar. Ten years as a special agent in charge. Ran a team of fifty Navy personnel."

"I'm familiar. So, what? You chased down sailors who jumped ship and solved murders on aircraft carriers?" I wiggled my hands in sarcasm. "Tough stuff there, buddy."

"It's more than that. We handled everything from terrorism to espionage. High stakes, high stress. And, yes, missing persons too."

I crossed my arms, the skepticism still lingering in my head. "And now you're what, a freelance hero?"

"I'm someone who can't turn his back on a pattern like this. Your sister, those girls, they deserve justice."

I sighed as the weight of his conviction pressed against my doubts.

"Fine. But if we're doing this, I need to know I can trust your judgment. No rogue missions."

"No rogue missions," he agreed.

I sensed a trustable promise in his voice, but he would have to work hard to convince me.

"Eight a.m. I'll bring coffee. And not this swill." He gestured disdainfully at his cup before taking a final swig.

"One more thing," I said. "Has someone in a black SUV followed you?"

He cocked his head to the side. "When did it happen?"

"When my kid was with me."

"You have a dash cam?"

"I have an eight-year-old basic Camry. I roll down my own windows."

He smiled. "I haven't had a tail, but let's keep a watch on that. If someone knows you're investigating this, we'll need to be prepared."

"This isn't new to me. I've arrested a lot of people. It could be any number of ex-cons or their family members looking to scare me."

"Anything else happen recently?"

I shook my head. "A few years ago, I think. Maybe last year. Nothing ever came from it."

"You think it's the same person?"

"I think it's a little too convenient, just like the blown tire I got on my way to pick Alyssa up earlier."

"Tires blow," he said.

"Especially when someone deliberately pounds three nails into them."

"Three?"

I nodded. "All in a row. A man pulled over and showed me. He said it looked like I'd pissed off an ex."

"Would your ex-husband do that?"

I laughed. "He's not an ex yet, but no. He'd never put our daughter in danger. How can it be about the case? I just got it."

"Because they're watching Jessica Steadman. She's got a lot of cash and will spend it all to find her daughter. She's said that multiple times on the air. Maybe they saw you at her place?" He glanced around the room again. "The boxes could be a hint."

"It's possible," I said. "But why wouldn't they just kill her to get her to stop?"

"You saw that place. It's like a fortress. The only thing it's missing is a moat." He added, "I'll see you soon. Be careful. You have my number if you need it," then closed the door behind him.

Sleep eluded me. My life had done multiple one-eighties, all in alternating directions, but Jessica Steadman dropping a bomb of an investigation into my lap gave me focus. Something I could sink my teeth into that might lead me to Molly's abductor. And with it came an unexpected alliance with a man who had seen the worst of humanity and still wanted to fight for free. I preferred to work alone. The GBI scarred me as a team player, but Parks knew the case, and he came off smart. If the cases were connected like he thought, I could use the help.

Could we bring a ghost into the light after all these years? The thought was a cold shower itself, shocking me into a grim determination. "Okay," I whispered to the silence. "I'm ready."

6

Parks had dug up the names of six persons of interest, all puzzle pieces he'd tried to somehow fit together but couldn't. If the man had the hours to cram together puzzle pieces, no wonder Steadman had canned him. Order was one thing, but investigators should never spiral down rabbit holes.

Bob vaulted onto the coffee table with the grace of a sumo wrestler, his front paws dancing on the edge of the box as he eyeballed its contents. Deciding the risk of a cardboard dive was worth the thrill, he cannonballed in, settling among my chaos like he owned it.

Elbow-deep in a cardboard sea, I scribbled notes on stickies and plastered them onto the file fronts before Parks made his second entrance. The knock rattled me. Our gated entrance hadn't offered the security I had hoped for with people able to skirt through it. I swung open the door, and there he stood, smirking.

"How did you get in here?" I stepped aside, more curious than annoyed.

"Morning to you too," he shot back, his smile a mile wide. "I'd spill, but then it wouldn't be my little secret anymore."

I uncontrollably cracked a smile, which I quickly inverted into a scowl. Hands over my heart, eyes rolling to the heavens, I played along. "Cross my heart."

How They Were Taken   49

"DoorDash," he confessed, as if disclosing the location of the Holy Grail. "My lost delivery guy works every time."

Then, as if to sweeten his less-than-desired arrival, he passed me a gas station coffee. Was it supposed to be some kind of peace offering for coming over in the middle of the night? Coffee from the land of convenience?

"Why not just buzz my apartment directly?"

"I live for the surprise factor."

"Thanks." I inspected the Styrofoam cup and smirked up at him. "You actually drink this swill?"

"Hey, give it a shot. It's a step up from Starbucks's charred beans, and your wallet will thank you." He drifted toward the couch, black coffee in tow. "Kept it black. Wasn't sure how you take it."

"Black suits me fine." I shuffled the sea of files to make space for him, then sank into my own chair fortress. "You put all these files in order like this? Got them talking to each other?"

"Me? Nah. My notes are all chicken scratch or voice memos. One of Steadman's people did that. She once called him a wizard who did the heavy lifting, though I can't say what that meant."

"It's impressive," I said.

"Impressive, sure, but what a time suck. There's a lot of information that should go in the dead file, but Steadman kept it all."

"What about the six suspects?"

He rolled his eyes. "All dead ends. Probably took them a little too far, but I wanted to make sure I ruled out everything."

I leaned back, pulling a knee up to my chest. "I figured that's why you got the boot. Too much tinkering, not enough detecting."

He corrected me with a shrug. "I wasn't fired. We just saw the end of the road on different terms."

I nudged further. "What was the breaking point?"

His gaze drifted to the mess of papers and back to me. "Told her the hard truth. Her daughter's either dead or..." His voice trailed off, hinting at darker fates we both understood all too well.

I searched his face for certainty. "And you're sure?"

"Do I have evidence to prove it? No. But put the pieces together. It's been a year. The police dropped the case on the state's golden girl into their cold case files months ago. Something's off, or they've hit a dead end."

The organized chaos in my apartment showed he was probably right. If I had to guess, I would have said the abductor murdered Emma too—or worse, like Parks had implied. They sold her off to the highest bidder. "Cold case or not, it looks like there's something alive in all of this mess."

"Glad we agree on something," he said. "My problem is I kept coming up with a bunch of nothing. I'm missing something, but I can't figure out what. There's a connection to the girls, more than their appearance."

"Serial killers usually have a type, but that type is determined by a reason. Could be our killer lost a sister or a kid with red hair, or someone with red hair hurt him, and he's trying to enact revenge this way."

"I've considered that," he said. "But I haven't been able to figure it out."

"If there's something to find, I'll find it," I said.

"Right," he said sarcastically. "So, did you have a chance to go through it all, or did you finish off the bottle of whiskey instead?"

Ouch. "Listen, let's get one thing straight, okay? If I choose to drink, it's on my own time and none of your business."

"I doubt your soon-to-be ex-husband agrees."

I lit up immediately. "That's the second time you've mentioned my husband. Did you run a background check on me?"

"Of course I did. Haven't you done one on me yet?"

No, I hadn't. In my defense, I didn't know he had struggled to give up his top PI spot on the case until late the night before, so I hadn't exactly had the chance. "I was busy going through your files that lead me nowhere."

"Touché," he said. "Then I'll tell you what." He leaned into the back of the couch. "Twenty questions. Ask me twenty questions, and I'll answer. Anything you want to know. Save you from running the check."

"That's ridiculous."

"Okay, I'll give you the 411 on questions I was asked when the CIA wanted me, and before you ask, yes, I got the job."

Any good investigator could ramble on about his successes for hours. "Ten questions."

"It'll be easier my way."

I exhaled. "Did you take it?"

How They Were Taken   51

"The job? No, I prefer to work without government restraints."

I could understand that. "Fine, but get a move on, please," I said.

He rubbed his palms together and smirked. Sitting up straight and altering his voice to sound persnickety, he said, "Question number one. Can you provide a summary of your most notable achievements during your tenure with NCIS?" He cleared his throat and spoke with a professionalism that surprised me. "Certainly. Throughout my time with NCIS, I spearheaded operations that unearthed espionage networks within the military, broke open international arms-smuggling rings threatening our national security, and solved complex murder cases involving high-profile military personnel. My team and I were instrumental in thwarting a terrorist plot aimed at naval assets, an operation that earned us commendations from the Secretary of the Navy. My personal dedication to these cases was recognized with the Meritorious Service Medal."

He looked at me. "Well?"

"I'm listening."

"What motivated your transition from NCIS to private investigation, given your successful career in solving high-stakes cases?" Another throat clearing. "After twelve years of service, I sought to apply my skills in a new context where I could still make a significant impact. Private investigation offered me the flexibility to choose my cases and the opportunity to help individuals seeking justice on a more personal level. However, my commitment to national security remains unwavering, which is why I'm here exploring opportunities to serve once again in a federal capacity."

"You wanted to be a paper pusher?"

"No, I wanted to be Jason Bourne, but I didn't have the patience to wait around to be promoted. Next question—"

I interrupted him. "Skip the question and just give me the answer, okay? We don't have all day."

"My NCIS background provides me with a unique skill set and perspective. I honed my abilities in forensic analysis, surveillance, and interrogation, all of which are invaluable in the private sector."

He spoke like he was applying for the job of my partner. Which he wasn't, because I didn't need a partner. Help? Fine, but definitely not equal footing.

"Moreover, the high-pressure environment of NCIS taught me how to navigate complex situations with discretion and integrity, skills that are equally important to my private clients. My experience has enabled me to approach cases with a meticulous eye for detail and a deep understanding of the legal and ethical considerations involved."

"And do you follow those legal and ethical considerations?" I asked.

"Not if they get in my way."

Hard not to like a guy like that, though I'd never admit it. "Has any of your experience helped in solving the Steadman case?"

"Not a damn thing."

I laughed. "Are you married? Any kids?"

"Divorced, and no. Wasn't married long enough."

"Okay," I said. "You pass. Now, can we get moving on this?"

He raised an eyebrow. "Isn't it your turn?"

"Fine, but keep it to a minimum. I've got a child abductor to find."

"I've never met a woman who asked me to be quick," he said with a smile. "Okay. What motivated you to use GBI resources in your search for your sister's abductor or killer, knowing it was against policy?"

Way to start with a bang. I cleared my throat and worked hard to play the game I knew was supposed to be played with questions like that. "My desperation to find answers about my sister's disappearance overrode my judgment at the time. I understand the gravity of my actions now."

"Hmm," he said. "That sounds like a practiced answer."

"It is."

"How did you justify breaking protocol to work to achieve your goals?"

"Given the personal stakes, I believed the ends justified the means. However, I recognize the importance of adhering to legal and ethical standards now and would not make that mistake again. I've learned the importance of maintaining professional integrity, even under personal duress, and the impact of my actions on my career and the organization."

"You memorized a speech, didn't you?"

"I have a gift. Well, a few, actually."

"Right. How do you handle high-pressure situations without resorting to unauthorized methods or drinking to get you through them?"

"Are you joking?"

How They Were Taken   53

"Answer the question."

"Whatever. I focus on thorough investigative work, utilizing my network and legal resources, and maintaining patience and persistence."

"And the drinking?"

I swallowed back the snark. "Still isn't any of your business."

"How do you balance the need for justice with the ethical constraints of the investigation process?"

Did he think I would go rogue? Break a hundred laws to catch the guy, only to ruin the case for the state? With my sister in the mix, it wasn't out of the picture. "I believe in working within the framework of the law to find justice, using my knowledge to navigate legal complexities ethically."

"What strategies would you employ to investigate the missing girl case, given its potential connection to your sister's disappearance?"

"I'd approach it with an open mind, leveraging all available resources and data, while ensuring my personal connection doesn't cloud my judgment." I sipped my coffee. "Is that enough?"

"Why not give me the answers you wanted to give?" he asked.

"You want those?" I asked. "Fine." I adjusted myself in my seat. "What motivated me to use GBI resources to search for my sister's killer?"

"Or abductor," he added.

"You said the girls are dead, and I agree."

"We're covering all bases for the questions," he said with a smirk.

"Fine, abductor. I purposefully interviewed for the job knowing I'd have access to information I couldn't get otherwise, and I fully intended to use it to find my sister from the start." I paused and added, "I didn't have to justify breaking protocol because I don't give a damn about protocol when it comes to missing and dead little girls."

"Good answer," he said. "What was my next one?"

"You asked how I handle high-pressure situations without being drunk."

"Well?" he asked.

"I never let booze touch my lips while on the clock. What happens after hours doesn't matter."

"Maybe, maybe not," he replied, his voice low and steady.

I felt the need to set the record straight, so I leaned in, my voice firm yet casual. "Just so we're clear, I don't wear the GBI badge anymore. I'm my own boss now, free to bend the rules as long as I stay out of handcuffs. And I can't promise I won't shy away from skirting the law if it means catching a killer." I wondered if that was how Leland described me to Steadman.

A hint of approval flashed in his eyes. "Good. You're exactly who I need," he said.

I smirked at the irony. "Funny, I thought it was currently my name on Steadman's checks."

His comeback was quick, accompanied by a smug tilt to his smile. "I've been on this case longer. It was mine first."

Parks and I waded knee-deep in paperwork, poring over every file, document, and evidence photograph stuffed in those boxes or saved on the laptop. Meanwhile, Bob decided Parks was the one. He made his move, climbing and sprawling all over Parks in a furry display of affection and rubbing his head against him to claim ownership. Parks didn't reciprocate the sentiment, which seemed to offend Bob's delicate sensibilities. So, Bob did what any self-respecting cat would do: he bit him.

"Ouch!" Parks yelped, the sounds of surprise and pain obvious in his voice as he scooped Bob up and unceremoniously dumped him on the floor. "Your cat just bit me."

I laughed a little chuckle at the absurdity of it all. "That's how he shows his love," I said, trying to explain Bob's complex emotional landscape.

Parks rubbed at the offended spot, eyeing Bob with a newfound wariness. "I prefer the kind of love that doesn't cause physical pain," he muttered, more to himself than to me.

I raised an eyebrow, the corners of my mouth twitching upward. "Then don't get married again," I quipped, unable to resist.

"Trust me, I don't plan to do it again."

"Rough divorce, I presume?"

"Aren't most?" He set a file on my coffee table. "My job became too much for me, and my drinking, too much for her."

"Sounds familiar," blurted out of my mouth.

He pulled a red chip from his pocket. "Two years a few months ago. Carry this with me everywhere I go."

Seeing the coin and knowing what it was humbled me. "Congratulations." I understood his concern over my drinking, but alcohol served a purpose, to relax. It wasn't an addiction.

"Thanks," he said earnestly. "Hardest and the best thing I've ever done. Too bad my marriage didn't survive."

"Is it, though? Is it too bad?"

He smiled. "A year in it was, but now? Nope." He handed me a file to review. "What about you? Still want your husband back?"

"As much as I want an STD." I kept blabbing on without realizing until I'd said too much. "I'm not sure our marriage ending bothered me as much as the fact that it wasn't my decision." I buried my head into a file hoping he'd miss the red splashing my cheeks.

"I understand." He tossed a file onto a pile and graciously changed the subject. "Twenty piles. If this were still my case," he said with a smile, "I'd say we circle back to the forensic information from the crime scenes. See if we can get a hold of anything instead of analyzing photos."

"All five of them?"

"Are you suggesting otherwise?"

"How are we going to get evidence from five cold cases, the military?" I asked.

"The military won't touch a civilian cold case, and one a private investigator is handling? Not a chance."

"I have some connections inside Atlanta PD. I can call in a favor or two."

"You have other connections as well."

I pushed a fallen lock of hair behind my ear. "You want me to use Leland."

He nodded. "Most of the cases were assisted or investigated by them at some point."

"And if they thought there was a reason to reopen them, they would have."

"Then be that reason, Wyatt."

We need to talk.

I stared at Nick's text like it was the plague sucking the life out of me.

About what?

Meet me at Dancing Goats Coffee Bar at 5:30. Don't be late.

Parks had just left with the promise of returning bright and early the next day. It was 3:30. Driving to Buckhead from Cumming could take two hours depending on traffic and accidents, and I would need to jump in the shower. Parks was right. I smelled like booze.

Is Alyssa okay?

She's fine.

Then what is this about?

Just meet me.

Make it 6:00.

Fine. Don't be late.

I dragged myself off the couch and to the kitchen, cracked open a can of cat food, then scooped it into Bob's bowl and set it on the floor. I didn't need to call him. He was already at my feet, wailing like the world was ending. "Your gourmet meal is ready." I eyed the bottle of whiskey staring me in the face on the counter. A shot or two would help me deal with whatever Nick spilled but wasn't smart. "Not now," I told it. I grabbed it and put it under the sink. I couldn't afford to smell like liquor in front of Nick.

Not again.

I showered and grabbed an outfit that hadn't appeared to be worn for multiple days in a row, something more suited for public viewing, and headed to the coffee shop, wondering what Nick could want to talk to me about.

I spotted him sitting at a table in the back corner when I walked in. Two coffee cups sat on the table. I pulled out the chair near the extra cup, sat, then pointed to the coffee. "Is this for me?"

"Yes. Black, but decaf so you can sleep." He responded with something he thought might tug at my heart, like always, when he wanted something.

He eyed the cup, a flicker of something crossing his face—annoyance? Regret? Hard to tell, but I wouldn't bet on regret.

Just as he opened his mouth to speak, Mr. Pendley, a previous neighbor from our Buckhead days, and an older man who had been living in the area

How They Were Taken   57

since before Ford created the first vehicle, wandered over. "Well, lookie here. Haven't seen the likes of you two for a time now. How's that sweet little girl of yours? What's her name? Allie? My memory isn't too good these days."

"It's Alyssa," I said. "It's nice to see you, Mr. Pendley."

He glanced at Nick. "Looks like you two have something important to discuss. Guess I'll be on my way."

"You're welcome to stay and talk," I said. He never stayed long, and I didn't mind yanking Nick's chain a little.

"Actually," Nick offered, "we are discussing something important, but maybe I'll come back in a few days and buy you a coffee. How's that sound?"

Did he want a medal or something? Pendley said he looked forward to that and shuffled out the door.

I got to it immediately. "What's going on? Is Alyssa sick?"

"She's fine. I'm here about something else." His voice was steady, but his fingers tapped against the tabletop, showing me he was uncomfortable or nervous.

The divorce. I should have known. I'd been sitting on the final details, dragging it out just to be a nuisance. Among other requests, he'd already agreed to fund my attorney, who I had worked a few cases for and was going to pro bono my divorce until I told him to swing something in it for him. Ethical? Probably borderline, but Nick had launched the first missile.

I played dumb. "What is it, then?"

"Heather and I are getting married."

As if I didn't already expect that. I gasped. "Oh, congratulations," I said with mock enthusiasm. "But gosh darn it, I can't make it to the wedding. That's the day I have to wash my hair." I leaned back, a smirk finding its way onto my face, my arms still crossed in a protective barrier, while my insides broke into pieces. It was one thing to expect to hear something, but another thing to hear it. I didn't want him back. I just didn't want her to have him either.

"You're only sarcastic when you're feeling insecure." He reached into his computer bag and removed a file, which he slid across the table toward me. "I need you to sign the divorce papers."

A hard-set jaw and sneer replaced my smirk. I stared at the file. "I'm not signing anything until we work out a custody agreement."

"I'm giving you every Wednesday and every other weekend. I still hold primary custody, but I've dropped visitation at my discretion."

Yippee. I would get to see my kid eight days a month. "You've got to be kidding."

He dragged his hand down the side of his face. "I need the divorce, Jen. Just sign the damn papers."

"What's the rush? Is Heather—" It hit me then. "Oh, my God, she's pregnant, isn't she? You got the home wrecker pregnant, and now you're tossing me Alyssa scraps to get me to sign the divorce papers so you can make her an honest woman." I cleared my throat; the bitterness and anger seeping into my voice made it raspy. "Way to make Alyssa a priority."

"She is my priority," he insisted. His eyes locked with mine and briefly revealed a flicker of the old Nick. "That's why I want the divorce now. I don't want her growing up thinking it's okay to have a child without being married."

"Really?" I asked, tapping my finger to my chin. "But cheating on your wife and moving in with a bimbo is acceptable behavior?"

"Read the document. I'm giving you everything you want. Including the house."

"I don't want the house," I said. The idea had lost all appeal the moment Heather and her truckful of commitment crossed the threshold.

"Fine. I'll sell it. You can keep what we make off it. I just want you to sign the papers."

"I'm sorry," I said, though my voice dripped with insincerity. "I'm going to have to read this over and then get with my attorney. I can't sign without fully understanding what's in it."

He exhaled loudly. "You talk a big talk, Jenna. Always saying you want more time with Alyssa, acting like she matters to you."

I cut him off. "She's the only thing that matters to me."

"That's BS, and you know it. Molly and a bottle of liquor are the only things that matter to you. If our daughter mattered, you'd sign the papers."

My heart raced. I clenched my fists. "You're clueless, you know that?"

"We're not getting back together, Jen." His tone was final, closing the

How They Were Taken   59

book on something I once loved but had known died the minute Heather barreled her way into our lives.

I said, "Thank God for that," through gritted teeth.

"It's a standard visitation schedule. It won't get any better. So just sign it."

"You wouldn't have offered that if you hadn't knocked up Heather." I pushed the envelope back toward him. "I deserve more than eight days a month with my kid. I'm her mother," I said, pressing my fingertip into my chest. "Me. Not Heather. You can't turn me into the fun aunt for a new happy family."

He stared at me for a moment before saying, "I'm not trying to make you anything. Alyssa knows who her mother is."

"And I'd like to keep it that way."

"I'm not giving you primary custody. Your career doesn't accommodate it, and even if it did, your drinking schedule certainly doesn't."

In a perfect world, I would have fought hard for just that, but he was right about part of that. Given my work, and its crazy schedule, I couldn't raise a child on my own without a village, but I wasn't much of an *it-takes-a-village* person. What I didn't want was Nick having power over my time with my daughter. And most importantly, I didn't want to be replaced. As for the drinking, I had never let that affect my daughter, and I wasn't about to start. "My drinking is irrelevant. It never impacted Alyssa's life."

"Right," he said. "You're living in a dream world, Jenna."

Screw you, buddy. I wouldn't back down. "I want equal custody. Fifty-fifty."

He closed his eyes and pressed his lips together before saying, "You don't have time for fifty-fifty."

"I'll make time." Alyssa meant the world to me, which was why I worked so hard to find the bad guys. She deserved a better world than the one we lived in.

"Go to rehab."

I clenched my fists under the table. "Do you really think I'm an alcoholic?"

"Maybe not yet, but you will be."

"Has it ever crossed your mind that I drink less now than when we lived together?"

That stumped him. "Honestly, no."

"You left our marriage a long time before Heather came around, Nick. I drank to fill the empty space."

A flash of regret washed over his face. It was the perfect emotion to leave him with.

"Equal custody, Nick." I stood, my chair scraping back loudly. "And then I'll sign."

Instead of sticking around Buckhead, I braved traffic heading north on 400 and drove to Alpharetta. I nudged my car to a dimly lit spot behind Smoke Jack, a place that, like me, embraced its own shadows as much as it did its patrons. I crept in through the back entrance, where no one would notice. I wanted to be alone, but I needed the buzz of the crowd to drown out the static in my head. The bar, with the low murmur of conversations, glasses clinking, and the occasional burst of laughter, would give me that. I found sanctuary in the only empty seat left, tucked away at the far end of the bar. For a moment, I pretended I was invisible, hoping to leave the weight of my own story and the stories of those poor girls behind if only for a few minutes.

The bartender, a guy with an easy grin and eyes that looked like they had seen too much, sauntered over. "What's your pleasure?" he asked, leaning in slightly.

"A shot of whiskey," I replied, my voice steadier than I felt, a trick I'd learned during my Harvard Law years. Weakness and insecurity weren't allowed at the prestigious college. If you showed it, they'd eat you alive.

"What kind?" His casual inquiry felt like a test.

"Decision making is a luxury I don't have at the moment, so, whatever's closest."

He reached under the bar and produced a shot glass with a magician's flair, then pivoted to grab a bottle of Maker's Mark from the shelf. He held it up. "This good?"

How They Were Taken 61

"That works."

He drizzled the shot into a glass and slid it toward me. I threw it back, feeling the liquid heat trace a path down my throat, giving me a momentary blaze of relief. Though not enough to dull the sharp edges of Nick's words, but I doubted another five shots probably could either.

Did I love Alyssa? More than life. But love wasn't the issue. The issue was Molly, and my failure wrapped in an endless loop of what-ifs. If I couldn't find her, couldn't bring her home, even just a slither of remains, how was I supposed to protect Alyssa? The fear gnawed at me, suggesting she'd be better off without me. But my selfishness, a fierce, primal thing, recoiled at the thought. Her life might be better without me. The problem was, I needed her in mine.

The bartender watched me with concern veiled behind professionalism.

I held up my finger. "One more, please."

He poured another shot. I knocked it back, the burn less shocking and more of a dull ache than the first. Pushing the glass toward him, I caught the briefest exchange of glances between two patrons further down, their curiosity likely intrigued by the solitary woman knocking back whiskey like water.

"Another one?" The bartender smiled with a touch of pity attached to it.

"I'm good. I've got some work to do." The words sounded hollow but necessary. I stood and set three crisp ten-dollar bills on the bar. The big tip a thank-you for the brief respite.

My resolve hardened within me as I stepped into the night. Nick's doubts, his skepticism, they fueled my determination. There was no way in hell I'd let him be right. Not about Alyssa. Not about me.

7

I woke up to my cell phone blaring on my nightstand. Bob, startled as well, jumped on my face to express his displeasure. I slid him onto my pillow, spit out a clump of his hair, and checked the caller ID.

Jessica Steadman. It wasn't even seven o'clock. I cleared my throat but still sounded like a woman who'd just smoked a pack of Kool Menthols in one sitting when I answered. "Jenna Wyatt."

"This is Jessica Steadman. I'm calling for an update."

At 6:43 in the morning? Who did that? Rich women, apparently.

"I've finished skimming through and reading the files. My first steps are to go back and review DNA and see if I can get my hands on any evidence from the abductions." I didn't mention Parks because I wasn't sure his removal from the case was mutual.

"That's all you've done? I told you I wanted to be your only client. Ms. Wyatt, I believed you could handle this, but if you can't, I'd—"

Nope. She wasn't going to can me after less than twenty-four hours of reviewing the mountain of papers she gave me. Heck, even the real-life Jethro Gibbs got more time than that. "Mrs. Steadman, with all due respect, you gave me over three thousand pages of material to review and a laptop overflowing with documents less than a day ago. I'm good at my job, but you've got to give me time to do it. If you can't do that, then yes, maybe I'm not the one to work with you." Billion-dollar paychecks be damned, I wasn't going to let her walk all over me.

She went silent, so I added, "As I said, today I'm moving forward with DNA from some of the crime scenes. Technology has improved since the girls' abductions, and we might find something putting it through testing again. If you're not interested, I can return the files in a few hours."

"No. That will be fine," she said, her voice a touch friendlier than before. "I can provide access to a DNA lab if necessary."

"Good to know," I said. "I'll tell you if I need it." I clicked end and stared at Bob. "Well," I said, picking him up and rubbing his head. "Thankfully, that went okay. Otherwise, we'd be sharing a can of Chicken of the Sea tonight." The truth was, I agreed with Parks. I needed that DNA information, but I would look good getting it myself instead of from her.

I dragged myself out of bed and hit the shower. An hour later, I texted Parks and told him to meet me at the Starbucks on 141 in Cumming.

Tapping into cold cases through the GBI wasn't easy. I couldn't guarantee Leland could help, and I didn't want to put him in a compromising position. But contacting my buddy, Drew Holland, at the headquarters lab was a bet I willingly took.

"Wyatt," he said. "Dude, good to hear your voice. You back on the job?"

"Not exactly," I said. "How's things behind the glass?"

"Same, yeah. Same. What can I do you for?"

Drew was somewhere in his late twenties, and though he came off as kind of a nerd, forensics was his native language. It had made him the most popular guy in the GBI.

"I'm working for Jessica Steadman," I said.

He sounded surprised. "Isn't that the rich woman whose husband was murdered and daughter abducted?"

"It is."

"Whoa. That's a solid score. Congrats." He cleared his throat and whispered into the phone. "You need something, don't you?"

"I do. Write this down." I gave him a second to get ready. "Elizabeth

Ryland, age five. Disappeared from her home on September 18, 1998. Zoe Bryant, age five. Disappeared after returning home from a festival on October 18, 2007. Lily Hansen, age five. Disappeared from her home June 18, 2018. Emma Steadman, age five. Disappeared from her home on April 18, 2023. And Molly Simpson, age five. Disappeared from her home April 18, 1999.

"Molly Simpson?" He cleared his throat. "That's your sister, right?"

"Yes."

"And you think they're connected? Like a serial killer? Cool! I haven't had one of those yet."

What Drew lacked in tactfulness, he made up for in talent.

"There are similarities, and I'd like to rerun any DNA we can get a hold of."

The tapping of fingers on a keyboard echoed in my ear. "You talked too fast. Give me the names again."

I repeated them.

"Okay, I'll see what I can do, but you know how it works with assists. No one wants to give us anything, and it could take months."

"It's still worth a shot, but it would be great if you pushed them to move faster."

"How come you didn't work any of these?" he asked. "The ones you were around for, I mean."

Because Leland kept me away from missing girls. "That's a question for management."

"Got it," he said. "Give me an hour or so. I can't say we'll have anything, but I'll call you back either way."

"Thanks, Drew. I appreciate it." I ended the call and fell onto my couch. Was it really happening? Was I getting a real shot at finding out what happened to Molly? I hoped so, because I needed it. I had to know what happened. I had to find her killer. Failure wasn't an option.

Jack Parks sat outside Starbucks with two to-go cups on the table. I greeted him by handing him a list of the victims he'd likely typed

How They Were Taken

himself, and a profile of the abductor, sat, then said, "Thanks for the coffee."

"What's this?" he asked, checking out the profile.

"It's an analysis of our suspect. Given the pattern of abducting five-year-old girls with similar physical characteristics on the same day of different months and years demonstrates a chillingly precise and consistent preference and suggests our abductor has a deep-seated compulsion or reason rather than opportunistic behavior. The guy is likely highly organized and plans each abduction meticulously to avoid detection and capture. The varied socioeconomic backgrounds of the victims indicate that his motivation is not driven by ransom or financial gain but either by opportunity, a specific psychological fixation, or a need that these children fulfilled. That's not to say there isn't a psychological fixation as well, just that it doesn't point to a specific one.

"His ability to kidnap girls from their homes while family is there suggests a chameleon-like adaptability and possibly a high level of intelligence and social engineering skills. He's probably had or has a job or hobby that provides a plausible reason for frequent travel or contact with children from different backgrounds, making him seem trustworthy to both children and adults.

"The lack of a discernible pattern in the timing and location of the abductions points to someone who is extremely cautious, perhaps paranoid about leaving evidence that could lead to his apprehension. It's possible he has a detailed understanding of law enforcement techniques and forensics, maybe through a background in security, law enforcement, or a related field, which helps him stay one step ahead of investigators."

"Wow," Parks said. "How did—"

"I'm not finished. He feels a sense of powerlessness or inadequacy in his daily life. The act of abducting and controlling these girls could be a twisted means of compensating for these feelings, asserting dominance in a domain he can control completely. He may have experienced significant trauma or loss, perhaps of a sister or his own child, around the age of five, leading him to fixate on children of this age as he attempts to recreate or rectify past experiences.

"He may have a place of containment that's isolated and under his control, where he can keep the girls away from the public eye without arousing suspicion. This level of planning and control suggests a deeply entrenched behavior pattern, indicating that he may have been contemplating or practicing these acts for a significant period before acting on them."

He smirked. "Is there some kind of online profiling software I don't know about?"

I sipped my coffee. "I've had a little experience in the subject."

He eyed me and studied my face as if he wanted the answer to appear. "Did you stay up all night doing this?"

"Close enough."

He nodded. "Well done, Ms. Harvard. That degree in criminology suits you."

Not surprised because that would show up on a background check, I replied, "Thanks. It's come in handy." I didn't tell him I had also graduated from the Harvard School of Law. It should have popped up on the report, but if he wasn't aware, I'd feed him that little nugget eventually.

"I have to admit, the change in your tone makes you sound like a professional."

"A professional snob, maybe."

"I didn't want to say that."

I laughed. "I learned a long time ago that the way you speak determines how intelligent people think you are. Most of the time I don't care what people think, but occasionally, I like to dial it up a bit."

"I already knew you were smart." He sipped his coffee. "What about the DNA? Any luck?"

"My contact is seeing what he can get. Hey, Jessica Steadman told me she had connections for DNA if I needed them. Why didn't you use her connections?"

"Mrs. Steadman has power, but she's not as powerful as she thinks. She tried. She couldn't get what I needed."

"Maybe things have changed?"

"In such a short time? I doubt it, but I guess it's possible," he said. "Can you make some calls first?"

How They Were Taken 67

"I'm planning to once I hear back from Drew. In the meantime, we need to start with the first victim like the abduction just happened."

"Elizabeth Ryland," he said. "Her parents still live in the same house. They both work from home."

I grabbed my things. "Let's go, but first I need a double espresso shot in this."

"Sounds like a long night."

"A long, sober night."

He held up his hands. "I wasn't thinking anything."

Parks had contacted the Rylands, letting them know we were headed over. His hands exuded calm as he steered us onto Ronald Reagan Boulevard, moving with the smooth assurance of a seasoned captain navigating through calm waters while a hurricane developed inside me. Diving head-first into the thick of things, getting my hands dirty in the real action, did something for me. Riled me up, maybe? Reading through files and piecing together the puzzles of cases I hadn't been physically part of was one thing, but being in the middle of the action? I thrived there, feeling the most alive.

We took the exit for Windward Parkway, the scenery morphing from commercial to residential.

"Elizabeth Ryland lived in Windward?"

He nodded. "On the lake side, not where you and Nick lived."

"He still lives there." With my kid and the woman living my life.

"Liz Ryland spent a decade searching for her daughter," he began, his voice steady. "She teamed up with John Walsh and the National Center for Missing and Exploited Children. Followed up on every lead." He paused, allowing for a moment of silence before he added, "It's all in the files."

"Yeah, I've read them a few times already," I replied, the stories within those pages echoing in my mind. I should have recognized the street.

"A few times?" He looked to me and then back to the road. "All twelve boxes full?"

"Mostly."

"It took me three days to get through the three boxes Steadman gave me."

"I'm a fast reader." Most of the time my photographic memory worked, but with so much information, I wasn't sure I could recall each detail.

"Clearly. Anyway, none of the leads panned out. It nearly broke her," he continued, the car turning smoothly off Windward Parkway. "She had a stroke in 2008."

"That's awful," I said, the words inadequate for the magnitude of her suffering.

"She's resilient," he assured me. "The stroke was minor, and she made a good recovery. But it was her husband who finally convinced her to declare their daughter dead. He said he couldn't bear losing another person to the monster who took Lizzie."

Nick had hinted at something similar once, but the full gravity of it hadn't sunk in until it was too late. "How did she take it, you digging into her daughter's case again?"

"She's grateful," Parks answered. He navigated through the community's maze of streets, each turn unveiling luxurious homes and lives lived behind closed doors, most probably with secrets that would blow up their images and marriages. "Grateful someone still cares enough to look."

We pulled up in front of a house that rivaled Mount Vesuvius in its grandeur. "Welcome to paradise," Parks announced, his tone bittersweet as he killed the engine. "Or at least, it would be. If Lizzie were still here."

The Rylands' house dwarfed the one Nick and I had shared. The community consisted of upper-middle-class and flat-out rich people, and the various home sizes proved that. Nick and I had lived in a smaller home on the other side of the lake.

A sorrow and a silence filled the air of the Ryland home and spoke louder than words. Liz Ryland appeared as her husband, Jacob, ushered Parks and me into the living room. She carried her grief with a heartbreakingly beautiful elegance. Jacob, on the other hand, had a stoicism that had already cracked some, revealing the depth of his pain. Their hands found each other's with a desperation I had seen in others who shared tragedies. I wondered how that kind of love and commitment felt.

I cleared my throat, completely aware of the enormity of the moment.

How They Were Taken   69

"Thank you for letting us come today. I can only imagine how difficult this is."

Liz offered a brittle smile, her voice a soft Southern lilt that belied the strength it took to speak. "We would do whatever it takes if it means finding out what happened to Lizzie."

"I understand," I said. I told them about Molly, adding, "I have a daughter now, and I can understand how hard it must be for you two."

"When was Molly abducted?" Liz asked.

"Seven months after Lizzie."

Her eyes widened. "From Alpharetta?"

I shook my head. "A little further south, but the details of the abduction are very similar."

"And did you find her?"

"Not yet," I said, "but there's always hope."

"My wife had a mild stroke in 2008. We made the agreement to have Lizzie declared dead. Liz has stopped actively searching, but we always said we would help if someone had information."

"Like Jack," Liz said. She looked at him. "I wish things could have turned out differently."

"So do I," Parks said.

I asked gently, "Can you walk me through that evening as best as you remember?"

Jacob took a deep breath as his hand tightened around Liz's. "It was an ordinary night. We had dinner, watched a little TV, and then it was bedtime for Lizzie. She was in her first week of kindergarten, full of stories about her friends and what she'd learned."

"I understand the security system was off," I said.

Liz sighed. "We felt completely safe here. Windward has its own security department. We just never imagined something so horrific would happen. We were so naive."

"It's not uncommon," I said.

"We had a racoon problem," Jacob said. "They kept setting off the detection devices and waking us. After the fifth night in a row, I hired a company to put out traps and shut off the security."

"I didn't want to see an animal get hurt," Liz said.

"The detective handling the case at the time checked with the neighbors," Parks said. "No one nearby had their cameras on, but there was one who caught a video of a black van coming from the home at approximately two a.m. the night before."

"Nothing came from that," Jacob said. "It didn't have a plate, and no one's seen it here since."

"Everyone made sure their security systems were on after Lizzie disappeared," Liz said, "and the police checked all the homes in the community. None had a van matching that one." She twisted her fingers together.

"Are you with the police?" Liz asked. She looked to Parks for direction.

"I'm former GBI," I said. "Jessica Steadman hired me to investigate the disappearance of her daughter."

"Jack told us the abductions might be related, but we weren't harmed like Mr. Steadman. We didn't even know Lizzie had been taken until the next morning."

"Not every abduction goes as planned," I said. "I was home when my sister was abducted, but I wasn't harmed either. It's likely Mr. Steadman walked in on his daughter's abductor and there was a confrontation." I left out the part about the man restraining me and sticking me in the closet.

"Do you think it's the same person?"

"I think the similarities are too many to ignore," I said. "Which is why I decided," I glanced at Parks, "to work with Mr. Parks on the investigation."

"He told us each girl was the same age as Lizzie and had red hair with freckles," Jacob Ryland said.

"As did my sister," I said. "Would you mind showing me Lizzie's room?"

"Of course," Jacob Ryland said.

They escorted us upstairs. Lizzie's room served as a time capsule of their lost daughter's life, with pink floral-papered walls, ballet slippers, and a shelf of well-loved books. It carried a sense of suspended animation, as if life had paused in 1998 and never resumed, for me an uncomfortably familiar feeling.

Liz's eyes misted over. "I couldn't bear to change it. Some days it feels like she might just walk back through that door."

"You said you weren't aware Lizzie was missing until the next morning, correct?" I asked.

How They Were Taken 71

"Yes," Jacob replied. "I needed to wake her for school. Her bed was empty and the sheets pulled back. Lizzie always tried to make her bed as best as a five-year-old could. At first, I thought she'd crawled into bed with us, so I checked, but she wasn't there. Wasn't anywhere." The anguish in his voice filled the room.

Liz's hands shook. "I remember calling her name, thinking she was hiding and just playing a game. But she wasn't, and the silence swallowed everything."

I noticed a ballet slipper on the shelf, slightly more worn than the other. "She loved to dance?" I asked, a lump forming in my throat. Alyssa's foot would have fit perfectly in that shoe.

"More than anything," Liz whispered, reaching out to touch the slipper. "She'd twirl through the house or walk on her tiptoes."

Parks looked up after scribbling notes on a notepad. "I realize we've discussed this before, but bear with me, okay?"

"I understand," Jacob said. "I've gone over everything multiple times. If your efforts provide even a miniscule amount of help, it's worth it."

I pressed, though gently. "I'm assuming the police questioned you." I turned toward Mr. Ryland. "And considered you a suspect?"

"At first, yes," he said. "But Liz verified I was home all night."

"They did their best," she said, but there was a hint of frustration in her tone. "But without leads, we were stuck from the beginning."

We moved back downstairs.

"Is there anything you think the police or even I might have overlooked?" Jack asked.

Jacob sighed. He'd been asked the questions before, and I knew he'd grown tired of them only leading to more questions. "We've gone over it a thousand times. The police, private investigators like you two. If there was something, it's long gone now."

"You mentioned in your initial interview having a recent verbal altercation with a man you'd found on your property a few days before," I said.

"Yes, and as I told the officers, I have no idea who he was."

"Did he mention your daughter?"

He shook his head. "He was just standing at our fence, looking in the backyard."

"I didn't see any sketches of a man in your file," I said.

"No one asked for one," he said.

I hated shoddy police work. The first thing they should have done was find that guy. People didn't just stand and stare in someone's yard for no reason. "Can you remember what he looked like?"

"I've tried multiple times, but given the circumstances a few days after, I really can't remember. I'm sorry."

"It's okay," I said.

He showed us the path the police believed the suspect took to abduct Lizzie. "Like I said, there were no signs of a break-in. It doesn't make sense."

"He had to pass right by our bedroom," Liz said. "I don't know how I could have missed it."

"And the door was closed?" I asked.

"Open. In case Lizzie wanted to sleep with us, which she did often."

"The guy had to have floated on air," Jacob said. "We didn't hear a thing."

"Barney would have heard," Liz said. She sighed. "He was our German shepherd. We didn't need a security system with him, but he got sick suddenly, and the vet couldn't save him."

We ended our interview after that, thanking them for talking with us and promising to be in touch.

I worked to connect the dots in the not-so-cozy confines of Parks's ride. "So, a couple days before Lizzie's abduction, the dad's out there, having it out with someone he didn't know and can't describe. Fast-forward a bit, and their dog's suddenly sick. Ends up having to be put down. Doesn't take a genius to figure this out."

"Right on the money," Parks muttered, easing the car past the last of the upper-class subdivision's sameness. "Smells like someone killed the dog to make the abduction easier."

I squinted at him. "They do any sort of autopsy on the pooch?"

"Nope," he shot back with his gaze fixed on the road.

I folded my arms as a theory brewed in my head. "How much do you want to bet that dog was poisoned?"

His side-eye told me everything. "Can't take that bet. I'm pretty sure he was, too."

How They Were Taken   73

"I don't recall the vet's information in the file," I said. "Any idea?"

"Midview in Brookhaven. It's in the file."

"Not sure how I missed it."

"You've read through over a thousand documents. Would be easy to forget more than you remember. Oh, and whiskey."

"Screw you, Parks." My cell phone buzzed in my pocket. "It's Drew," I said. "Forensics at GBI." I answered. "You're on speaker with another PI. Talk to me."

"Nothing," he said. "I got nothing. They're not willing to cough up anything. You're going to have to charm some of the badges to get what you need."

Parks glanced at me, raised a brow, and mouthed the word, "Charm?"

"I'm texting you the list of badges now. I'm sure you have them, but I figured this would be easier to access."

"Thanks, Drew. I appreciate it."

"No worries. Hey, I know Jessica Steadman has connections, so if she gets what you're looking for and you want me to test it or whatever, I'm in."

"What about your boss?" I asked, referring to Leland.

"I hear he likes you."

"We'll see," I said and disconnected our call just as his text message came through.

"You don't want to use the GBI, do you?" Parks asked.

"I'd rather no one get burned because of me."

"Understood. I think we ought to nix interviewing the victims' families for now. Didn't give us anything new. Want to hit up the detectives?"

"Steadman is looking for an update. I need to tell her something."

"Let's go to the vet, then we'll figure out what to do next."

"I didn't see anything in the files about pets. Did any of the other families have them?"

"The Hansens did."

"How did it die?"

"It got loose and ran into traffic."

I cringed. "That's awful, but it could be the way our perp is removing obstacles." I treaded carefully. "How did you miss that?"

"The dog got out a month before the abduction. It didn't fit the time frame."

"Maybe we should reconsider that," I said.

"Maybe you can use some of that charm you're rumored to have and get something I couldn't."

"I'll do my best."

He smiled. "Can't wait to see what this charm thing looks like."

"What you see is what you get. Hey, can you call the Rylands?" I asked.

"Sure. Why?"

"They might still have the dog's remains."

8

We repeated the entire shebang of entering Jessica Steadman's estate as I had before. The look on her assistant's face when she saw Parks with me had me almost bust a gut laughing.

We waited in the same office, Parks looking like he had just lost a big bet while I stared at the same masculine decor, wondering if she would ever change what had very likely been professionally designed for her husband.

"What is he doing with you?"

Her voice shocked me out of my thoughts. "Mrs. Steadman," I said, standing.

"Jessica," Parks said.

Jessica?

"I'll ask again," she said, ignoring Parks completely. "Why is he here?"

"I've got a house filled with files and a computer full of videos and other documents. Mr. Parks spent almost a year on this investigation. He knows the case and is a valuable resource."

"I hired you because he and I couldn't work together."

"And you don't have to," I said. "He's working with me. If it suits you, I won't bring him to our meetings, but two investigators are always better than one."

She looked at me, not Parks. "Does he expect to be paid?"

"I want to find the person that did this, Jessica," he said. "I don't need to be paid."

She walked over to the desk and removed the same large check register as before, scribbled on a check, ripped it off, then walked it over to Parks. "I don't deny you are a valuable resource, and I won't have you working for free. Perhaps Ms. Wyatt is correct. Two investigators are better than one. This, however, is a trial. If we don't get results soon, I'll stop payments."

He didn't move to take the check. "I don't need or want the money, Jessica. I'm just here to help."

She eyed him suspiciously. Was there something more to their relationship? What was I missing?

"Fine." She ripped up the check, then walked behind the desk and sat. "Update me."

"I need your DNA assistance," I said. The Rylands did still have their dog's remains and had allowed us to borrow them for testing. I removed Brutus's container from my bag. "We need this tested."

"What is it?"

"The remains of a German shepherd that died in 1999."

She glanced at Parks and asked, "Is this the Rylands' dog?"

He nodded.

She knew the case, of course. That could go either way for me.

"Is it possible to get DNA from cremated remains?" she asked. "Especially after this long?"

Thank God she didn't know everything. "Sometimes. Are you aware of how cremation works?"

She crossed her arms. "Enlighten me."

"The body is subjected to temperatures in the range of fourteen hundred to eighteen hundred degrees Fahrenheit, which typically destroys most organic materials, including DNA."

She sipped a cup of tea her assistant had brought in. "Please continue."

"Even with the high heat, it's possible to find fragments of bone or teeth that may contain trace amounts of DNA."

"Has it been done before?"

How They Were Taken 77

"Yes, ma'am," I said. "The success depends on several factors, including the conditions of cremation and the remains themselves."

"And how difficult is the extraction process?"

"Complicated, to say the least. The bone fragments must be pulverized into a fine powder, which takes a highly sophisticated process. If the DNA recovered is highly fragmented and degraded, obtaining a complete genetic profile will be difficult."

She angled her chair to the side and crossed her legs. "And what are you looking for in a dog's DNA that might lead you to my daughter's abductor?"

"Actually," I said, "we're looking for poison, which may show up in the fragmented teeth and bones, but the odds of finding it are slim."

"And if successful, you think it will help how?"

"These missing girls were investigated by different departments. To the best of my knowledge, they didn't share information, which is common with cases like these. The abductor could be connected to the dog's death, and if it is, that could be the break in the case we've been looking for."

"How so?"

"Dogs act as an alarm and deterrent for criminals."

She glared at Parks. "Why didn't you suggest this?"

"There is only one other family with an animal, and it was hit by a car over a month before their daughter's abduction. I considered the connection, but given the time frame, I didn't pursue it further."

"Then you should have." Her face reddened.

Ouch, that felt personal.

"We are now," he said, his face stoic.

"I don't have an animal," she said to me. "Did you?"

"No, ma'am, but he didn't abduct the girls because they did or didn't own a dog. It's merely a way to further link the girls' abductions."

"Fine," she said to me. "I'll take a portion of the remains and have them delivered to my contact."

I handed her the remains. "I'd like their information, please," I said.

"I'll get that then as well. Please keep me informed." She stood and walked out of the room.

I looked at Parks and whispered, "Are we done?"

"We need the rest of the remains back first."

A few minutes later, one of her staff returned with the dog's remains.

"Now can we go?" I asked.

"Yes."

"So, how many rounds did you two go?" I asked quietly.

Parks, bless his evasive heart, wouldn't even grace me with a side-eye. "How many rounds of what?"

I snorted and purposefully rolled my eyes so hard I saw my brain. "Oh, come off it, Parks. I can spot a jilted lover from a mile away."

We walked toward the vendor entrance.

"Let me guess. You slept with her, and then gave her the old heave-ho?" I couldn't keep the snickers at bay. "Don't tell me you had the audacity to ditch the wealthiest woman in Georgia."

Outside, he focused on the driveway as if it held the secrets of the universe. "To be fair, one must actually be in a relationship to qualify for dumping privileges."

We climbed into the car.

"Playing Twister in the sheets and working for the woman qualifies as a relationship in my book." I shook my head, trying to hide my amusement. "Listen, whatever soap opera you've got running with her, if it's going to throw a wrench in my investigation," I shook my thumb toward the window, "then it's time to hit the road, buddy."

"It's a non-issue," he insisted. "It won't interfere."

"Whatever you say," I said with a smile.

"Question," he said, changing the subject. "How'd you know the forensic stuff?"

"Uh, former GBI here, remember?"

"I'm aware, but it didn't sound like an agent talking. It sounded like a forensic scientist."

"I took a few forensic classes in college."

"Man, you must have a photographic memory or something, because that sounded like it was straight out of a manual."

"That's the gift I mentioned before, photographic memory. Though it's not always consistent."

He looked at me and blinked. "You're kidding, right?"

How They Were Taken   79

"About having it or its inconsistency?"

"Both."

"Neither. If I'm reading a lot of material quickly, like the millions of case files Steadman gave me, it's not as good."

"That's incredible. The GBI must have loved that."

"Not when I used it against them."

He laughed. "I bet. The detective who handled Lizzie Ryland's investigation retired about ten years ago. I met with him, but he didn't have much to say. I'd say we could give it a shot, but it might be worth it to head to that department first, see if we can get our hands on any evidence from the scene."

"You want me to use my former GBI status, don't you?"

"Former NCIS didn't work, but what's to lose?"

"Let's give it a shot." Nick's text tone echoed from my bag. "Great." I read the message.

Not signing the papers won't stop me from getting divorced. I'll just have my attorney tell the judge you won't cooperate because you're bitter.

"Something urgent?" Parks asked.

"Just the almost-ex bullying me to sign the divorce papers." I tossed my phone back into my bag.

"Why the rush?"

"Heather, my soon-to-be ex-husband's girlfriend, is pregnant."

"Ouch."

"I don't care. I just don't want her baby making Alyssa second-rate."

"I doubt you'd let that happen. Does he want to marry her?"

I nodded.

"And that doesn't bother you?"

I looked at him as he glanced at me. "This is a missing persons investigation, not a therapy session, Parks. Let's stick to business only."

He saluted me. "Yes, ma'am."

The lobby of the Alpharetta Police Department echoed the affluence of the surrounding community—gleaming floors, modern furnishings, and an air

80 CAROLYN RIDDER ASPENSON

of polished professionalism. Yet, behind the protective barrier of bullet-proof glass sat an officer, his young face marked by a hint of cynicism unusual for his age. Some would consider it entitlement, but I recognized working for law enforcement could take its toll on a soul fast.

"From 1998?" he asked. "I was two. I'd say most of the guys that covered that are dead or retired."

His remark hung in the air and soured my mood. Someone clearly hadn't taken their happy pill that morning. "We'd like to talk to the chief, please," I managed to say, keeping my tone as prim and proper as I could muster. Gone were my days as a GBI agent, where a flash of my badge would have sufficed, replaced by the need for charm, which was not something I kept readily available in my toolbox.

"I'll give him a call. Not sure if he'll see you or not," the officer replied with a nonchalance that grated on my nerves.

"Thank you," I replied, my teeth grinding into that fake smile.

"Hey," Parks chimed in after the guy walked away. "Try not to bite their heads off. We might need them later."

"You haven't seen me growl yet, let alone bite," I shot back, half joking.

He blanched. "Good to know."

An officer escorted us to Chief Reginald Baxter's office moments later. The room was an even more impressive statement of the community's wealth—spacious and impeccably decorated. Mahogany bookshelves filled with an array of law enforcement accolades and personal memorabilia lined one wall. The picture window's panoramic view of the meticulously landscaped grounds balanced the likely brutality of the cases discussed within the walls.

The chief himself carried the air of someone accustomed to power but wearied by the burdens it brought. Given his size, somewhere above six feet and built like a boxer, he wasn't someone to mess with.

"I'm assuming you're here about the Merritt investigation?" Chief Baxter began, his voice betraying a hint of resignation as he motioned us to sit. He cleared his throat, looking slightly discomfited. "I've had two other PIs here looking for information. Y'all are fighting like bucks trying to win the client on that one."

The Merritt case was the talk of the town—a brutal, high-profile crime

How They Were Taken   81

that had everyone on edge. But we were there for something just as important and far too neglected.

"I don't take cases without a contract," I stated firmly, cutting through the assumptions.

"Neither do I," Parks added quickly.

"We're here about a missing girl case from September 18, 1998," I clarified. I watched his face change as he processed the date. "Elizabeth Ryland, age five. She was abducted from her home here in Alpharetta. The Windward subdivision."

His eyes widened slightly. "I remember the case, but that's a while back. May I ask why?"

"We're working with Jessica Steadman to locate her missing daughter," I explained, watching him lean back in his chair and stroke his chin thoughtfully.

"That must bring you in a pretty penny," he remarked, scanning us with a discerning eye. "She thinks you're experienced enough to handle the investigation?"

"I'm former GBI," I responded, with pride and assurance steady in my voice. "Ten years on the job. Last three as the assistant special agent in charge." There was no need for further justification or to tell him Leland canned me.

"Former special agent in charge, NCIS," Parks stated succinctly, letting his record speak for itself as well.

Baxter nodded. "What do you need from the file?"

"We have the documentation in the file," I said, hinting at our preparedness and the leverage it gave us. "But we've come across some new information, and we'd like to borrow the evidence from the scene or at least look at it here."

His eyebrow arched. "Exactly how did you get copies of our case files?"

"Jessica Steadman is a powerful woman." Parks's response implied more than he stated.

Baxter's demeanor showed both resignation and curiosity. He stood. "That she is." His attempt at a smile faltered. "Give me a moment, please."

"You think he'll give it to us?" I asked.

"Nope. He'll let us look at it with him babysitting."

"Control."

He nodded. "Some people think control is power."

"Sometimes it is," I said.

He returned a few minutes later, sat behind his desk, and leaned back in his chair. I figured he had probably put in a quick call to someone over at the Steadman residence to double-check our credentials. When he finally settled back in, I noticed a hint of resignation in his tone. "I've got an officer retrieving the items you requested. They're not gifts, mind you. They're part of the official case file."

I suspected he let us take it because Jessica Steadman wielded so much power. "Of course," I said.

"In return, I'd appreciate any new leads you might uncover on this investigation."

"Your cold case," Parks pointed out.

Baxter's gaze fixed on Parks. "Are we in agreement?"

"Absolutely," I cut in before anything could escalate. "We're all playing for the same team here. If we solve it, we'll let you know that as well."

Back at my apartment, Parks and I spread out the evidence bags on the living room floor. I took meticulous notes on each item while Parks handled the photography.

He held up a small, bloodstained shirt with a puppy face on it. "Her mother confirmed she went to bed in this."

"Why would her abductor switch her into a clean shirt and leave the one with his DNA? To keep the blood off himself or his car?" I mused, more to myself than to Parks.

"He probably took her without a shirt. I doubt he had enough time to find a new one."

I scanned the notes. "I don't see anything saying they tested the blood on her shirt." I leaned my head back and sighed. "Why the hell not?"

"DNA testing took a long time back then," he said. "They probably didn't want to wait for the results."

I gave him a deadpan stare. "That's idiotic."

How They Were Taken 83

He shrugged. "Didn't say it wasn't."

I examined the shirt carefully. "We need to test the blood."

"The guy broke into the home and abducted the child without getting caught. You think he's going to switch out a shirt with blood on it by accident?" he asked.

"No. I think he got blood from a bank and splashed it onto the shirt to keep suspicion off himself." I held the shirt up for him to examine. "Look at the blood pattern. It's not much. He could have laid the shirt out flat and flicked blood at it."

"Good point. He also might not have considered the future of DNA retrieval. With more criminals in the system now, maybe we'll get a hit that we can link to the abductor."

"I'll drop it with GBI's forensic guy and see what he can do," I said. Just then, my apartment buzzer sounded, though I wasn't expecting anyone. "Give me a sec," I said, heading over to the door. I peered through the peephole and swung the door open after seeing my regular mail person wave. "Hey, Mr. Martin, how are you?"

"As good as it gets," he replied, his voice dry as he handed me a certified letter. His fingers in a pair of his usual latex gloves. "Got something important for you here."

I took the envelope, noting the lack of a return address. After signing for it, I thanked him and closed the door. I turned the envelope over in my hands cautiously, knowing it had to be from Nick.

"You always that suspicious?" Parks quipped from the couch.

"I don't usually receive certified mail without a return address, so yes," I retorted.

"Probably about your divorce," he ventured, immediately coughing slightly. "Sorry, that sounded insensitive."

After closer examination, I realized it wasn't from Nick's lawyer; they always printed their address in bold, black letters. I carefully opened the envelope and immediately regretted not donning gloves like Mr. Martin. Inside, a chilling note lay flat with only two sentences:

Your daughter is beautiful. I especially like her in her ballet shoes.

A shiver ran down my spine, the words echoing ominously in my head.

"Someone's watching my daughter."

9

"Let me see," he said. "Got gloves?"

I flicked my head toward the kitchen. "In the pantry. Second shelf."

He slipped on a pair of latex gloves, gave me a pair, and carefully took the letter while I put them on. "Okay. Let's not panic."

My pulse hit a dangerous number. "Not panic? A psycho is watching my daughter. Hell, Parks, should I just grab a beer and chill?" I pointed to the letter. "That's a threat because I'm looking for Steadman's kid."

"We don't know that yet. Let's talk it through, make sure there are no other possibilities before we go balls to the wall on it, okay?"

Bob sat on the dining room table, watching me closely.

I paced from my couch to my deck door, going back and forth and running every horrific scenario through my brain. The maniac taking Alyssa during ballet. At school. The playground.

"This has to be from the person in the black SUV. They're stepping up their game." I exhaled. "I need to call Nick."

"Jenna, take a breath. You don't want to do that yet."

"He needs to keep her with him at all times." I went for my cell phone on the coffee table, but Parks got it first. "What the hell? Give me my phone."

"What if it's someone you put away messing with you? You go to Nick,

How They Were Taken   85

and he won't let you within five feet of your kid. Doesn't matter who sent the letter."

I rubbed my temples. "I'm hiring someone to watch her. I've got the money."

"That's a good idea," he said. "I know the perfect PI." He handed me my phone and pulled his from his pocket. "I'll call her now."

An hour later, we sat at a small coffee shop in Dunwoody with Tiffani Bateman. If you searched "stereotypical Southern woman" on the internet, Tiffani's picture would have appeared at the top of Google. She waltzed in like she had just stepped out of *Southern Living* magazine, all charm and pearls, with a smile that could melt the heart of a grizzly bear. Parks had said she was forty-two. I would have guessed younger from her polished look that screamed cotillions and sweet tea, her perfectly coiffed blond hair and pastel dresses more suited for a garden party than a stakeout. She spoke in a syrupy Southern drawl typical of every former beauty queen.

I'd wanted someone like Jane Rizzoli from *Rizzoli & Isles*. Instead, I got Suzanne Sugarbaker from *Designing Women*. Fire and brimstone she wasn't. Lipstick and hairspray was more her thing. I wondered if she could protect my daughter when the chips were down or if she would just offer the bad guys a slice of pecan pie.

She leaned back in the chair and smiled at me. "Are you done assessing me, darlin'?"

Parks laughed. Had he warned me of what was coming, I could have controlled my facial expressions.

Instead of skirting the issue, I decided to be honest. "You resemble what every girl from my high school looks like now."

"Listen, I get it. For the record, I am a former beauty queen. I know I look like I just stepped off the set of *Gone with the Wind*. But don't let the exterior fool you, sweetheart. I'm not just a pretty face with a charming smile." She flashed that charm at Parks.

"She's right," he said.

"Thank you, darlin'." She looked back at me. "I spent fifteen years with the FBI, and I was damn good at what I did. Need more?"

The FBI? Doing what? Serving coffee and donuts to the agents? "Yes," I said. "This is my kid we're talking about."

"Understandable," she said, continuing. "I was a top-tier profiler, specializing in behavioral analysis and counterterrorism. I've taken down cartel leaders, tracked serial killers, and dismantled human trafficking rings. I know how to read people, find patterns in chaos, and anticipate moves before they happen. Not only can I watch your daughter, but I can also tell you what you need to know about the person threatening her."

We shared similar traits, but none in fashion. "I think it would be hard to take on a possible killer in," I pointed to her dress and heels, "that outfit."

"I don't wear the stilettos on the job. Just a standard pump." She smiled.

"That helps," I said with sarcasm.

"Trust me, sweetheart, I can handle myself in a fight. I've got advanced hand-to-hand combat training, Krav Maga, and a black belt in tae kwon do. I've faced down suspects twice my size and walked away without a scratch. I'm an expert marksman, trained with everything from handguns to sniper rifles. I don't miss. Ever. High-speed pursuits, evasive maneuvers, precision control—I've done it all. If someone tries to run, I guarantee I'll catch them."

Okay, she had begun to impress me. "What about your surveillance techniques?"

"Surveillance and countersurveillance are second nature to me. I can follow someone for days without them ever knowing I'm there. Especially dressed like this. I can easily gather intel and get the evidence we need to put someone away for a very long time. I'm also a whiz with technology. Cyber forensics, hacking, and data retrieval—I can dig up secrets people think they've buried deep. I can find anyone, anywhere, and make sure they have nowhere to hide."

Was she for real? "You sound like a law enforcement genius, and too good to be true."

"I have an analytical mind. Genius level. I understand we share that trait."

I couldn't deny that. "What's your record with the FBI?"

"Ninety-seven of one hundred and six. It's lower than I would have liked, but the highest on record. The Clementine case. Johnathan Spain. The Ray murders. I led and closed them all, along with my team, of course. Shall I go on?"

How They Were Taken   87

The Clementine case shattered anything I'd ever investigated. A seventeen-year-old sociopath slaughtered a family of twelve in cold blood. This kid excelled as the top student in his class and slipped through law enforcement's grasp like a chameleon. Until he didn't.

"The Clementine case took over a year to close."

"My team took it over and closed it in three months. Verify if you'd like."

"I can verify that," Parks said.

"Thank you, hon." She smiled at Parks and then directed her attention back to me. "I understand all the skills in the world won't stop you from worrying about your daughter's safety, but let me at least try to put your mind at ease one more time. I'm not just capable—I'm the best damn protection she could ever have. Anyone who tries to get to her will have to go through me first, and trust me, that's a battle they're guaranteed to lose."

Admittedly, someone who looked like her would not be on my radar if I were into crime. "Okay," I said. I filled her in on the situation, which included our investigation and how it was likely the reason for the letter.

"Got it," she said. "What about your ex? Are you telling him?"

"I haven't decided."

"Would you like my opinion?"

"Sure."

"Don't. His behavior and demeanor will change and will make it harder for me to do my job."

Nick would lose his mind if I didn't tell him, but she was right. He could make it harder for her, and I wanted my kid safe. "I won't, but if things get out of hand, I'm going to have to."

"Understood," she said.

"Why did you leave the FBI?" I asked.

"Let's just say we no longer used the same moral compass."

"Wyatt," Parks said, "her input could help us with our investigation."

"Can you get DNA tested?"

"I can, but it would be under the table, and I can't guarantee something happening."

"That's my issue as well."

"We can use the DNA company Steadman's got," Parks said.

"Only if we have to," I said.

Tiffani's experience helped me worry less about Alyssa, but not enough to lower my heart rate to something near normal. I texted Nick, asking to have her call me when she got home from school.

Why?

Because I'm her mother.

I threw my phone into the cupholder of Parks's car and called Nick a few choice names.

"So, that went well?" Parks kidded.

"As well as a priest texting an atheist. I don't want to talk about it."

"Okay, let's talk this case through," he said. "We're investigating the abduction of the daughter of the richest woman in the state, and probably the southeast, if not the country."

I didn't bother reminding him that I was investigating, and he was assisting. "Really? I didn't know."

"I'm not finished."

My eyes shifted toward him. "Go on, then."

"An abduction that is very likely connected to four other abductions, one being your sister."

"Tell me something I don't know, Parks."

"How many of the victims' parents received notes from the abductor?" he asked.

"None that we know of, but the guy could have changed his MO."

"I never noticed anyone suspicious while I worked the case alone," he said.

"That doesn't mean he wasn't stalking you or keeping tabs on the other families."

"You've been involved in multiple criminal investigations, some making national news," he said. "Anyone with a computer could research your background. It wouldn't be hard to put it together. Former GBI agent's kid sister went missing in the nineties, now she's investigating the abduction of the wealthiest woman's daughter. Let's mess with her."

"For what? Shits and giggles?"

He laughed. "You sound like my grandmother saying that. My point is,

How They Were Taken

we can't guarantee the note is from our guy, and we can't be sure the person who wrote it is even planning to make a move on your kid."

"I know, but I'd rather not sit on it and hope for the best."

"I wouldn't either. I just think it's important to keep things in perspective."

I made eye contact again. "You still agree with Tiffani? You don't think I should tell Nick?"

"I don't see the need until we know more. Why create panic and maybe stop you from seeing your kid because some a-hole thought it would be fun to mess with your head?"

Why was my first thought that Heather the home-wrecking whore sent the note?

Parks laughed.

"What's so funny?" I asked.

"Your face." He laughed again. "The note. You think his fiancée sent it."

"I do not."

"Nice try, but it's all over your face."

Was I that transparent, or was he that good? The answer sucked either way. "Yeah, well, I wouldn't put it past her. She's taken my house, my husband, and my kid for the most part. What's stopping her from taking it a step further and making it a permanent deal?"

"Fear."

"What's that mean?" I asked.

"You scare the hell out of me. Imagine what you do to her."

The drive from Dunwoody to the Georgia Bureau of Investigation regional office in Conners, Georgia, took over an hour on a good day without traffic. But a good day without traffic or accidents in the metro Atlanta area didn't exist. We hit two car accidents on 285, but with some skilled, slightly reckless driving, Parks got there in an hour and twenty minutes, while I white-knuckled the passenger door handle the entire way.

"I saw my life pass before me multiple times on that ride," I said.

"Come on, Jenna," he said with a smile. "Grow a pair."

I offered him a middle finger in response. I stared at the unassuming building. "Here we are, back at my former home base."

"You drove here daily? I'm surprised you're still alive."

"I have excellent defensive driving skills."

The building, a squat, one-story unassuming thing, sat among a cluster of pine trees, with a parking lot half full. Most GBI staff worked out of the office.

"Ready for this?" I asked, stepping out and slamming the car door shut.

Parks nodded as he adjusted his sunglasses.

"Let's just hope Leland's in a good mood," I said. Though Leland would do most anything for me, if he'd had a hellish day, the odds were he would take it out on me with an assaultive lecture. Venting was his superpower.

We walked up to the entrance and into the utilitarian and bureaucratic lobby, with its linoleum floors that squeaked underfoot and beige walls lined with official notices. The receptionist gave us a cursory glance, said, "Wyatt," and returned to her work.

"Pearson," I said. "Is Leland available?"

She contacted his assistant without another word as we walked over to the small metal chairs near the front door.

"She's a Georgia peach," Parks said. "Seems to like you."

I smirked. "About as much as she loves everyone. Pearson isn't rainbows and sunshine."

"Really? I hadn't noticed."

An agent walked us to Leland's office a few minutes later. He looked up from his cluttered desk as we entered. His hair had grayed since we'd begun working together, but his eyes still had that piercing intensity that made him both respected and feared.

"Jenna." He smiled and moved as if he wanted to stand but backed off at the sight of Parks. "Parks. I don't think either of you are here just to say hello. Is this about the Jessica Steadman investigation?"

"Yes and no." I held up the bag with Lizzie Ryland's shirt. "This shirt belongs to Elizabeth Ryland. She disappeared from her home on September 18, 1998. We need it analyzed as well as a cremated dog's remains."

How They Were Taken 91

Leland leaned back in his chair and rubbed his temples. "You know I can't just hand over GBI resources for private investigations."

"I know, but I don't know if Steadman's DNA labs are as good as Drew. Please, Leland. Think of it as aiding an important investigation."

"You've got to understand the position that puts me in."

"I do," I said. "You do remember recommending me to Steadman, correct?"

"There you go, throwing my good deeds in my face." He smiled at Parks. "Try to help a friend and look what it gets me."

"She made me drive here," Parks said. "She's the boss."

I laughed. "Right."

Leland eyed me, then looked back at Parks. "Congratulations for making it here alive. Rule number one: Never drive with Jenna Wyatt on the highway."

"What's rule number two?" he asked.

Leland smiled. "You'll find out soon enough." He turned to me. "Fine, get it to Drew, but do me a favor, keep a low profile. Last thing I need is a bunch of questions about why I'm helping a couple of private eyes."

"Thanks, boss man." I called him by the name I'd called him for ten years. "I owe you one."

"Yeah, yeah. Just get out of here before I change my mind," he grumbled and waved us off.

We headed to the forensics lab in the basement of the building.

Drew greeted us with a broad smile. "Wyatt!" His voice went up an octave from his surprise. "Can't believe you've got the balls to show up here."

Parks chuckled.

"Oh, you know what I mean," Drew said, blushing.

I introduced Drew to Parks, then handed him the evidence bag and dog remains. "We need a DNA test on this shirt, please, and the dog in this container."

His eyes widened as he glanced at the container. "There's a dog in there?"

"The remains of one," Parks said.

"Like I said before, I'd love to help, but I need the boss's approval."

"Already got it."

He examined the shirt. "Shouldn't be a problem. Was it tested before? I can compare results."

"There's nothing in the files," I said.

"Seriously?" He noted the date on the bag. "This was a long time ago, but damn, that's just poor police work."

"Don't have to tell me that," I said. "The dog remains will be harder."

"I love a challenge. Don't worry. It's all good. We've come a long way since 1998. Back then, DNA testing was archaic. They needed large samples and took forever to get results. Thank God it's better today. With advancements like polymerase chain reaction and short tandem repeat analysis, we can get accurate results from even the smallest samples in a matter of days."

"Can you say that in layman's terms?" Parks asked.

I glanced at him. "PCR is a laboratory technique that allows scientists to take a very small sample of DNA and amplify it to a large enough amount to study in detail. STRs are small sequences of DNA that repeat multiple times in a row."

"The number of repeats can vary greatly between individuals, making them useful for identifying people," Drew added.

"Oh," he said. "Got it."

Drew led us to his workstation, where sleek computers and high-tech lab equipment lit up with activity. "Do you want to stick around and watch me do my thing?" he asked. "I can do it now. It's a slow day. Just two samples to work on so far."

"That would be great," I said. I knew Drew well enough to know it was important to him to show off his skills, and they were impressive.

"Cool," he said. "I'll start with the shirt first." He smiled at Parks. "Want me to explain as I go?"

"Sure," Parks said.

"Okay, I'll start by extracting the DNA. This involves breaking open the cells and isolating any DNA I can find. If I find some, which I'm sure I will, I'll amplify it using PCR so we have enough to work with."

Parks watched intently as Drew explained the steps. "How reliable is this process compared to the old methods?" he asked.

"Oh, dude. Much more reliable," Drew replied. "In the late nineties,

How They Were Taken 93

they relied heavily on RFLP. It's restriction fragment length polymorphism analysis, which required a lot of high-quality DNA. I'm sure you know how hard that is to get most of the time. It took forever. Once I have enough DNA, I'll run it through an electrophoresis machine, which will separate the DNA fragments by size. This creates a unique DNA profile, and I can then compare to any known samples or databases."

Drew's hands moved with practiced precision as he carefully prepared the shirt for testing, using swabs to collect potential DNA from the fabric.

"This process also includes checking for any contaminants," he continued. "Modern techniques can differentiate between multiple sources of DNA, which is incredibly useful in cases involving multiple individuals."

"How long do you think it'll take to get results?" I asked.

"Like I said, given the current workload, I'd say about forty-eight to seventy-two hours," Drew said, sealing the samples and labeling them meticulously. "I'll prioritize this for you, though. Should have something sooner if all goes well."

I explained what we needed from the dog remains.

"That could take a while," he said.

"Understood," I said.

"Thanks. We really appreciate this," Parks said, clasping Drew on the shoulder.

"No problem. Always happy to help out, especially for a good cause," Drew replied with a grin. "I'll keep you updated."

Jessica Steadman sat at her monstrosity of a desk and judged me like I was a waste of time. "The dog's DNA was useless." She slid a report across the highly glossed wood top. "See for yourself."

I scanned the document, then handed it to Parks. "It was a long shot, but one we had to check. We're having another forensic specialist look at the remains as well."

"Then it most certainly was a waste of my time and an abuse of my personal relationships with the lab."

"Did they say that?" I asked.

"Wyatt," Parks mumbled.

Steadman blanched. "They didn't have to. What's the point of testing the DNA from an animal in the first place? You yourself said it would be a miracle if we could find something."

I hadn't said that exactly, but not in the mood to deal with her pompous entitlement, and even though aware she could fire me on the spot, I leaned in and said, "Mrs. Steadman, maybe I'm wrong, but I would think nothing that could lead us to finding your daughter would be a waste of time. If you don't agree, then perhaps I'm the wrong investigator for this job."

The side of her mouth twitched. I half expected her to lean forward and slap me across the face like in old black-and-white movies.

She didn't. Instead, she jotted something on a piece of paper and handed it to me. "The lab will work directly with you from now on. I expect reports as per our previous discussion." She glanced at Parks, then back at me. "Is he still beneficial to your investigation?"

"Yes, ma'am."

She opened her drawer, removed that same large check register from before, and scribbled out another check. Ripping it from the book in one swift motion, she then set it on the desk in front of Parks. "I pay the people who work for me."

He didn't bother looking at it. "I don't work for you."

Well. The air in the room had gone from 1940s flick to daytime soap opera. If we stayed there much longer, someone would end up dead or a long-lost twin.

"It's the second time she's offered," I blurted out. "Just take the damn check." I looked at Steadman. A smile threatened to curve on her lips.

Parks took the check.

Parks ripped it up the second we climbed in the car. "I only took it because you threw a fit."

"I threw a fit?" I laughed. "I don't know what happened between you two—well, I know, but I need the 411. I have to figure out how to handle the two of you together."

"I told you, we don't have a relationship."

"Fine. Your previous relationship."

"It's not relevant to the investigation."

How They Were Taken 95

"Like hell it isn't. She can't look at you without wanting to scratch your eyes out." I failed to mention that I thought she might get off on that kind of thing.

"Nice, Wyatt."

"I'm not kidding. I can't let whatever happened between you two screw this up. Either tell me what happened so we can figure out how to deal with it, or we're done."

He exhaled. "Like I said, we slept together a few times. It was no big deal."

"Seems like it was to her." I paused, then added, "She thought you two were in a relationship, but you didn't. Is that it?"

"If you ask her, yes, that's it."

"Hell no. I'm not touching it with her." I let out a breath. Great. That would be a constant pain in the butt for the investigation. "So, I was right. You dumped her."

"I didn't have to dump her. As far as I was, and still am, concerned, we weren't a thing. We had sex a few times. People do that, but that's it. It doesn't matter. She figured out how I felt, and I guess it ticked her off."

"I know I'm going to regret this, but how did she figure it out?" I hoped it would be something like he had made it clear from the start, but she couldn't accept it, though I doubted that was the case.

"Because she busted me in bed with someone else."

I leaned my head back and groaned. "She fired you when she found you with the other woman, didn't she?"

He nodded and cleared his throat. "Lost that client too."

"Jesus, Parks. You sleep with all your clients?"

He told me to go to hell.

"I'll take that as a yes."

"It's not what you think," he said.

"It's absolutely what I think." I ran my hand through my hair. "Listen, you're a decent-looking guy. She's rich and hot, and you're both single. No judgment from me. Just keep it away from the investigation."

"You're lecturing the wrong person."

"Maybe, but she signs my checks."

10

The black SUV with the California plates appeared on 141 in Cumming as I drove to the Barnes & Noble across from the Collection. I switched lanes and swerved to turn left into the parking lot across the street. I aimed for the Starbucks drive-through first but changed my mind and parked. I climbed out of my car and watched without fear as the SUV pulled up and backed into a spot near Rosati's.

It wasn't one of my previous arrests or even their family. It had to do with Emma Steadman. They thought I knew something. If I did, I wasn't aware of it.

Then, watching traffic, I headed inside and watched them out the window. As cars crowded in the lane to wait for spots, I hurried back out to mine, jumped in, and gunned it out of the lot, crossing through the light into the Collection and parking near the pizza place. I rushed into Barnes & Noble, watching for the SUV, but I didn't see it.

It was quiet in the cafe area, so I scoured through missingkids.org, searching for girls who looked like our victims while I waited for Nick to arrive. Though I had asked to meet, I hadn't decided what, if anything, I would tell him about the note, but I did need to find out if he'd noticed anything strange around Alyssa. I also wanted to know why she hadn't called me.

How They Were Taken 97

He slid into the chair in front of me. "Are you going to sign the papers?"

"Are you going to stop being an asshole? I asked you to have Alyssa call me."

The aroma of freshly brewed coffee and the scent of new books created an almost comforting backdrop to our tense conversation. Almost.

"I forgot. I'm sorry." He leaned back and exhaled. "Why can't you just do it? You know we're not getting back together. Why won't you get on with your life?"

I smiled my biggest smile and flashed him my pearly whites. "I am getting on with my life. I've got a great job working for myself. I'm making more money than I know what to do with, and I'm investigating the biggest case since the Lindbergh baby. You're the one pretending to be a happy family in a home that still smells like me."

His face reddened. "What's your problem?"

As if he didn't already know. "My problem? What's my problem? How about you cheating on me, for starters?" I eyed the store but kept talking. "Oh, and telling me you want a divorce through a text message. Could that be my problem? How about moving your mistress into my home? Oh, and not only did you hand yourself to her on a silver platter, but you're letting her raise my daughter, and you want to know my problem?"

His eyes shifted around the large store. "Keep your voice down."

"Oh," I whispered. "I'm sorry if my calling you out embarrasses you, but deal with it."

"We're not getting back together, Jenna. Move on."

I laughed. "Get over yourself, Nick. I wouldn't take you back if you begged. But this divorce isn't happening on your terms." I leaned back and jabbed my thumb to my chest. "It's happening on mine."

He dragged his hand down his five-o'clock-shadowed face. "I'm not giving you custody of Alyssa."

I hated to admit it, but I knew in my heart that wasn't an option. Half of the reason Nick cheated was because I wasn't available. I wasn't present. He thought I cared more about my cases, about my sister, than I did my family. He was wrong, but I hadn't worked hard enough to prove that. He might have cheated, but I opened the door and pushed him out. And working the hours I did, the job I had, it wasn't safe for Alyssa. The note proved it.

"I know I can't have full custody. I'm not asking for that. I want two nights a week, every other weekend, and alternating holidays."

"Your job is dangerous."

"So is every other divorced cop's, but somehow they get shared custody of their kids."

"What about your drinking? Is it worse?" He leaned forward and sniffed.

"I'm not an alcoholic, Nick, but fine. If it makes you feel better, I won't drink when I've got her." As if I would have. I crossed my arms. "I'm not asking for money, my share of the house, or anything I should have. We both know Georgia is an equitable division state, so be happy, because I could get a lot more than I'm asking for."

He stared into my eyes, but before he could say anything, I added, "And I need you to promise me this new kid isn't going to turn Alyssa into some modern-day Cinderella. She deserves to be treated as an equal member of your new little family, and I want to talk to Heather about that without you there."

"I'm not letting you talk to Heather on her own."

I smirked. "I won't rip her apart. I promise."

"You really are bitter, aren't you?"

"I never claimed to be perfect."

"Fine, I'll arrange it." His tone was more resolved than angry. He would get what he wanted, and he knew it, but he had to do it my way, something Nick never liked doing.

"How's our daughter? Does she know about the baby?"

"Not yet. We're waiting until Heather's further along to say anything."

At least there was that. I tried to speak in a casual voice. "Have you noticed anything different when you're out with Alyssa?"

He narrowed his eyes at me. "Different how?" Nick knew me too well.

"I'm just wondering about my kid, Nick."

"What's going on? Is this about the Steadman girl? If Alyssa's in danger, I need to know."

"Chill out. I'm just covering all bases. You know how my job works."

He shot me a look that could cut steel. "I know how you work. Tell me what's going on."

How They Were Taken 99

"You want everyone in town to know? Keep talking loudly."

He glanced around, saw the curious eyes ogling him, and whispered, "Spill it."

I sighed, glancing at the growing line of customers waiting for their lattes and scones. He was Alyssa's father, and no matter how much it would mess things up for me, her safety had to come first. I gave in. Leaning in, and lowering my voice even further, I said, "Someone sent me a note saying they liked her in her ballet shoes."

Nick's eyes widened but then narrowed into slits. He didn't hold back. "Someone's watching my daughter?"

"Our daughter," I corrected.

He pursed his lips, glanced around the store, then said, "That's it. You're not seeing her until you drop this case."

"I'm not dropping the case, Nick. You know I don't work that way."

He shook his head. "Doesn't matter. Being with you puts our daughter in trouble." He stressed "our" when he said it.

I couldn't argue that.

He took a breath. "When were you planning to tell me this?"

"I just did. Listen, I just got the note. Don't worry. I've got eyes on her. A former FBI agent. She won't let anything happen to our daughter."

He leaned back in his chair and shook his head. "Jesus, Jen, a woman? If this is connected to the Steadman case, you really think a woman can handle it?"

Well, that was insulting. I clenched my fists under the table to try to keep my cool. How had I missed the jerk in him? "Jessica Steadman hired me to find out what happened to her daughter. In case you forgot, I'm a woman. One who gave you a child that will be a woman someday too, remember?"

"Come on. Let's be real here. It's been a year. No one's finding that girl, and now her abductor might be watching Alyssa?" He pounded his fist on the table. "Why couldn't you just work at some boutique and be in the PTA?"

"You know why," I said through gritted teeth.

"Molly's never coming back, Jenna. She's dead. You want that to be Alyssa too?"

I resisted the urge to sucker punch him. "Watch it, Nick."

He exhaled. "You really think this FBI chick can keep her safe?"

"Former FBI agent, and yes."

"What about Heather? Can she keep her safe too?"

"If she's with Alyssa, nothing will happen to her either."

"I want someone watching Heather, too."

"I can give you a list of PIs to call," I said, "but she's not my concern."

"She's carrying my baby."

"Whoever this is is after me, not you. Hire a PI and tell Heather to keep her head down, and she'll be fine." Maybe.

"I can't tell her that. She's already worried enough about the baby."

"Then don't tell her."

"She needs to know." His face softened. "What should I do?"

"Are you seriously asking for relationship advice about the woman you left me for?" I shook my head. "Un-freaking-believable."

"You're the expert here. As someone with experience in law enforcement, do I tell her or not?"

"If you think it'll change her behavior, then don't." She wasn't smart enough to catch a tail on her back, so I didn't bother with that. "We don't need our note-writer thinking we've got eyes on him."

He nodded. "Yeah, that's a good idea." With the sincerest and most concerned look for me I had seen in ages, he asked, "How are you holding up? I know it's got to be hard."

I wasn't sure how to handle that kind of concern from him. I hadn't seen that side of him in a few years. I squirmed in my seat. "I'm fine. I've got help. We'll find the guy soon enough."

"Help? Is Leland working with you?"

"No."

His eyebrow went up. "Then who?"

"A former NCIS guy. He worked the case before. We're working together now."

"So, he brought you in. Not Steadman."

"No. Would it matter anyway?" I asked.

"I just want to see you successful at this, Jen. You need to get your life together."

How They Were Taken 101

"My life is together, Nick, and for the record, I'm not the one that blew it apart. And not that it's any of your business, but Jessica Steadman did hire me. The NCIS guy works for me."

He snickered. "Poor guy."

That sucker-punch thing looked even better. Having said what I came to say, I stood to leave, but of course, I couldn't just walk away without having the last word. "Nick, I can promise you Alyssa will be safe, but your pregnant girlfriend isn't my problem. Like I said, if you're that worried about her, you should consider hiring your own security." I flicked my hair behind my shoulder, pivoted on my heel, and headed toward the exit before he could explode.

Parks held open the door. "Surprise."

I stepped back, then snarled. "Are you following me?"

He flicked his head toward Nick. "That the ex?"

I glanced back and caught Nick watching us, so I grabbed Parks's arm and dragged him outside out of Nick's view. "Why are you here?"

"Because I like to see you stressed out." He handed me a file. "I missed something, and since you didn't mention it, I think you did too."

I took a seat at a table outside the coffee shop when I saw what was in the file. "How did we miss this?"

"The photos were small. Not clear. Before I got fired, I brought them to a friend who could improve them. I just got them back."

"This can link our killer to three of the missing girls."

"All but your sister and Lizzie Ryland."

That didn't deter me. It was possible the guy wore the shoes out. Sixteen years is a long time for a pair of shoes. Even ones worn just to abduct little girls.

I examined the footprints.

Parks leaned in closer, his eyes narrowing on the images. "It's him, Jenna. No doubt. These prints match too perfectly."

A faint spark of excitement rushed through me. "I agree." I spread the photos out on the table, my finger tracing the patterns on each of them. "Best I can tell, the first prints are identical." I pointed out the details. "Same wear patterns, same scuff marks. He's been using the same pair of shoes for years. The shoe imprint is slightly different in the other picture."

"Probably kept the original pair just to kidnap the girls." Parks tapped the photo taken from Emma Steadman's crime scene. "Same style, but it's not the same shoe. Look at the heel, the outer edge—it's newer."

I leaned in to examine the enhanced images. "The wear on the right side of the heel is less pronounced, and the outer edge isn't as rounded. This shoe hasn't been worn as long."

Parks nodded. His jaw tightened. "Why switch shoes?"

"After sixteen years, he probably thinks he's untouchable, or he wanted to mess with law enforcement," I said quietly. "Wearing the same shoes all this time? That's confidence, maybe even arrogance. Getting away with this for more than twenty-five years will do that to a person. Who analyzed the prints for you?"

Parks leaned back, his metal chair creaking from the weight. "Stan Belflower. He's with Counter Forensics inside the perimeter."

"I know Stan."

"Then you know he's good."

"He's not just good. He's top-notch. GBI used him as an expert in multiple cases."

"He's former NCIS, which is also why I use him. He said he used advanced imaging techniques to bring out details the police missed. He agrees that the first two prints show uniquely equal wear and tear, consistent with long-term use. The last prints lack that history. It's clearly a replacement."

"Right. So, we're dealing with someone meticulous enough to stick with the same brand and model but smart enough to change shoes when needed," I said.

"He's cocky, like you said. Cocky enough to think no one would connect these abductions."

"Because no one did," I said.

"But he didn't count on us."

I took a deep breath as my mind raced. "We need to cross-check every purchase of this shoe model in the past two years, no, since Molly's abduction, starting with areas around the crime scenes. Someone must remember selling a new pair."

Parks jotted down notes. "From sixteen years ago?" he asked. "You think

How They Were Taken   103

the same people work at the shoe stores? I doubt most of them are even open now. You read the files. We can't even talk to witnesses. Based on the reports, no one saw anything."

"It's worth a shot." The world narrowed to those photos. Sixteen years of abductions, shattered lives, and finally, we had something tangible. The shoe prints, once just smudges, were our golden ticket. I hoped. "Sixteen years," I murmured, my fingers grazing the edge of the first photo. "And finally, a real lead."

Nick's deep voice snapped me out of my thoughts. "Is this your partner?"

"Nick. I'm sorry. I thought we finished our conversation."

"If you call throwing my fiancée under the bus and then walking away an ending, I guess we did."

Parks barely stifled a laugh. He stood and extended his hand. "Jack Parks. I'm working with Jenna on the Steadman investigation. You are?"

Nick didn't bother with the hand gesture. "Jenna's ex-husband."

"Not quite my ex," I corrected.

Nick ignored me and focused on Parks. "Is my daughter at risk?"

Parks glanced at me. I nodded to let him know Nick was in the loop.

"We have eyes on her. Probably the best in the business, in my opinion."

"Why should I trust your opinion?" Nick shot back.

"Nick, knock it off," I warned.

"No," Parks said. "It's okay. I'm happy to tell your husband how well our eyes, a former FBI agent, performed on joint investigations with me during my time serving our country and with NCIS." He smiled at Nick.

Slam. I almost burst out laughing.

"Just keep her safe," Nick said. "And my fiancée as well."

"That's above my pay grade, sir," Parks replied. "You'll have to get approval from my commander." He pointed at me.

Maybe Parks wasn't so bad after all.

"On that note," I said, "let's get back to work." I locked eyes with Nick. "I'll keep you posted."

"Sign the damn papers, Jenna."

Parks smiled at me as Nick stomped to his car. I knew the man's every move, from his gentle touches to the way he walked when angry, to his true feelings when he told me—after sending me a text about it—that our marriage was over. But at that moment, he wasn't just angry; he was pissed. And that was his problem, not mine. "That was priceless," I said.

"You're welcome."

I gathered the photos with a renewed energized resolve. We had found a lead, a connection spanning sixteen years. Was it a long shot? Yes. But it was more than we had ever had before. With advancements in forensic techniques, we were finally in a position to catch the bastard.

"Holy hell," I said. We had gone back to my place to work. I reviewed the information on Nike and summarized it for Parks. "As of 2023, Nike's shoe lineup includes a total of seven hundred and seventy-three different footwear options. Men have three hundred and forty-two, women three hundred, and there are a hundred and thirty-seven unisex styles." I rubbed my temples. "We'll be looking forever."

"You're forgetting the other brands," Parks said. He poured himself a glass of OJ. "I don't even know how many there are these days."

"Nike's the most popular brand. We start there, the odds are we'll find the shoe."

"Know anyone at their corporate location?"

"I don't even know where their corporate location is," I said. I tapped onto the laptop keyboard. "Beaverton, Oregon."

"Beaverton? Is that a joke?"

"Really? That's where your mind went? What are you? Twelve?"

"Sometimes I act like it."

"Obviously."

"Steadman has stock with Nike. A lot of it."

"How do you know that? After-sex bonding?"

"Something like that. My point is, she's got connections."

"I'm not asking her for a name until I try first." I grabbed my cell and dialed the number for Nike World Headquarters. They connected me to their legal department.

"William Stuart," the man said when he picked up the line.

How They Were Taken 105

I explained the situation, told him we worked for Jessica Steadman, one of his company's top investors, and asked how to have the prints checked.

"Could you please forward the photographs in question to my email for initial review?" he asked. He spoke like how lawyers wrote briefs. "Upon receipt, I will consult with our team to ascertain whether they can confirm the origin of the item as ours from the available evidence. Please be advised, however, that depending on the findings of our preliminary assessment, we may not be able to fulfill your request in its entirety. Should we be able to proceed, I will ensure that you are informed of the outcomes relevant to your inquiry. It is important to note that all disclosures will be subject to the constraints imposed by our obligations under applicable laws and any confidentiality agreements that may be in effect." He then gave me his email.

"Thank you," I said, sending the photographs over and giving him my contact info. After disconnecting the call, I said to Parks, "That was easier than I thought."

"Name-dropping is an effective means to an end," he said. "You got an extra bedroom in this place?"

"Not for you," I said. "For my kid."

"Who your ex won't let stay here anytime soon."

"I didn't ask, but you're probably right."

"We need to pin the photos onto whiteboards and map out the crime scenes from the photos. See if we've missed any other similarities."

"You mean see if you missed any," I said. "I just got the case."

"Whatever."

"I don't mind the whiteboards in this room," I said. "It's not like I'm entertaining anyone but you these days."

"I won't tell you how pathetic that sounds."

"You don't need to. I already know." I checked online for the nearest office products store with DoorDash delivery and placed the order.

"They'll deliver the whiteboards? How do you know that?"

"Let's just say DoorDash and I go way back."

"I'll take Emma. You take Molly."

I swallowed. "I might be too close to Molly's abduction to see anything."

"I'd think you knew the scene by heart by now," he said.

"I do, which is the problem. I'm so used to studying the pictures, if something stood out, I'd have caught it by now."

"Just give it a shot. We'll switch when we're done."

The hours ticked by slowly as we worked. I reevaluated the photos from the night of Molly's abduction after laying them next to each other on the floor. The memories flooded like a tsunami, causing me to catch my breath as I did every time I traveled back to that time in my life.

We lived in a modest home with a small porch and an overgrown garden, captured in grainy photos that brought back feelings I didn't want to remember. Two of my childhood home could fit into the Steadmans' garage. The dreams of a teenage girl hoping to be famous someday, with her own sprawling mansion in Buckhead, with pristine landscaping and modern security cameras, had no idea what would happen, but those photos reminded me they had killed her dream.

Bob wandered over. His nose twitched as he sniffed at the pictures.

"Different worlds, aren't they," I asked him.

He meowed and climbed onto the couch.

"Our guy was methodical about who he chose," I said, staring at the line from Emma's sprawling mansion back to the modest outline of my childhood home. "Emma's place and mine? Might as well be different planets. Yet he picked similar girls and found a way into both homes."

Parks raised an eyebrow. "We've already established that," he said.

"I know. I'm talking through my thoughts," I said. "It's my process."

"Got it. Go on."

I massaged the growing ache forming at the base of my skull. "It wasn't about the neighborhood or how fat the wallets were. It was personal. Like we said, about the girls themselves, but also about him, his need."

He leaned in. "Because their appearances triggered something in him?"

Nodding, I set another photo on my map as a chill ran through me. "All redheads, similar build, same age when taken. He's chasing a ghost— maybe someone from his past. A sister, a friend?"

"A daughter?"

"Right."

We sprawled the photos and notes across the makeshift workspace. I sketched out the quiet, tree-lined streets of my old neighborhood, pinning

How They Were Taken 107

down the exact location of my house and the shadowy paths leading into the woods—a place a younger me had believed was magical, not menacing.

Parks took a methodical approach. His notes on Emma's neighborhood were precise, much like I would have expected from someone in the military. He charted the security-heavy layout of the gated community, the strategic placement of cameras, and the trails leading to the stables—a favorite haunt of Emma's away from prying eyes.

"The timings exactly the same," he murmured, his voice lower than normal. "Most of the abductions shrouded by the silence of a sleeping house, one with a murder, and then you there in the late evening hours but before you went to bed. How did he get in without making a sound?"

I shook my head, the memory of that night always too sharp, too raw. "It was normal one minute, then the next, I'm tied up, and then Molly was gone."

Parks nodded slowly. "He knew the layouts, had the run of the place. He'd been there before. Maybe a handyman, a delivery guy? Anyone like that come to mind from back then?"

I shrugged as my frustration simmered. "Teenage me wasn't exactly tuned into that stuff. I was more worried about school dances and friend drama."

"I get that," he said, jotting down another note. "Do you remember it being hot or cold in your house? It was April, right? Maybe the furnace needed repair?"

"I don't know. I know we didn't have an air conditioner, but I'm not sure if the furnace worked."

"What about your plumbing? Could you flush your toilets?"

"Yes. It didn't work well, but it worked."

He tapped his pencil on the floor. "We can't rule any service company out, but if it's the same guy, age is a factor now. He'd be much older."

"Which brings us back to it being more than one person," I insisted, my mind ticking over every case file I devoured late into the night. "It might be a twisted sociopathic inheritance. Not unheard of. Rare, but it happens. If a kid found out his dad was behind something like this, it could warp him, set him on the same dark path."

"Continuing what Daddy couldn't finish," Parks finished grimly.

"Exactly. Same patterns, and other than my place where he kicked the door in, all unknown methods of entry. It's all too familiar, too practiced."

"Maybe Daddy showed him the ropes," he said.

My gaze drifted to the photos, to the tangled web of yarn. "This isn't just random—it's a legacy of horror. And we're going to end it."

"If it's a family thing, and Daddy didn't hand over the reins, the replacement had to know what was happening and took over after his father stopped."

"Right," I said.

Parks rubbed his chin. "We need to think outside the box here. What if we're looking for a connection that isn't direct? Like a franchise or a company that could have employed different people over the years under the same training or standards?"

"That goes against what you just said."

"I know, but it could be a mentoring situation or maybe idolizing. It's just a thought."

"But we have the same brand and size shoes. The only difference is their wear pattern, which points to them being related."

"Right," he said. "Like a father-and-son company. Bob and Son's HVAC Repair. We service your A/C and take your kid."

"Sounds about right." I reopened my laptop and tapped in a search for longstanding repair and service companies in the areas where each girl was abducted. "I'll start with plumbing and pull up any company that's been around for over forty years."

The search churned out a handful of results, but only three companies that appeared family owned back then. We dove into comparing the company histories with our timeline but found nothing.

"Try HVAC," Parks said.

"Already on it."

After the same process, I noticed one name kept popping up—a family-owned heating and cooling service that had been in business since the '70s.

"Look at this." I pointed at the screen. "This company was founded by a John McAllister Sr., then it passed down to another John McAllister, then James McAllister." I pulled up a state map, cross-referencing the addresses

How They Were Taken 109

with the company's listed service areas. "They cover all the right places. If not directly, then close enough to not rule them out."

"That's a big territory," Parks noted, leaning in closer to squint at the names. "John and Jim, father and son. Fits our theory."

"Let me see what I can find." I clicked through to the company's website, looking for any archived service calls or employee lists. As expected, the digital paper trail was thin, but a contact form on the site offered a glimmer of hope. "I'm going to ask for historical employee records, see if they bite."

"Good luck." Parks continued to scan the other names while I filled out the inquiry. "We need something solid to connect them to all our victims, though," he said, frustration evident in his voice.

"I know. Everything feels like a long shot," I admitted, clicking send on my request. "But right now, they're all we have."

We revisited the whiteboards as we waited for a response, pinning up everything we knew about the other victims.

"Did you ever look into the vendor angle?" I asked.

"I asked about vendors coming by, but nothing specific. You know how it is. Traumatic events tend to erase the daily minutiae."

He had a point. "They've got to be linked somehow. Maybe this way, maybe not, but we're onto something, I can feel it," I muttered. My eyes traced the lines of yarn crisscrossing the boards.

Parks didn't respond immediately. After a long pause, he finally spoke. "What if we're wrong? What if it's just a coincidence, the way the girls look alike?"

"I don't believe in coincidences," I replied. "They're all too similar to be random."

"But it's still possible."

"How?" I pressed. "Convince me."

"What if it's about the families, the houses? Something that ties them to the places, not just the people."

"But the girls all looked similar."

"Doesn't mean that wasn't a fatal flaw our guys didn't see."

My mind raced at the suggestion. "Okay. I'll go with it. Like what? Land disputes? Previous ownerships? Shunned relationships? Maybe the owners talked down to the repair guy?"

"It's all possible," he said.

Parks was right again. We had to expand our view, to think about what connected these families beyond the obvious. "You just piled on another twenty-four hours of work, but we can't rule that out."

"We can't spend every day playing tag with bullets on the streets."

"Thank God for that." I let out a wry chuckle, acknowledging the grim reality of our less glamorous detective work. "We'll follow what we find and detour when necessary."

We were far from the end, but every new angle brought us closer to the truth, no matter how many long shots it took.

Hours later, we'd done our due diligence but couldn't find a connection through real estate information, legal disputes, or anything else we considered. It was well past midnight. We had ground through details and leads for hours in my cramped apartment, surrounded by papers, whiteboards, and cold coffee cups, making some headway but nothing earth-shattering.

Parks yawned. "Our best bet is a service company."

"I'm not opposed to digging deeper into them, but I don't want to go balls to the wall and forget everything else."

"Never said we would, unless it gives us something."

"Right." Exhausted, I uncorked a bottle, ready to pour myself a generous glass of wine. "You mind if I have one?" I hoisted the bottle slightly. "I don't want to drink in front of you if that bothers you."

"Really?"

"Sometimes I'm less bitchy than others."

He laughed. "For me, I'm fine if you have a glass. It's you I worry about." He straightened up from where he leaned against the kitchen counter. "I don't think drinking on the job is a good idea."

I appreciated the concern, but that didn't stop me from pouring myself a glass. "It's after midnight," I countered, walking into the living area and collapsing back into the cushions of the couch. "I'm definitely not on the

How They Were Taken

job." A groan escaped me as I stretched my legs. "Man, I've been thinking about Jessica Steadman and her attitude today. I bet that woman can give a beatdown better than most."

Parks followed. "She married the richest man in town. I'm sure she had to have some grit." He crossed his arms and watched me with those analytical eyes of his.

I took a swig of my wine. "She wants miracles from us. It's only been a few days. She can't expect much yet."

"It's been a year for her. She wants to know what happened to her daughter," he said, his voice dropping a notch. He continued studying me. "What's going on?"

"Nothing," I said. "Why?"

"Your mood. Is it about your meeting earlier?"

"What do you mean?" I asked, my voice sharper than I intended. I knew exactly what he was getting at—my meeting with Nick where he had laid down the law about me seeing Alyssa again until I either found the Steadman girl or dropped the case. Right or not, it infuriated me that he controlled my time with my kid.

"Do you have a good lawyer?"

Parks's question snapped me back into reality. "I do, but as much as I hate it, Nick's right. Alyssa isn't safe with me. Whoever took these girls knows I'm looking for him." I ran a hand through my tangled hair. "He aimed for my weak spot and nailed it. I can't risk my daughter's safety or her life. Not even if it means never finding out what happened to Molly." A lump formed in my throat. "God, I'm a horrible mom. I should have dropped this Molly search the day I found out I was pregnant."

"You're not a horrible mom," Parks reassured me, his tone firm yet gentle. "You're protecting your daughter and teaching her to be strong."

"By obsessing about my missing sister? We both know she's long dead. Does what happened to her really matter?" The question hung in the air heavier than the humidity. The fact was it did matter. To me. As much as I hated it tormenting me and destroying my life, it still mattered.

"To you, yes, and that shows the kind of person you are," he said quietly. "Someone who cares enough to keep going until the job is done."

I chewed nervously on my fingernail, suddenly very aware of my vulnerabilities laid bare in front of Parks, a guy I barely knew. In a moment of self-doubt, I chugged the rest of my wine.

"We're going to find the guy, Jenna. Neither of us will stop until we do," he stated with conviction.

"Let's hope," I murmured, the wine emboldening my resolve a little.

"What happened at the bureau?" he asked, changing the subject.

I appreciated the diversion, but that wasn't a subject I was eager to dive into either. "I failed to uphold GBI standards."

"I know that. What standards is my question," he pressed, leaning in.

"The kind that say you can't beat the crap out of a suspect to get him to admit to killing a kid," I confessed, the bitterness of the memory mingling with the aftertaste of the wine.

He nodded as understanding colored his features. "The Blake case."

"You know about it? GBI kept the incident under wraps."

"Incident?" He laughed. It was a short, humorless sound. "You broke his nose. Everyone in the field knows about it."

"Great," I muttered, sinking deeper into the couch.

"And we all were glad someone took that MF'er down. He kidnapped and shot a fifteen-year-old boy. He deserved more than a broken nose."

"He'll get life, and we both know what prisoners do to kid killers."

"Actually, they love doing kid killers," he paused. "Right before they shank them."

Parks left a while later, after I'd finished off the first bottle of wine and uncorked another. He'd said something about getting sleep and starting again in the morning, but we both knew I wouldn't sleep.

I re-corked the wine and set it on the kitchen counter. I didn't need it. It would only serve to further numb me and blur my mind. Besides, I didn't want to prove Nick or Parks right. I wasn't an alcoholic. I drank to cut the fire inflaming my nerves, but I didn't need it.

And I didn't want to need it.

I jumped into the shower and let the cold water wash over me and send me sprinting back to sobriety for the night. I tossed on a fresh pair of jeans

How They Were Taken 113

and a T-shirt, then got in my car and headed over to Nick's. I didn't plan to see them, but I wanted to stay close to keep an eye on the area and my daughter.

The early morning air carried a chill of unease that had settled deep in my bones. I gripped the steering wheel as my car hugged the curves of the quiet suburban streets of my old community. The neighborhood no longer offered the safety and comfort of before but had become a stage for a sinister play in which my daughter, Alyssa, and I were unwilling actors.

I became less Jenna, the private detective and mother behind the wheel, and more Jenna, the GBI agent on high alert. I slowed to well below the speed limit, my eyes meticulously scanning each vehicle parked along the street, categorizing them by make, model, and any sign of recent use: a fleeting shadow in the driver's seat, an abruptly dimmed interior light. The yards stretched out like dark chasms, potentially hiding anyone with a view into Alyssa's bedroom, but I wouldn't give up. If someone was there, I'd find them.

I imagined the eyes of each resident scrutinizing me from behind their facade, judging me for letting my marriage fail, maybe? Get over it, I told myself. It wasn't all about me and my failures. The problem was each mistake impacted my daughter, and it was hard not to beat myself up over them.

I cleared my thoughts and refocused on the task at hand, checking each house, looking for the twitch of a curtain, hoping for a telltale heartbeat of something amiss. I noted everything—the way the streetlight flickered over the Hendersons' driveway, the strange new sedan outside the McGraths' that hadn't been there last week, the stillness that hovered over the neighborhood like a bad omen.

I spotted the silver SUV parked directly across from Nick's house, its engine off but its presence screaming volumes in the otherwise silent night. Tinted windows—too dark, illegal even—gave away nothing of who or what might be inside. I felt my heartbeat kick up a notch. It wasn't right.

I parked a few houses down and reached for my phone with a shaky hand. I dialed Parks while keeping my eyes fixed on the SUV.

"Hey," he said.

"Hey, sorry. I know it's late, but I'm outside Nick's place, and I've got a suspicious SUV sitting on the street. It's not the one that's tailed us. Windows are too dark to see anything. I'm keeping my eye on it," I murmured into the phone, my voice low and threading through the stillness of my car.

"The silver SUV?"

"Yeah," I said. "How'd you—"

He cut me off. "Because it's me."

"You own a silver SUV? Why didn't you tell me that?"

"I didn't know I needed to give you a list of my belongings, but I'll make one after I get some sleep."

"You're keeping an eye on Alyssa." I meant that as a thank-you, not a statement. "I mean, thank you."

"It's the right thing to do. I watched you ready to dive into your second bottle of wine. I figured you'd be out in less than an hour, so I came by to check things out."

"Not that it's any of your business, but I didn't drink it."

"That's good."

"Wait, did you come here from my apartment?"

"After switching cars, yes. I don't want another girl to disappear, Jenna. Especially your daughter."

He had left me speechless.

"Listen, go home," he said. "Take a shower and get some sleep. We need to step it up first thing tomorrow."

"I just took a shower."

"Then just get some sleep," he said, and ended the call.

11

I woke up a few hours later from a fitful sleep to a text message dinging from an unknown number.

Ms. Wyatt. My name is Lisa McAllister. I am John McAllister's daughter and Jimmy McAllister's sister. I work for the company and saw your inquiry. Please call me before eight.

My heart raced. I replied immediately. *I can talk now. Is that good?*

My cell rang a few seconds later. I picked it up, put it on speaker, flicked on my bedside lamp, and grabbed a pen and paper from my nightstand.

"This is Lisa McAllister."

I reminded her of my email.

She spoke with a forced professionalism that bordered on inconvenience. "May I ask why you need the information?"

So much for cooperation. I was so used to saying I worked for the GBI that I blurted it out. "Let me correct that," I added. "I am a former GBI agent, now a private investigator. I'm looking into the abductions of five girls, one being Jessica Steadman's daughter, Emma."

"The rich woman in Buckhead? I saw that on the news, but I didn't know they hadn't found the girl yet."

"We're following every lead we can," I said.

"And why does this concern my family's company?"

116   CAROLYN RIDDER ASPENSON

"We're ruling out service companies that service the area."

"Service areas change and grow for most heating and air companies. May I ask who else you're talking to?"

"I'm not able to discuss them, but I can assure you we're telling them the same."

"Oh, okay. So, you're looking for service records for how far back?"

"1998."

"Oh, wow. I wasn't born until the next year, but I'm sure we've got them in storage. My family saves everything."

"I'd like to read you the names. Maybe your father or brother mentioned them?" I asked her to keep our conversation private for the time being. I couldn't guarantee she would, but I had to risk telling her to get what I needed.

"I honestly wouldn't know," she said. "I just started with the company a few months ago, and my father's no longer with us." Her tone balanced between hurt and angry.

"I'm sorry for your loss."

"Don't be," she said. "He was a son of a bitch."

I hadn't expected that. "May I ask when he died?"

"Not soon enough," she said.

I knew a *mind your own business* comment when I heard it.

We scheduled a time to meet and discuss my request for later that morning. Though exhausted, I couldn't go back to sleep, so I showered again, also in cold water to shock my body into functioning, guzzled three cups of java as I dressed, fed Bob a saucer of canned tuna, then headed out.

I called Parks on the way. "Got a call back from Lisa McAllister. We're meeting in an hour at Starbucks off 92 in Roswell."

"I'll be there."

Parks arrived a few minutes after me.

"You didn't sleep," I said. "I got a little."

"Nope." He scanned the room. "Do you know what she looks like?"

How They Were Taken 117

"I think that's her," I said, pointing to a young woman who could pass for a high school freshman shuffling through the door.

"How do you know?"

"She looks like how the girl I spoke to talks," I said.

"I'm not even going to ask you to explain that. I'm sure it's logical in your mind. Somehow."

"Wouldn't have said it if it wasn't. I'll bet you twenty bucks I'm right."

"All right," he said. "Deal." He tugged his wallet out of his back pocket, threw a twenty on the table, and smiled. "You're good, but that's a stretch."

"We'll see," I said, layering a twenty on top of his.

I watched the girl as she stood in the order line with her head sunk down toward her phone. Her appearance defined mousy—dishwater-blond hair pulled back into an ill attempt at a ponytail and round glasses that dominated her small face. She clutched her phone like a lifeline as she navigated her way into the queue. Talking to people on the phone gave her confidence, but being around them in person showed me she lacked it most of the time.

"Did you find anything last night?" Parks asked.

"Just processing. You?"

"There are eight billion variations of sneaker shoe soles online, in case you're wondering." He shrugged. "Watching a sleeping house gets boring. I had a lot of time to search the internet."

"That gives me a headache just thinking about it."

"Which part?"

"Both," I said.

One of the baristas yelled, "Grande coffee with double espresso for Parks."

I smiled. "Ordered on the app. Smart man."

"Technology is convenient." He strutted to the counter.

After ordering, the young woman I believed to be Lisa McAllister had positioned herself near the pickup area, her body language shrinking as if to take up the least amount of space possible. She scanned the room intermittently, her eyes skimming over faces until they locked with mine. I smiled and gave her a slight wave. Her eyes brightened.

With her drink—a towering concoction of whipped cream and syrup—

securely in hand, she navigated through the maze of tables and chairs and finally sat across from me.

Parks sat beside her. "Jack Parks. I'm her partner."

Partner? Not exactly. I slid the two twenty-dollar bills toward me and stuffed them into my purse, all while smiling at Parks.

"I'm not sure I'm comfortable talking with you about the business," McAllister said. She twisted her fingers into a knot.

I treaded carefully. One wrong word and the poor girl would run. "As I said on the phone, we're trying to rule out your company."

"But if I help you, you could find something."

"Are you afraid we will?" I asked.

"Are you saying you think my father and brother kidnapped the little girls?"

Was that a spark I saw in her eye or just my imagination? "Not at all." I repeated what we needed. "As I mentioned on the phone, I'd like to get a hold of your service records and, if possible, your employee records, for 1998 through now."

She sipped her drink. "So, that is what you're saying. You think my family is involved in their abductions."

"Lisa, don't be alarmed. We're talking to every company with a similar service area."

"One of our techs could have done it. Some have been with us a long time."

"It's possible," I said. "And we would like to rule that out as well."

Parks added, "Each of these instances occurred under circumstances that suggest the abductor had a good understanding of the victims' homes, knowledge that someone working in a service capacity might have."

She nodded. "It really feels like you think someone from our company did it. Like an employee?"

She had asked that question multiple times, in multiple ways, but we couldn't give her the answer she wanted. I gave her points for her persistence.

"Right now, we're doing our due diligence," I said. "We believe exploring all possibilities includes looking into past service records and any

How They Were Taken 119

employees who might have been working in those areas at the times of the incidents."

Lack of sleep and the weight of Jessica Steadman's assumption I would succeed ate away at my patience.

"It's a lot to process. I understand the need for thoroughness, though. I'm the company's business manager now. I handle everything from billing and scheduling to human services. My aunt Linda used to do it, but she wanted to retire and only works part-time."

I made a mental note of that.

"Will you help us?"

"I want to prove my company wasn't involved."

"Thank you. I know it's a lot of work, but we really need the records back to 1998."

"Back then, my grandpa owned the business. He gave it to my father, and when he died, it went to Jimmy. My aunt handled the records until recently. If I can't find what you need, you won't get it."

"We can talk to your aunt," Parks said. "If you give us her contact information."

She shook her head. "She would kill me if I did that. Besides, she won't talk to you."

"Why is that?" I asked.

"My dad's family isn't nice."

Undeterred, I said, "It's worth a shot."

"We can wait on it for the time being," Parks said.

I gave him a look that clearly said, *What the hell?* "How about your grandfather?"

"He's dead. I think I said that?"

"I mean was he nice?"

She laughed sarcastically. "No one on his side of the family is nice. He was meaner than the rest of them. My mom said that's why my dad was the way he was, and part of the reason she left him. She said he learned to be an asshole from Grandpa." She blushed. "Sorry."

"Don't be sorry," I said. "I know a few assholes too."

She stared out the window, then asked, "You'll give me addresses and dates?"

"The dates, yes. We aren't able to provide the addresses." I had already written the dates down, and handed her the information. Giving her the addresses could have posed a serious problem. She didn't strike me as involved, but if her family was abusive, and she had decided to work for them, she could be easily persuaded to give them information about us. "Anything on these dates or around them would be great."

She looked up at me, surprised. "All services for these days?"

"How many employees do you have?" I asked.

"Right now, over twenty-five. I'm not sure about the dates you gave me, though."

I nodded. "We would appreciate everything you've got for those days, yes."

"Okay, but that's going to take a while."

"We understand," I said.

Parks said, "These were planned incidents. We're assuming the abductor would have gone to the home sometime within the month prior."

She nodded. "So, you want me to look a month back on each of these dates too?"

"Yes, ma'am."

She exhaled. "Okay. I'll pull anything we've got, but it's going to be a while. I'm not comfortable doing it during business hours. Too many people come in and out."

"We understand," I said. "Thank you. Oh, one more thing. Did your grandfather and father make service calls?"

"My dad, yeah. My grandpa? I mean, probably. If he did, his name will be on the paperwork."

"Good to know," I said.

She studied the room, then looked back to me. "Will you be honest with me?"

Leaning forward, I rested my arms on the table, giving the impression of casual interest and professional detachment. I wanted her comfortable, but not too much. "That's part of my job," I said, my tone steady. "Unless it's something that could interfere with our investigation."

My last sentence appeared to hit a nerve, because her eyes flickered

How They Were Taken   121

away briefly before locking back onto mine. "Do you think my dad kidnapped any of those girls?"

I leaned back, crossing my arms and raising an eyebrow slightly, then pushed the question back into her court without accusation. "Do you think he did?"

She swallowed hard as her gaze dropped to her hands clasped tightly in her lap. "I'm not sure."

I prodded gently, trying to peel back the layers. "Why?"

She shook her head as a visible shiver ran through her. "He was abusive. I'd rather not say anything else." She whispered so softly, the other customers drowned her out.

I nodded, letting the silence hang for a moment. "When did he pass?"

"A few years ago in June." She maintained a steady voice, but it included a hint of relief.

"And how old was he?"

"Sixty-two." She looked up, her brow furrowing slightly. "Does that matter?"

"Everything matters," I said with a slight emphasis, trying to convey the importance of every detail. "Was he in good health?"

"Yeah, I guess. I mean, we didn't expect him to die." She seemed to relax slightly, the topic less personal, more factual.

"So, he wasn't ill?" I watched her reactions closely.

"No. He was still working." Her response was quick, almost defensive.

I paused, letting her digest the questions before diving deeper, hoping she would add more details. When she didn't, I asked, "How did he pass?"

The words caught her off guard. Her eyes widened. "Someone broke into the office and shot him." Her eyes watered.

The shock was still there, raw and fresh. No matter how abusive the person, someone always loved them. But I hadn't expected to hear he had been murdered. I maintained my composure, keeping my expression schooled to neutrality.

"Do you happen to know their shoe size?" Parks threw the question out there casually, as if it were just another routine query.

"Whose?" She blinked, taken aback. "My dad and grandfather?" She shook her head. "Do people know that about their family members?"

"It's always possible," he replied. He shrugged, I assumed to keep the atmosphere light but investigative. "What about your brother?"

"His shoe size?" She shook her head. "They're all about the same height, or were, but I have no idea about their sizes, even clothes."

"You never bought them shirts or something for their birthdays?" Parks asked. "My sister-in-law gets me shirts every holiday." He chuckled. "Hate to tell her they're not my style."

"We're not like that. I don't like being around my family. I only took the job because my aunt insisted. I'm not that close to any of them except for my mom, and I doubt she would know the answers. I'm not comfortable asking her anyway."

"Why not?" Parks's tone was curious but gentle.

"Everyone in my dad's family hates her. She's never said it, but I think they did things when she left him."

I angled my head to the side. "Things like?"

"I don't know."

I leaned back, my face softening as I made my decision on how to proceed. "I'll tell you what," I said, my voice low and reassuring. "You get what you can for us, and give me a call."

"You aren't going to talk to my aunt, are you?"

"No," I said. I thought, but didn't add, *Not yet.*

"Thank you," she said in an unsteady voice. Her brow smoothed, and for the first time, her eyes didn't dart around like she was bracing for bad news. "I don't want to get in any trouble."

"We don't want that for you either."

"I think we should talk to a few more parents," Parks said. "Let's start with Zoe Bryant's mother. She lives in Gwinnett County."

"Divorced?" I asked.

"Widowed."

"Before or after the abduction?"

"Are you asking if the husband's death is a direct result of Zoe's disappearance?"

How They Were Taken

123

"Is it?"

"I can't say for sure. He shot himself a few years ago."

"That's not in your notes."

"It's not relevant to the investigation, and I didn't know I would have to share the investigation with someone."

"Let's go, then." I understood. Investigations stuck with most investigators whether they liked it or not. "Mind if we drop my car off at my apartment first?"

"No problem."

I thought about what Lisa said while driving back to my place. I regretted not giving Alyssa a sister or brother, but listening to Lisa talk about her family showed me it wasn't a bad thing. As Leland always said, you can pick your friends, but your family is always a roll of the dice. In her case, he was right.

My cell phone rang seconds after I climbed back into Parks's car. I answered on the second ring. "Wyatt."

"Ms. Wyatt, this is William Stuart with Nike. I have some information for you about our discovery, but it warranted a call before sending you the results."

I hit the speaker button while Parks drove. "Great. What can you tell me?"

The attorney spoke with measured professionalism but read a practiced response. "I am pleased to inform you that we have conducted a preliminary review regarding your inquiry. I am prepared to send you the pertinent information via email. However, I must stress that this information must remain confidential until it is determined to be a critical element in your investigation. Should this information prove pivotal, please notify us immediately so that we may take appropriate steps to address any ensuing legal or public relations concerns."

He continued ensuring clarity and adherence to protocol. Lawyerspeak always used too many words. "Furthermore, before sending the information, we will require you and anyone affiliated with this request to sign a nondisclosure agreement. This agreement stipulates that you will not discuss the findings with anyone outside of your investigative team. For our records, and to ensure compliance with our legal responsibilities, please provide a list of the law enforcement personnel involved in this matter."

I hit him back with a shot of his own medicine, that lawyer-esque speak where, if words cost a buck each, he could have fed the starving children in Ethiopia. "Certainly. I appreciate the necessity for confidentiality and will adhere to all stipulated legal protocols, that is, if doing so does not impede our investigation. However, it's imperative to underscore that this matter concerns the abduction of five young girls. While I recognize your company's apprehension regarding potential litigation, our paramount concern is the safety and expedient recovery of these individuals. Rest assured the information will be managed with the highest level of diligence and discretion by my team." I took a breath, surprised I got that all out without hesitation.

"Then I must inform you of a possible suit filed against you for such actions."

"It wouldn't be the first time I've heard that, Mr. Stuart, and I suspect you would file against Jessica Steadman as well."

"Jessica Steadman?"

"My client."

He exhaled as if I had tested his patience. I did not care. "This concerns her daughter?"

"Yup."

"May I have the names of your other team members, then? If you sign the NDA, that's all I need for now."

I rattled off Parks's name. "What's your email?" I whispered to him. I repeated it back to the attorney.

"Thank you, Ms. Wyatt. I'll have those documents to you immediately."

I disconnected the call and tipped my head back on the headrest. "I hate attorneys."

He laughed. "How do you look at yourself in the mirror, then?"

I smirked. He had done his homework. "Who told you?"

"I might not have a law degree, but I know how to research."

"Why didn't you mention you knew before?"

"Why didn't you?" he asked.

"Touché."

How They Were Taken 125

"Ever practice?"

"I never intended to practice law. I just wanted to understand it."

"So why not just read a few books?" he asked.

"I wanted more than that. I passed the bar and applied to the GBI the next day."

"You wanted that law degree to help find your sister."

I nodded.

A few minutes later, I checked my email, signed the electronic document, then navigated Parks's cell for him to do the same as we sat at a red light on the way to Zoe Bryant's mother's.

My phone alerted me of an email from the attorney. I read it to Parks. "Ms. Wyatt, after discussing this with the rest of our in-house legal department, we are declining to provide you with the information you have requested. At this time, Nike requires a warrant or subpoena for the information you have requested and any other information you might require of us in the future." I dropped my phone beside me. "Not surprising."

"We had to try."

Mrs. Bryant lived in Buford, near the Mall of Georgia, a place a million bucks couldn't convince me to shop at. Malls might have been my thing as a teenager, but their appeal had disappeared with Molly. "Traffic here sucks."

"It sucks all over the metro area," he said.

He turned into an older complex of apartments without balconies and in dire need of a new paint job.

"Why did they build these things without balconies?" I asked. "They could get more money from renters."

"Not in this area," he said. "Who wants to breathe in exhaust?"

"I know, but just having them would have helped."

"They cater to a specific crowd."

"Got it," I said.

12

Stephanie Bryant didn't look a day under fifty-seven, but bless her heart, according to Parks, she had just turned forty-seven. Her pale skin accentuated the deep creases in her face, etched like canyons, ones I assumed had been carved by the relentless grief of losing her daughter. Her cheeks, hollowed and gaunt, told tales of tough times and a few too many pills. Her hair, a tangled mess of grays and dull brown, had ends so split they begged for a decent pair of scissors. Not that I was there to pass judgment. I saw that same look of slow decay mirrored in my mom after Molly's abduction. Despite all my so-called successes, those deep lines etched between my eyebrows might as well have been carved in stone, marking every ounce of my own grief. Her physical appearance would have been enough to recognize her addiction, though seeing the mess inside her apartment, the empty whiskey bottles, the overfilled ashtrays, and drug paraphernalia confirmed it.

She caught me looking and said, "That's not mine."

I wasn't judging her, but her appearance had given her away even without the used syringes and spoons on the coffee table.

"Mrs. Bryant," Parks said. "This is Jenna Wyatt, former agent with the GBI. She and I are working on the disappearances together now."

She gave me a once-over so intense my skin itched. "This is the one you

How They Were Taken

told me about?" She puffed a cigarette, then flicked the ash into one of the overfilled ashtrays.

"Yes, ma'am," he said.

She looked me in the eye. "You need to eat more. You run down some meth head, he'll break you in two, you're so skinny."

"Thanks for the advice," I said. "I'll consider it."

Her upper lip twitched at the side. "Didn't get a chance to clean up before you came," she said as she shoved a pile of crap cluttering the couch onto the floor. "Don't get many visitors these days. Have a seat."

"I prefer to stand," I said.

She eyed me. "Wait. Don't tell me." She picked up a plastic tray with what looked to be rotting microwavable lasagna and held it toward me. "You don't like mess, do you?"

She wanted to test me, to see if I was tough. I refused to show reaction. "It's your business, not mine. We're here about your daughter, Zoe."

"I don't have anything else to say. I've said it all, and look where it got me." She splayed her arms as if her apartment was her kingdom. "I'm a daughterless mother and a widow hooked on drugs, living in this dump." She finished the cigarette and smashed it, still lit, into that plastic tray, then lit up again. "Zoe's dead. Probably nothing but dust by now, too."

I swallowed. "Mrs. Bryant, my sister, Molly, was also abducted. I'm sure Mr. Parks has told you that your daughter and my sister are two of five missing girls, including one abducted this past year. All redheads with additional similar characteristics. All five years old."

Pain flashed over her face momentarily, but resignation quickly returned. "That's terrible, but it doesn't bring my baby or my husband back. They're both dead."

"No, it doesn't, and you're right. It's highly probable Zoe and the rest of the girls are dead. But we can get justice for them by finding the person responsible."

"Justice?" She laughed, then her face turned angry. She took another puff on her cigarette. "What the hell good does that do me? Justice can't bring back what I've lost, and even if it could, you think I'm good for my angels like this?" Her hands shook as she lifted the cigarette to her lips again. "I'm just hoping I'll OD and not have to face life without them anymore."

I believed my mother had felt the same. Desperate and alone. Hopeless. "I'd like peace too," I said. "As would the families of the other missing girls."

"Well, good luck to them," she said. "The only thing that will give me peace is death. I just don't have the strength my husband had to kill myself intentionally."

"Mrs. Bryant," Parks said. "Don't let this guy win. Help us find him. Let him pay for what he's done."

She exhaled. "Look at my life. He's already won."

"We can throw the ace on the pile," I said. "We can take back his win if you help us."

"Just answer a few questions," Parks said. "Can you do that?"

She shrugged. "I guess I don't have anything better to do."

"Whoever abducted these girls knew how to get in and out of the homes. They knew the layout. We think they were there before, maybe left a window unlocked or something to gain access again," he said. "Can you remember having anyone at the house in the few weeks before Zoe disappeared?"

"You mean like friends?"

"Friends. Family. Repair companies. Delivery people. Anyone."

"We were doing some work in the basement. We had people there, but the police already knew that."

"Yes, you were finishing the basement," I said, recalling the information from the file.

She nodded. "I don't remember who we used. My husband was cheap."

"Did you already have heating and air in the basement?"

"I don't think so, but even if we did, we got a new system so it would be strong enough for the basement." She stared at the wall. "Back then, we had one of those big houses with the walk-out terrace level. We wanted it for the kids. I was expecting my second child, and the thought of two kids messing up my living space made my skin itch." She laughed. "Bet you wouldn't think that now, would you?"

I wondered where that kid was. "Do you remember the name of the company?"

She shook her head. "My husband handled those things." Her arms shook slightly. Either she was coming off a high, or she needed another hit. "Can't you find it in the reports? God knows the cops wrote everything down."

There had been nothing about service companies in the report, just the construction. Thinking back, I wasn't sure law enforcement had asked my mother or me about repairs or people coming to our home either.

"Do you have records from the remodel?" I asked. "Maybe something about the air-conditioning company?"

She let out a rueful laugh. "I have a few photos of my family, and that's it." She flopped down on the couch, swiping at more clutter before making herself comfortable. "I was raised in a small town. I never imagined I'd see the day where I wasn't pinching pennies after paying the bills, much less snag a good husband and land a big house. I didn't deserve any of it, which must be why the good Lord decided to take it all back and leave me with memories so bitter they're drilling a hole through my head. You really think I'd remember something like an air-conditioning company?"

It was worth a shot, but Bryant had done enough drugs to dull her emotions and push her to forget the past. Once we left, she would take a hit of something to calm her jitters.

Walking to the car, I said, "What happened to the other child?"

"She lost the baby a week after Zoe went missing."

My heart hurt for her. "Oh, God. That poor woman."

"She was eight months pregnant. They had to bury a child they hadn't met and couldn't find the child they knew to bury her."

I could only imagine how horrific that had been. "Was she like this the last time you saw her?"

"Every time." He clicked the key fob and opened my door for me. "I keep hoping she'll get help."

"You heard her," I said. "She wants to die. She's actively trying to kill herself without pulling the trigger." I shut my door as he climbed into the driver's seat. "She can't help us. She's trying to forget, and helping us will make her remember."

"Maybe that's what she needs?" he asked. "To remember."

"It's not our job to heal the broken, Parks."

"Really? Isn't that what we do? Provide closure to the victims and their families? That's a step in the healing process."

I couldn't argue that.

I pulled up traffic on Waze. "Traffic's reasonably normal. Feel like taking a drive to the Bryants' old house?"

"I went nine months ago. The owners wouldn't let me in."

"I love a challenge," I said. "Maybe they'll let you in if you're with me."

"Right." His lip twitched. "Because you're all rainbows and sunshine."

Parks pulled to a stop in front of the home. "This is it."

The Bryant family's old estate unfurled in front of us like something out of a Southern Gothic novel, all wrapped up in Peachtree City's posh trappings. Honestly, had I been blindfolded and dropped there, I would have bet my last dollar we were in some ritzy part of Alpharetta or another well-heeled Georgia enclave. Every wealthy community looked the same.

My gaze fixed on the red brick façade, white columns, and the grand porch embracing the place. The expansive home revealed a side of Stephanie Bryant I would never see. "Hard to square this place with her now."

"Tragedy has a way of reshaping people," Parks said, his voice a low rumble beside me.

I drew a breath, steeling myself for what came next. "Remember, I'm lead. I'm sure she'll like me more than you."

He gave a nonchalant shrug. "Don't matter who does the talking. I just want to look around and get inside."

I straightened my shoulders as we made our way to the front door. I grabbed the lion-headed brass knocker, the perfect guard for the place, and gave it a good rap to announce us. The sound echoed ominously as we waited.

A minute later, the door swung open, and there stood a woman, mid-fifties, looking like she'd had one too many lip injections. She planted her hands on her hips before I could even get a word in. "You people just don't

How They Were Taken 131

get it, do you? We don't allow solicitors here," she snapped. "I'll report you if you don't leave."

"I assure you, we're no solicitors, ma'am," I began, doing my level best to keep my tone even. "My name is Jenna Wyatt, and this is Jack Parks. We're investigating the abduction of Emma Steadman and—"

"Emma Steadman? The girl who vanished when her father was killed?" she interjected, her tone softening into something like recognition.

"That's right," I confirmed.

"And what's that got to do with me?" She landed an accusatory but sharp stare on me.

"We believe Emma's case is linked to four other missing girls, one of whom vanished from this house."

"The Bryant girl," she muttered, eyeing Parks. "I remember you. You were here a few months back, asking to come inside my home."

"That's correct, ma'am."

She pushed her hair behind her ear. "You'd think a private investigator would know better than to expect a woman to let a strange man into her house alone."

Hoping to bridge the gap, I said, "That's precisely why I'm here. We'd like to walk the property and, if possible, look inside."

She squinted at us. "May I see some identification, please?"

I fished out my wallet with practiced ease, accustomed to the weight of it from my GBI days. "I'm a former GBI agent. I can get you in touch with my direct supervisor for a reference."

She scrutinized my ID and then Parks's, but her expression remained unreadable.

Sensing her hesitation, I pressed gently, "We're just here to review the scene of the abduction. It won't take long."

"The house is different now. They haven't lived here in years." She looked every bit the skeptical guardian with her arms crossed. "I'm not sure this is a good idea."

I leaned in slightly, softening my voice and hoping I sounded trustworthy. "Mrs.?"

"Levenworth," she supplied.

"Are you a mother, Mrs. Levenworth?"

Her eyes widened, and she nodded.

I tapped into that motherly protection to push her to yes. "Do you have a daughter?"

Another nod. Her facade melted a bit.

"What if it was your daughter? Wouldn't you want someone to let investigators into the home where she disappeared? Mrs. Levenworth, Zoe Bryant was only five when she went missing. Her disappearance broke her family—her father ended up taking his own life, her mother lost a baby at eight months pregnant and now struggles with addiction, hoping each time she uses that it'll be her last." I let the weight of my next words hang between us before asking, "Will you help us, please?"

Her throat bobbed with a swallow as her posture slumped. "All right. Come in."

"Thank you so much. We'll be quick."

She stepped aside, allowing us to enter the house. The interior's grandeur matched the exterior, with high ceilings, polished wooden floors, and an air of timeless elegance.

Mrs. Levenworth, hot on our heels, watched us closely as we climbed the stairs. She was still wary, but her initial hostility had faded.

"Do you know anything about the previous owners?" I asked.

"You mean the Bryants? They were two previous owners before us. The neighbors used to talk about their daughter, mostly just telling me what happened, but it hasn't been mentioned in a while."

"Her room is at the end of the hall," Parks reminded me.

We stood in front of the door. "May we?" I asked.

She nodded.

The room defied any trace of a little girl's charm. Masculine furniture dominated the space, and male lacrosse player posters screamed boy, not girl. Two windows framed the outer wall.

"Did they break in?" Mrs. Levenworth asked.

"There was no sign of forced entry."

"They'd need a ladder to go through the window."

"We believe they gained access during a previous visit and secured a return," Parks said.

Her eyes widened. "And walked through the house, up the stairs, and all

How They Were Taken

the way to the end of the hall?" She placed her hand on her chest. "Then repeated that to leave with the girl? How did her parents not hear it? I hear every sound my children make, asleep or awake."

"She didn't disappear at night, ma'am," Parks said.

"The Bryants were getting the basement finished," I said. "I imagine it was loud. The police report says Stephanie Bryant was down there talking to a worker. Because it was during the day, Mr. Bryant was at work."

Her tone turned judgmental. "I can't imagine letting a five-year-old out of my sight like that."

"Life happens," I said. "Do you have any documents from the remodel? Mrs. Bryant mentioned they had recently replaced the air conditioning unit. Maybe you have something from that?"

"Oh, actually, I do. It's in the office. Follow me."

We needed another minute examining the space, so she headed to the office without us.

"It would take a good thirty seconds to get the girl down the hall and stairs," Parks said. "In the middle of the day, it had to be risky," he mumbled. "People coming in and out, probably through the garage." He glanced at me. "The safest way out would be on the back side of the house."

We took the stairs back to the first floor, stepped into the office, and asked to see any back doors to the home.

"There's the one in the kitchen and one in the main living area. Both go to the deck, which does have stairs." She removed a file from the desk. "Go on. Have a look."

The kitchen door led to an expansive deck with stairs down to the terrace level.

"How could he get her out without anyone seeing?" I asked. "This place is stacked with windows."

"Maybe it wasn't this way," he said. "It's a big risk going out the front, but he couldn't go through the basement with the construction workers and Zoe's mother."

"He was watching from somewhere," I said. "He knew the exact moment to come in."

"That's what I'm thinking."

We walked toward what we assumed was the basement door.

Mrs. Levenworth caught us before we made it all the way down. "We used the company who installed it to service it. I have their information."

"What's the name?" I asked.

"McAllister Heating and Air."

Parks had made it halfway down the stairs, spun around, and hustled back up, his boots thumping softly on the wood.

Mrs. Levenworth peered at me with her brows knitted. "Does this help?"

I ignored her question and followed her into the kitchen as I read the service report. "Where's your outdoor unit?"

"Both units are on the left side," she said, gesturing toward the deck doors. "You can head out this way."

I stepped outside and rounded the corner to the units. I leaned in close to each, checking the manufacturer's stickers for any sign of a service tag.

Bingo! Each unit featured a metal tag holder displaying a list of all service information. I pumped my fist. "Yes!"

Parks rounded the corner and stopped short when he saw my grin.

"Check these out," I said. "We got it."

While climbing up the deck stairs, I said, "If we can connect McAllister to the other victims, we're golden."

"Not golden, but close."

"Right."

Inside, Mrs. Levenworth gave us a small, worried nod as we thanked her.

"Your help's been crucial, ma'am," Parks said. "But for the sake of your safety, we suggest you keep this to yourself."

The shadow that flickered across her face carried regret. "I'm sorry I didn't help earlier."

13

Parks and I rolled through the less trodden parts of suburban Atlanta with our eyes peeled on the traffic, but more focused on that golden ticket we'd just found.

"We've got a friend," Parks said.

I dropped the visor and used the mirror to check behind us. "The black SUV. How long's it been there?"

"It just moved behind us a few miles ago." He glanced in the mirror again. "Can't say for sure how long before I saw it."

A flash of worry ripped through my veins. "They could have followed us to the Levenworths' place."

"If so, they saw us near the air-conditioning units."

"And the Levenworth family could be at risk," I said, kicking myself for not considering that first.

"I've got a friend with the local police department here," Parks said. "I'll call him and let him know what's going on, but first, I need to lose this guy."

"Don't go to Steadman's," I said. "Go to a police department."

He laughed. "I'm not a woman on my own. I'm not driving to a police department." He swerved to the right and took a turn on a road unfamiliar to me.

I gripped the handle above the window as Parks took a sharp left, and his tires screeched against the pavement. I glanced behind me, not caring if the driver saw. Parks's turns had already said everything they needed to know.

"Nice Sunday drive, don't you think?" He drove through an empty lot to the cross street, hopped back onto the road, and headed south twenty miles above the speed limit.

"Keep driving like this and we'll lose them."

"Isn't losing the guy what we're trying to do?" He glanced back at the SUV just a car length behind us in the right lane. "Hold on!" He jerked the wheel to the right and pressed down on the gas.

I gripped the *oh shit* handle above the door and held my breath as he sped through a red light.

"You're going to get us killed!"

He whipped the car to the left and took the side street. "This should take us out just north of the intersection. If we're lucky, he's still sitting at the light."

The SUV driver's decision not to run the light caught me off guard, but it also showed he hadn't intended to hurt us.

Parks yelled, "Damn it!"

I checked the mirror and caught the SUV two vehicles behind us. "Gun it. We've got two car lengths on him. You can lose him."

Parks took a turn, cutting off a group of people crossing the street, putting some distance between us and the SUV when it had to stop for the pedestrians.

The streets blurred together as Parks maneuvered through Atlanta's web of roads, turning onto side streets and occasionally cutting through a parking lot or two. The SUV matched our moves at every turn, its dark windows giving nothing away.

"Try the alley up there!" I pointed to a narrow passage between two buildings.

Parks nodded and swung the car into the alley, the shadows enveloping us momentarily.

The SUV hesitated, then entered behind us, its engine growling in the confined space.

How They Were Taken 137

"He's still on us. Ideas?" Parks asked, his voice steady despite the adrenaline I knew pumped through his veins.

"Head toward Atlanta Highway, then double back on them. It's risky, but it might work," I suggested, my hands clenching tighter, knuckles white.

"Ten-four." Parks shot out of the alley, back onto a main road, and then executed a series of complicated turns that had me dizzy and confused. We darted down Atlanta Highway, then slipped through a residential area. Parks drove through someone's backyard, narrowly missing a garden gnome, and hopped the curb back onto the road.

"I think we lost them." I panted as I craned my neck to look behind us. No black SUV in sight.

Parks let out a long breath, slowing the car down to a normal speed. "We need to be more careful. No telling who else they might be watching."

I called Leland for a favor while Parks called the PD near the Levenworths' home and received payment for the favor owed to him.

"You want me to run full reports on the three McAllister men," Leland said. "On a hunch."

"It's more than a hunch," I said, explaining about the service records on the units. He finally agreed and said he would get them to me via email.

We headed to Jessica Steadman's place since we had lost the tail.

"I'm staying at your place from now on," Parks said. "This guy's watching you, and now me. We'll do better as a team."

"I'll be fine on my own."

"It's not a question," he said.

Leland called as we walked up to Jessica Steadman's door.

"I thought you were sending them through email?"

"John Jr. has a few domestic violence calls, but nothing came from them."

"Anything else?"

"Senior's daughter Mary disappeared in 1967. He found her a few months later in a shallow grave."

Parks and I made eye contact. "What?" he asked me.

138 CAROLYN RIDDER ASPENSON

I held up my finger and mouthed, "One sec." To Leland, I asked, "I'm assuming they never caught the person who did it?"

"Not that I can find."

"Do you have any information on the girl? How old she is, maybe? Hair color?"

"There's a black-and-white photo of her from the paper, but it's not clear. Other than that, the article describes her as the same age as the other girls, as well as having red hair. I'm sure there's detailed files with the PD that handled the investigation. It's just too far back for digital."

"Got it. Thanks for letting me know."

I pulled Parks to the side and filled him in.

"Was she a redhead?" he asked.

"The newspaper article said she was. Leland said there's a photo."

"This is good." He ran his hand through his short hair. "We can work with this, but we need to talk to Steadman first."

Jessica Steadman sat on her expensive sectional couch staring at me with an air of snobbery well beyond my comprehension. "You think it's an air-conditioning serviceman?" She looked at Parks. "Why didn't you discover this on your own?"

I had no patience for the scorned woman's hissy fit even though she signed my checks. "Mrs. Steadman, what matters most is we've made a connection, but we need your service information to confirm what we believe."

"And the others?" she asked. "Have they confirmed it's this McAllister company that's involved?"

"One case has been connected, but we have reason to believe our theory will pan out."

"How so?"

I dodged the question. Telling her all we knew, client or not, could compromise the investigation, especially given her connections. "Do you have records we can check?"

"You're not going to share the details?"

How They Were Taken 139

"Ma'am, we don't want anything getting out."

"And you think I'll tell someone?"

"I think it's possible you'll use connections to help, and we can't risk that."

"Very well," she said. "I will allow this for now." She called for her house manager to get the records and then said, "But these abductions were years apart. Wouldn't the person be old now?"

"Possibly," I said, "but the owners are family. Grandfather, son, and then grandson."

"And you think they were in on it together?" She shook her head. "I can't imagine that would be true."

"Mrs. Steadman," I said calmly. "Based on our collective experience, I believe we have a much clearer idea of the depths of psychosis running in families."

She blinked. "You're telling me three men from the same family worked together and abducted little girls. For what?"

"I'm telling you it's a theory, and one we need to keep quiet until we have more information. The motive is still to be determined."

Her house manager returned with a file. Steadman examined the papers inside and then handed it to me. "It's the same company." Her voice shook, but she gathered her resolve quickly. "What happens next?"

I scanned the documents and handed them to Parks. "We continue investigating."

"Do you have records from your home?" she asked. "Isn't it abandoned?"

I kept my tone professional to hide my feelings. "Yes, but it's possible the A/C unit is still there."

She nodded. "Very well. Keep me up to date, please." She eyed Parks with a look that could cut steel.

My cell phone rang as we walked outside. I checked the caller ID and answered. "Drew, did you get anything?"

"It's cow blood," he said. "Your guy work on a farm, maybe?"

"Don't think so," I said. I climbed into Parks's passenger seat. "Thanks for checking it, though."

"Any time. Listen, Leland called in a few favors. He has evidence from the Lily Hansen case. It was just some hairs. DNA isn't in the database, but if you want, I can send it out to make sure I didn't miss anything. Leland's cool with it. It'll take a few weeks, though."

"I'm hoping we've caught our guy by then, but go ahead, please. Just in case."

"Sure thing. This place is a morgue right now. Feel free to keep me busy."

"You're going to regret saying that," I said.

"Not at all."

"We were right," I said to Parks. "It wasn't human blood. The abductor wanted to make it look like someone bled at the crime scene."

"He wanted the police to think it was a different person?" he asked.

"That's my professional guess." I chewed on my finger for a moment. "We don't have any prints, so we can't compare them to anyone from the McAllister company. We need something more than the A/C company link as evidence."

"Mary McAllister's death could be motive."

"Revenge is a powerful thing. Think now is a good time to visit the Hansens?"

"Their daughter's missing. Any time is a good time."

"How far is it?"

"They're in Buckhead."

Not far. "Let's go."

Parks contacted Mrs. Hansen on the way as I worked through what we knew.

"She's home," he said.

"Good, since we're already heading there."

"We could have checked the unit without her."

"True," I said. "Two homes with the same company. A dead daughter for John McAllister. Similar footprints that could belong to different family members. A not-so-nice family according to Lisa. It's all fitting together, but we're still missing the center piece of the puzzle that makes it complete."

How They Were Taken

"The without-reasonable-doubt evidence," he said.

"Yes." I stared out the window the rest of the way, wondering what that could be and if we would ever find it.

We arrived at the Hansen home twenty-five minutes later. Mrs. Hansen greeted us like she hadn't seen another human in months.

I had never been to high tea, but given the spread laid out in her great room, I suspected she had.

"Thank you for coming," she said. Her deep Southern accent and casual attire of jeans and a T-shirt contradicted everything about her home. She stretched out her hand. "Lila Hansen."

"Jenna Wyatt. I'm sorry we're meeting under these circumstances."

"You will never interrupt me when it concerns my Lily."

"Understood."

"I threw together a small snack. I hope you like tea."

"That will be fine," I said.

She smiled at me as she poured us each a cup. "It's Earl Grey."

"Perfect," I said, though I had never tried it.

"I understand you're working for Jessica Steadman now." She glanced at Parks. "Have you found anything new?"

"Possibly," he said. "We have a few questions."

"Of course."

"Is Mr. Hansen coming?" I asked.

"I'm afraid he's out of town, but we can call him if necessary."

"I'm sure it's fine." I got to the point. "Do you recall having your HVAC unit looked at around the time of your daughter's disappearance?"

"Our air conditioning?" She sipped her tea. "I don't recall, but I can check our records. Would you like me to do that?"

"That would be great."

She stood. "Then please excuse me for a moment."

I studied the place while she disappeared into a room near the entrance. "This place could give the Steadman home a run for its money."

"The Hansens are old money. The home's been in the family for years."

Even though my family had left me guilt and tragedy, it didn't make me want the responsibility that came with money. Old or new. "Was she as courteous and polite when you first came here?"

"I don't think she knows how not to be. People like this pretend life is great when most of the time it isn't."

"I think that's the case for a lot of people. Did you meet her husband?"

He shook his head. "I'm not sure he really exists."

"Interesting."

"Ahem," he said.

Mrs. Hansen returned with a file. "We did have a company service the air-conditioning units in May, but that was a month before our sweet daughter disappeared."

Her composure concerned me. People could only hold in so much before they burst. "McAllister?"

She glanced at the paper in the file. "How did you know?"

"Is the serviceman's name listed in your file?"

"Yes, James McAllister." She looked at me. "What does this have to do with Lily?"

"We're not sure yet." Parks and I made eye contact. "May we see her room?"

She shifted her attention to Parks. "Is this necessary again? I don't want her things disturbed."

"A fresh set of eyes is always a good thing," he said. "And we'll be respectful of Lily's things."

"We'll make sure everything stays as is," I said. "I'm more interested in the path the person took to abduct your daughter."

"Of course," she said. "Follow me."

She led us up the circular stairs and down the hall. The hallway included four additional doors, three before Lily's. Two on the left, one on the right just before her room, and one with double doors at the end.

"Are these other bedrooms?" I asked.

"Yes. Ours is this one," she said, pointing to the room at the end of the hall. "Our son Quinton's is the last room on the left, and the other two are guest rooms."

The hall stretched just as far in the other direction with the same layout. "What's on the other end?"

"A playroom, the nannies' rooms, and the upstairs laundry."

How They Were Taken 143

"Did you have nannies at the time of Lily's disappearance?" The file said yes, but I needed confirmation.

"We had two from Poland, but they had both returned home for visits."

"Understood," I said.

"They checked out," Parks said.

I nodded. "I remember."

"We haven't changed a thing," Mrs. Hansen said as she opened the door to Lily's room. "We want Lily to come home to the same home she left."

She said it as though it was possible, though the chances were slim.

Parks filled me in on the predicted path.

"The security cameras were disabled, correct?" I asked.

"Destroyed," he said. "Shot out."

Since the home was older, it didn't have a terrace level. "Where do you think they accessed the home?"

"Through the back. There is a set of stairs from the kitchen," Parks said.

"And you didn't hear anything?" I asked the woman.

She shook her head. "I took Ambien that night. I was having trouble sleeping."

"And Mr. Hansen was out of town?"

She nodded. "And Quinton didn't hear anything as well."

"He was a teenager," Parks said. "They sleep like rocks."

I hadn't, though sometimes I wished I had.

We covered the route Parks believed Lily's abductor had taken. In the kitchen, I asked Mrs. Hansen if she had turned on the alarm that night.

"I hadn't," she said with regret. "I never did when my husband traveled. Not that I didn't want it on, but he was the one who did it on the other nights, and I had simply forgotten."

I suspected the guilt from that would never go away. "I understand. When had the dog escaped?"

"In May." She pursed her lips.

"Do you remember the date?"

"Yes. Memorial Day. We had a gathering that day and thought someone had accidentally let him out."

"Was it a big party?"

"Aren't they always?"

"How many guests?"

"Oh, I don't remember exactly, but our gatherings are rarely under one hundred guests."

I smiled. "Thank you. May we walk the property before leaving?"

"Of course." She turned toward Parks. "Will you let me know what's going on?"

"Yes, ma'am. When we have something concrete, you'll know."

On the way back to my apartment, I said, "That's all but the Rylands and my family. Do we know if they had central air?"

Parks merged onto 400. "I'll call them." He called through his Bluetooth and explained the situation to Mrs. Ryland.

"Let me check. May I call you back?"

"Please," Parks said. He disconnected the call and said, "Molly could have been a convenience grab."

"Or maybe it was too much work to hunt for houses when so many were right under his nose."

"Did Leland do a deep dive on the McAllisters?" he asked.

"Not that quick. I can ask if he will, but he's already put his job at risk."

"Steadman is close to the governor. If something happens, she'll fix it."

"I'm not telling him that, but it's worth a shot."

I dialed Leland's cell.

He answered on the first ring. "I doubt you're calling to say you miss me."

"That's always the case," I said, and I meant it. "But I have a favor." I hit the speaker icon.

"Didn't doubt that."

Parks chuckled.

"Can you do a deep dive on the McAllisters?"

"You do remember we don't work together anymore, yes?"

"You fired me. How could I forget?"

"Never going to let that go, are you?"

How They Were Taken 145

"Have you paid for health insurance through the marketplace?" I asked. "It ain't cheap."

"Aren't you still on Nick's until the divorce is final?"

"Technically, yes, but I don't want him knowing anything about my health."

"I think she means her mental health," Parks said.

Leland laughed. "I'm pretty sure he knows that status."

"Okay, this isn't pick-on-Jenna day. Can you help or not?"

"Have I ever said no to you?"

"Multiple times."

"I'll get back to you. Where are you in your investigation?"

Parks's radio blared, "Call from Elizabeth Ryland."

"Leland, I have to go. Call me when you find something."

Parks answered the call. "Hi, Elizabeth. Did you find anything?"

"Yes, the company was McAllister. The service person is listed as J. McAllister Sr."

"Thank you," he said.

I gave him my gate code as he turned into my apartment complex. "Don't use it again without my approval."

"I can't guarantee that."

We climbed the stairs arguing about my privacy and how it rated against his desire to make sure I was okay.

Standing outside as I unlocked my door, he said, "I was raised to protect."

"I can kill you with my hands. I don't need protection." I shoved the door open and stopped dead in my tracks. "Shit."

My apartment mirrored a battlefield. Shredded papers blanketed the floor like confetti from chaos. Several meticulously organized boxes had disappeared without a trace. The whiteboards mapping our investigation lay shattered, jagged edges mocking the order they once held. Broken frames and crushed markers littered the scene, smeared ink obliterating our painstaking notes. My heart pounded, and fury surged hot and unchecked through my veins.

Someone had torn through the place, hell-bent on annihilating every shred of evidence tied to the investigation.

"What the hell!" My voice shook with raw anger.

Parks stepped in behind me. His body tensed, but he didn't waste a second. Without a word, he scanned the wreckage, his eyes wide and every muscle alert. "Stay here." He removed a gun from the back of his pants and held it in position.

I examined my lock as he moved through the chaos, disappearing down the hallway toward the bedrooms.

They knew. Whoever took the girls knew we were close to IDing them. They had been in my home and tore apart our work. What if Alyssa had been there?

Bob.

I instinctively ran, gun ready, toward the bedrooms.

Parks walked out of mine cradling Bob, who looked disheveled and wide-eyed. "He was under your bed," Parks said, his voice steady but tight with tension.

I exhaled sharply, trying to calm the whirlwind inside me. "Is he okay?"

"He's fine. A little shaken, but nothing serious." Parks set Bob down, and the cat darted to my side and pressed against my legs.

I knelt, stroking Bob's fur, my touch shaky, then picked him up and held him tight.

"How did they get in?" Parks asked.

I walked over to my small deck, but the door's lock hadn't been touched.

"Maintenance. They must have contacted maintenance and pretended to be me." I hurried to the kitchen. "They should have—yup. Here's the work notice."

"They snuck in and hid," he said.

I scanned the service report. "The caller reported a leak in the guest bath. After a thorough examination, no leak found." I exhaled. "If the service guy had his head under the sink, they could have walked right by him without him seeing."

Parks kept his hand hovered near his gun. "They know we're getting close. They're getting desperate. It's sloppy and rushed." He picked up a bottle of whiskey lying on the floor, rolled his eyes, and added, "At least they're feeling the pressure."

"Good," I growled, my anger sharpening into resolve. "Because when I catch them, they'll regret ever coming into my home."

"We can't tell Steadman about this. She'll lose it."

"We need to know what's missing," I said.

"That's not going to be easy," he said. "But I've got copies of everything, including the files on the computer."

We headed back to the living area.

I dropped an f-bomb when I saw the laptop and my computer screens busted. "They didn't come here to take anything, or they would have found a way to take it all. They wanted to trip us up. Piss us off."

"Right," he said, nodding.

I sipped a cup of coffee while sorting through the mess. We had spent several hours reorganizing everything and had only made it halfway through by dawn. I leaned against the bottom of my couch and yawned as I studied Parks's perfectly organized space across my small living area. On the floor he had laid out folders, stacked papers in each, and made other stacks in neat piles beside them. "I'm type A to almost an obsession, but you're off the charts."

Without looking up, he said, "The military will do that to you."

"Apparently. Are you hungry?"

"I could eat."

"Waffle House work for you?"

"I'll never turn down clogging my arteries with an order scattered, smothered, and covered."

I laughed at the Waffle House order reference. "Did you work there or just love the food?"

"I've spent many mornings at their counter listening to the servers and cooks. I've cracked their code." He headed down my apartment building's stairs before me. "Let me check outside first."

His protectiveness had begun to grow on me, though he didn't do it because he cared. Our training had become second nature, regardless of who we were with.

"If the car is in plain sight, the guy's an idiot," I said.

He scanned the parking lot. "Sociopaths resemble idiots sometimes."

"Valid point."

"Looks all clear," he said. "I'll drive."

"Yes, sir."

My cell phone rang as we pulled into the Waffle House parking lot. I didn't recognize the number but still answered. "Wyatt."

"This is Linda McAllister. I want you to stop harassing my niece and stay away from my company, you hear me?"

"It's nice to meet you," I said with a touch of sarcasm. I hit the speaker icon so Parks could listen in.

"You think this is funny?"

"Let me be clear. I don't consider anything funny about my job."

"We got nothing to do with those abductions. Now back off before I get the law involved."

How I wished I could still say I *was* the law. "Ms. McAllister, under Georgia law, investigating a crime is not considered harassment, but if you would like to report us anyway, please feel free. I suggest contacting Leland Seymour with the Georgia Bureau of Investigation. Would you like the number?"

She said, "Just let us be or you'll live to regret it," and killed the call.

"Bet she's fun at parties," Parks said.

"How did she find out Lisa talked to us?" I asked.

"Maybe she told her?"

I shook my head. "She said she didn't want her to know." I chewed my bottom lip. "What if she's got the lines tapped?"

"Didn't you talk to her on her cell?"

"Yes, but I emailed her at the company email. Shit. I hope Lisa's okay."

"Call Lisa and check on her."

How They Were Taken 149

I called and left her a voicemail. "Auntie Linda's covering her ass."

"It's possible," he said.

We walked into the diner and took the only open booth at the far end of the place.

The server took our order and returned a few minutes later with our plates. I'd barely taken a bite of my waffle when the sound hit us—less a sound, really, and more like the world splitting open. A booming, guttural eruption that punched through the air and sent a jolt through me that resonated deep in my bones. For a split second, everything in the Waffle House suspended in animation, the syrup mid-pour from the bottle, the laughter from a nearby booth cut off sharply.

Then, chaos.

The front windows blew inward, a cascade of glass shards showering the diner in deadly confetti. I instinctively ducked, as did Parks, as the sound of the explosion morphed into the screams and cries of shocked patrons. My ears rang, the initial blast replaced by a high-pitched whine that came from everywhere and nowhere.

As I squinted through the settling dust and debris, the outside world looked like a scene from a war-torn city. Parks's car—or what was left of it—was engulfed in flames in the parking lot, black smoke billowing into the early morning sky. The air smelled acrid, and burned rubber and gasoline stung my nostrils.

"Son of a bitch!" he yelled.

A woman screamed, "Fire!"

Parks just stared in disbelief at the flaming wreckage of what had been his polished, carefully maintained vehicle. His face, usually so composed, mirrored the horror that tightened my chest.

Turning back to the diner, I took in the full scene of devastation. A man lay near the counter, a twisted, jagged piece of Parks's car protruding grotesquely from the right side of his head. Blood pooled around him, staining the cracks of the tiled floor, as his chest rose and fell in shallow, labored heaves.

"We've got injuries." I quickly dialed 911 and gave them the location. "Hurry. He needs medical attention." After disconnecting, I shouted, "The man by the counter," my training propelling me forward.

Parks followed right behind me, checking on others. I knelt beside the injured man, my hand automatically going to his neck to check for a pulse. It was there, faint but present. "I need towels over here! Now!"

A waitress heard and ran toward the kitchen. A few seconds later she returned with a stack of towels.

"Okay," I said to her. "I need you to take those and wrap them around the shrapnel in his head. Be gentle, but you need to press enough to slow the bleeding."

She stood there, staring at the metal, her entire body frozen.

"Now!"

"I don't think I can. I don't want to hurt him."

I grabbed the towels and did it myself. "Now hold it there. You can do it."

She replaced my hands with hers.

"Good. The paramedics will be here soon. Just keep pressure around the shrapnel. We need to slow the bleeding. Okay?"

She nodded. "Okay."

I turned toward Parks as he helped an older man to a chair. "Hey! Help me clear space," I instructed, trying to keep my voice steady. "The paramedics need access to this guy."

The man's breathing slowed. His clammy skin looked pale under the fluorescent lights. I tilted his head back to clear his airway and listened. Nothing. His shallow breathing had stopped. I checked his pulse again but couldn't find one. "He's not breathing and doesn't have a pulse!" With no time to hesitate, I started CPR, counting the compressions out loud, trying to detach from the horror of the situation. "One, two, three, four..."

The blood he had lost slickened the floor, making it hard to stay in place. I adjusted my position, wiped my brow, and continued. "Stay with us," I muttered between compressions. "Don't you die on me! Help is on the way."

Time slipped into a murky lull, measured only by the rhythm of my compressions and the distant wail of approaching sirens. I was dimly aware of other patrons being helped, of crying children and soothing voices, but everything appeared far away, secondary to the heartbeat under my hands I fought to sustain.

How They Were Taken

The paramedics burst in with a flurry of motion and efficiency. "I can't get a pulse," I said. "I think it's been a few minutes."

"I can't stop the bleeding," the woman holding the towel said. A paramedic told her she would take care of the man and pushed the waitress to the side. As they took over, lifting the man onto a stretcher with practiced ease, one of them clapped a hand on my shoulder. "Good work," he said.

"There's a girl over there." Parks pointed to the end of the counter. "She's stable but needs attention." His voice remained calm.

As they wheeled the man out, Parks pulled me into a tight embrace. "You okay?" He glanced at my shoulder. "You're bleeding."

The pain hit me then. A pulsing, intense slamming in my shoulder in a rhythmic beat.

He shouted to a paramedic, "Hey, we need some help here."

14

I lay on the hospital bed in the emergency room, feeling only slightly better than I had when I arrived a few hours before.

Parks walked in with a mile's worth of gauze wrapped around his right hand. "The man is in surgery," he said. "The doctor said you quite possibly saved his life."

"I'm glad."

He sat in the chair beside the bed. "How's the shoulder?"

"They took X-rays. I guess they're waiting to see if there's anything inside."

"Like a piece of my car."

"I'm not really sure," I said, though I suspected he was right.

"Didn't you feel it?"

"I was a little busy to notice."

He grinned. "Does it still hurt?"

"Only when I talk to you."

"You're funny, Wyatt." He checked his watch. "When do you think you'll get out of here?"

"No clue. I can get a ride home. Don't wait on me."

"I'm not leaving. I don't want you suing me because you've got a piece of my bumper inside you."

I laughed. "I'm sure I don't. I keep telling them it's fine, but they want to make sure before they stitch me up. That was a warning, you know."

He nodded. "We wouldn't be talking if it wasn't."

"They've always got someone on us. How is that possible?"

"They have help," he said. "At least two people."

"Linda McAllister had just called."

"Lisa?"

I shook my head. "My gut says she's not involved. The bomb was already in the car."

I sat up and cringed. The pain shot through my shoulder and forced me to lie against the back of the bed. "This is my fault. I should have hidden my meeting with Jessica Steadman."

"I don't think that would have mattered," he said. He handed me a newspaper. "Page two."

I read the headline. *Wife of Deceased Real Estate Mogul Hires Ex-GBI to Find Daughter.* "You've got to be kidding me."

"Check the date. Things will make more sense."

I glanced at the date in the top corner of the page. "Three days ago? How didn't we know about this?"

"Keeping up with the news wasn't exactly tops on our to-do list," he said. "I checked the paper's website. It's on there as well."

"Nick or Leland had to know. They should have told me."

"They probably assumed you knew. I'm sure that's the case with my friends."

"You have friends?" I smiled.

"Contrary to what you think, I'm a decent guy."

"Yeah, I'm sure all the women you've slept with would agree."

He laughed. "The list isn't as long as you think."

The doctor walked in. "Ms. Wyatt, I'm Dr. Priest. I've taken a look at your scans, and I don't see anything out of the ordinary."

Parks said, "Not even a door handle? I was hoping to save something from my car."

I laughed, but Dr. Priest didn't have a sense of humor.

"I'll send in a nurse to stitch you up. She'll give you the after-care directions, and then you're free to go."

"Thank you, Doctor." After he left, I asked Parks to hand me my phone from the cart behind him, then sent a voice text to Nick and one to Leland asking if they had heard or read about me handling the Steadman investigation.

Leland called, and I put the phone on speaker. "Your involvement with her made the news a few days ago," he said. "I saw the news about the car bombing at Waffle House. Please tell me that wasn't you."

"It wasn't, but it was Parks's car."

"Is Parks okay?"

"We weren't in it," I said. "Thanks for asking about me first."

Parks laughed. "I'm good, Leland. Thanks. But we're at the hospital for Jenna."

"What? How bad is it?"

"Not bad enough that I couldn't call you. It's just a few scratches," I said. "We were inside the diner. Ten minutes earlier and we'd be burned toast."

"Damn."

"The explosion destroyed the dining area of the place. Multiple injuries. One man almost didn't make it."

"You don't think it was random." Leland wasn't asking a question.

"Someone's been tailing us for a while now. They've even passively threatened Alyssa."

"Alyssa? What happened?"

"It was passive-aggressive. They sent a note saying they liked her in her ballet shoes."

"Son of a bitch. Is she okay? Does Nick know?"

"She's fine. Nick knows, but he's not happy," I said. "And he blames me."

"It's not your fault, Jenna."

"Isn't it, though? I took this case. Every case I worked I brought home in some way. Everything is because of me."

"Stop beating yourself up. You don't have time for this."

I exhaled. He was right. I could save the emotional beating for after we nailed the McAllisters. "Listen, I need another favor."

"Shoot."

"I've already got eyes on Alyssa, but I need some on the McAllisters. I'll

How They Were Taken   155

pay them." If I had anything left over from my medical bill. "Can you hook me up?"

"I can't give you any of our guys, but I know the owner of a private security company. His people are all vets."

"Titanium?" Parks asked.

"That's the one. They don't come cheap, but they're good. I'll give them a call now. You want to meet with them or get them started?"

"We need eyes on them now. The aunt, Linda McAllister, the office manager, Lisa McAllister, and one of the techs, James McAllister."

"Expect a call from Vincent Hallowell, the owner. He'll confirm." He killed the call.

"His guys are good," Parks said. "Seal Team Six, Rangers, all specialized and tough. They'll have our backs if we're being watched."

Nick finally replied, saying he hadn't read the paper. I let him know what had happened and watched the blue dots as he responded with what I knew would be a string of cuss words and complaints.

I wasn't wrong. Ignoring them, I suggested he take our daughter and stay at a hotel in another town. I assured him I had eyes on our kid and gave him Tiffani Bateman's contact information.

Parks called her and let her know. "Put them in the Four Seasons," he said to me. "It's already high-level security, and Tiffani knows the security manager."

I let Nick know, fully expecting his call.

"The Four Seasons. Are you joking? I can't afford that."

"I'm paying," I said. "I'll even spring for the home-wrecker to stay with you."

"Nice, Jen. Real nice."

"Listen," I said as the nurse came in and prepared my arm for stitches. "We're close, but we can't take any chances, especially with Alyssa."

"Do you know who took Molly?" The concern in his tone sounded genuine.

"I'm closer than ever."

"Send me your credit card info."

"Are you at work?" I asked.

"Yes, but I'm heading home once we hang up."

"Make it quick and head straight to Jessica Steadman's place. They'll give you the cash unless I tell you otherwise." I had planned to ask Jessica Steadman for an advance since I didn't have access to the money she had already paid.

He sighed. "You really need an office job." He disconnected the call.

Parks had left the room. Tough military guy couldn't handle watching a nurse stitch my shoulder? Wow.

She finished and left to get my discharge papers. I peeked through the privacy curtain and searched for Parks. He walked through the double doors, phone in hand.

"You can't handle a needle and thread?" I asked.

"Yeah, that's it."

"How'd you make it through the military?"

He rolled his eyes. "Jessica Steadman is booking the penthouse at the Four Seasons and putting it in Nick's name. She's sending a driver to Nick's to take them there and wants me to tell you it's all on her dime. Also, the man with my car in his head is stable, but that's all they'd give me."

"You called Steadman?"

He nodded. "Did you really think I couldn't handle seeing the nurse stitch up your wound?"

Vincent, or Vince, Hallowell met us at 9 Mile Station, a restaurant and bar located above Ponce City Market in Atlanta. Parks led me to the bar where a man the size of Alan Ritchson sat drinking an iced tea.

After our introduction, he led us into the kitchen and through a door. I eyed Parks, who looked at me and nodded. We walked down a hallway to another door, which required a handprint to enter. Hallowell pressed his hand on the box, and the door opened. "Welcome to Titanium," he said. "As you can see, we like our privacy."

The space had no windows but multiple offices and a large conference room on the side. Hallowell's office was on the far left. Viewing from the outside, I would have assumed it was part of 9 Mile Station.

"Nice," Parks said.

How They Were Taken 157

Hallowell sat behind his desk and motioned for us to sit in the chairs in front of it. "My team is already in action. I have assigned three people to James, Lisa, and Linda McAllister. I will say they have not been able to locate Linda, but it hasn't been long enough for concern, so of course they will continue looking."

"Have they identified the one tracking us?" I asked. "It's a black SUV with California plates."

"As I said, it's only been a few hours, but the men assigned to you have not reported any activity. They will stay close until further notice."

"Men assigned to me? I don't want men on me," I said.

Parks narrowed his eyes at me. "You're kidding, right?"

"No. Having them watching the McAllisters is enough. I don't want to trip over them."

"I don't recommend that," Hallowell said.

"Duly noted."

"I agree with Hallowell," Parks said.

"You can walk away anytime."

He shook his head. "You know I'm not going anywhere."

"Then we're doing it my way." I smiled at Hallowell. "Got it?"

"Yes, ma'am."

"They must have backed off after the explosion," Parks said.

"I suspect that is the case," Hallowell said. "I have a basic understanding of your investigation, but I would like more details. My people need to know what to watch for."

Parks and I explained what we knew, how we learned it, and what it led us to believe.

Hallowell tapped a pen on his desk and looked at me. "Molly Simpson is your sister, correct?"

"Yes."

"And the reason you took the case."

"Partly," I said.

"I understand Tiffani Bateman is protecting your daughter, Alyssa."

"Yes, but we have moved her and her father to a secure location."

"The Four Seasons," he said.

"How did you know?"

"Ms. Bateman and I have been in contact. I have added additional members of my team to assist her."

"Thank you."

He provided us with photos and descriptions of his team members, letting us know to whom they were assigned, the addresses of each suspect, and what we could expect. I didn't normally trust people easily, but Leland trusted him, so I did as well. The man knew his job, and he did it well.

I scanned the surrounding area while walking back to the Mercedes Jessica Steadman had provided.

"You're looking for Hallowell's men, aren't you?"

"No," I lied.

"You refused security. No one's covering us, but if they were, you wouldn't see them. They hid from terrorists and took them out. Watching us would be nothing."

"You can take me home," I said.

He moved in front of me and blocked my path. "You're planning something."

I blanched. "No, I'm not. It's been a long day, my shoulder hurts, and I'm tired. I'm going home, taking a shower, and going to bed. I'll see you in the morning."

He eyed me up and down, then said, "I'm not sure I believe you, but you look like you got hit by a truck, so I'll take you home."

I had told Parks a half-truth. My shoulder did hurt, I was tired, and I wanted to take a shower. The going-to-bed part would have happened, eventually. I needed to steady my brain, and cleaning always did that.

The glass crunched under my feet as I swept my kitchen floor, the last vestiges of the break-in that had been an attempt to stall an already chaotic investigation. I had managed to stack the files Parks and I had organized against the wall, but the rest of my apartment? It still looked like a cyclone had danced through it and took my sanity along for the ride.

Bob navigated the glass with an ease I would expect from a ballerina. He climbed onto the counter and meowed.

How They Were Taken

Treat time.

He must have come from a home with other cats because he only ate on the counter. I grabbed his treat jar and dropped a few moist squares beside my cell phone.

My phone's ring from an unknown caller pierced the silence. I froze, broom in hand, staring at the device vibrating violently against the cold, hard granite. Unknown caller. The suddenness of it made my pulse spike. It was past midnight—too late for telemarketers and political calls. The ringing seemed louder in the stillness, a sound out of place, wrong. I stared at it, every instinct screaming at me to let it go. Don't pick it up. But I didn't listen.

"Yes?" My voice sounded far steadier than I felt.

The line crackled with static, the hiss filling my ear. For a split second, I thought I'd made a mistake answering. Then, a faint, small sob—so soft I almost missed it—made my heart stutter. That sound. I knew it, deep in my bones, a primal recognition I couldn't explain.

"Alyssa?" The broom clattered to the floor, my grip failing as the chill of dread crept into my limbs. "Baby, is that you?" My voice cracked, became jagged, sharp, and alien even to my own ears.

"M-mama?" she whimpered. Her voice was shaky but unmistakable.

"Mama, I—I'm scared. A bad man made Daddy and Heather go with him."

My stomach lurched as my world imploded. "What?" The word was barely a breath, but inside, my heart roared. "Are you at the hotel?" My mind spiraled into a tangled mess of worst-case scenarios, each one clawing at me with more terror than the last.

Where the hell was Tiffani and Hallowell's men?

"I'm with the other man. Mama, I'm scared." Her voice, frayed with fear, felt like a gut punch.

I forced myself to breathe, but my chest tightened, and I couldn't get enough air. My heart hammered against my ribs so hard it hurt. "Where are you, sweetheart? Can you tell me what you see?"

"I don't know. It's dark. I can't see outside. There's just a little window, but it's so high up." She choked on her words, then her sobs came faster, each one escalating in panic.

I gripped the phone so tight my fingers went numb. "Okay, baby, stay on the phone with me. I'm right here, all right? Are you hurt?"

"No," she whispered, her breath hitching. "But they hurt Daddy."

Panic. Raw, wild panic clawed at me, but I refused to let it take over. I needed her to keep talking, to stay with me. With my other hand, I fumbled to send a text to Parks. "Daddy's tough. I'm sure he's fine." My voice sounded like a poor imitation of reassurance. "I'm going to find you, okay? Just hold on. Do you remember anything about how you got there? Anything at all?"

"We were playing Candy Land," she sobbed. The innocence of it made the horror that much worse. "Then a man came, and everything went really fast, and now I'm here. Mama, I'm scared." Her voice, once so strong, broke into a keening wail. The sound shattered me.

The call cut out.

"No, no, no!" I scrambled to redial, my fingers trembling too much to hit the right buttons. The room spun as the panic I'd fought so hard to contain finally exploded and pushed me into action.

I called Tiffani Bateman and added Vince Hallowell to the line. "What the hell happened?" My voice tightened and my breath hitched as I yanked on a pair of jeans. Time slipped away, each passing second piling weight onto the dread clawing at my throat.

"Who has been taken?" Hallowell's voice remained calm, almost too calm for the chaos burning inside me.

"My daughter, her father, and his fiancée. Under your watch. Where the hell are they?" It was the first time I had used that word *fiancée*.

"They're not gone," Bateman said. "We're in the penthouse suite together. They're in their room. It cannot be accessed through any door but the one from the main area, and we have men there. No one has taken your family."

"Ms. Wyatt," Vince Hallowell said. His tone clipped as though he was finally grasping the gravity of the situation. "I've just confirmed with my team. Ms. Bateman is correct. Your family is safe with them as we promised."

My thoughts scrambled to catch up. "Are you sure?" I stood frozen in

How They Were Taken 161

the middle of the room with my jeans half-buttoned as my mind couldn't believe their words.

"Let me call them with you on the line," he said. "Hold on."

I gripped the phone tighter, whitening my knuckles and causing the stitches in my arm to pulse. A minute passed like an eternity. Every tick of the clock echoed in the suffocating silence.

Finally, Nick's voice broke through. "Why do you need to talk to me after midnight?" The familiar irritation in his tone almost grounding me—almost.

"Is Alyssa okay?" I demanded. My knees buckled. I collapsed onto the edge of the bed as my body finally gave in to the overload of fear and relief warring inside me.

"What? Yeah, she's fine," he replied with a groggy voice. "She's sleeping. I was too. What's going on?"

Hallowell filled him in as I worked to control my emotions.

"Ms. Wyatt called after receiving a call from someone sounding like your daughter. She contacted me immediately, and we wanted to verify that you're safe."

Nick's breath caught in his throat. "Listen," he said, "I don't know what the hell is going on here, but we're doing what your men tell us to. I can't take this much longer. My fiancée is pregnant, my kid needs to be in school, and I have a job to get back to."

"Yes, sir," Hallowell answered, but Nick cut him off.

"I wasn't talking to you," Nick growled, the tension in his voice tightening with every word. "Jenna, fix this." And with that, he hung up, leaving me reeling in the aftermath.

"Nice guy," Tiffani muttered.

"Not really," I said. "But he's the father of my child." I cleared my throat. "What the hell just happened? I could've sworn that was Alyssa on the phone."

"Ms. Wyatt," Hallowell said with a guarded tone. "It would appear whoever contacted you has been able to access recordings or videos of your daughter and has augmented her voice using artificial intelligence. It's a common scam used to elicit money from people."

"AI?" My brain struggled to catch up, to wrap around the sudden shift. "They don't want money. They're trying to scare me."

"I believe so," he said quietly, but the weight of the unknown hung between us. "What cell service do you use?"

"Verizon. You can't get anything from them without a warrant." I walked through my apartment and paced between the kitchen and the couch.

"We have before, but I can't guarantee we will again."

"Thanks," I said and killed the call.

A knock on the door jolted me out of my thoughts. The sound reverberated through the quiet apartment, feeling too loud, too sudden. I glanced toward the door as my body tensed, bracing for a threat.

"Jenna, it's Jack. Open up."

I exhaled. I should have known. I dropped my phone on the counter and hurried to the door, peeking through the peephole before unlatching the deadbolt. When I opened it, Parks stood there, his face lined with concern, but even so, a flicker of annoyance shot through me. "I told you not to use the code again."

His eyes scanned my face. "I thought this was important."

I forced a sigh, then apologized to him and thanked him for coming by.

Parks's presence filled my small apartment after he stepped inside. "What happened?" His voice was low, steady. Too steady compared to my nervous system. "Is Alyssa okay?"

My words tumbling out in a rush, as I, barely able to keep my own panic in check, filled him in.

"AI. It's the latest and greatest tool for scammers."

"That's basically what Hallowell said," I muttered as my mind continued spinning. How close had I come to losing everything?

Parks moved closer and brushed a stray hair from my cheek with a tenderness that caused my skin to prickle. "Are you okay?" His voice softened, and for a moment, I wanted to let myself collapse into the safety of what that question implied. That someone would take care of me.

But I couldn't. My eyes met his, and I took a step back as that familiar unease slithered into my gut. "I'm fine," I lied. "You can go now."

His gaze swept over my apartment. "You work fast." There was some-

How They Were Taken 163

thing in his voice—an edge that he tried to hide. "I think I'll stick around. I want to be here if you get another call."

"Parks, I'm a big girl. I don't need you to babysit me."

"I didn't say you did, but you texted me about Alyssa. That means you trust me. Let me stay, just in case."

I hesitated for a second, but I couldn't shake knowing how my mother had felt after Molly's abduction. That crushing pain that brought me to my knees, that blocked my rational thought—this had been her reaction too. Maybe I had overestimated my strength. "Fine," I said, barely above a whisper. "We'll keep each other safe." I walked into the kitchen and downed a shot of vodka.

15

I hadn't slept, choosing instead to research John McAllister Sr. That the abductions began during his reign and he had been at one of the homes helped to solidify my theory. Getting the service records from Lisa would be even better.

Parks hadn't slept either.

I sipped my coffee and stared at my phone as I sat on the chair next to my couch. "John McAllister Sr. was a moose."

He glanced up from a file. "Is that a reference to his size?"

"No, Loyal Order of the Moose," I said. "Have you heard of it?"

"Fraternal organization for mostly blue-collar men, right?"

"Yes."

"And?"

"You know anything about them?"

"Not really."

"They do a lot of good things," I said. "But like the more prestigious fraternal organizations, rumors claim it's filled with criminals."

"Criminals bad enough to accept child abductors?" he asked. "I guess it's possible."

"Anything's possible."

"Are you doing a deep dive?" he asked.

How They Were Taken 165

"I am." I checked the Fulton County Assessors website and confirmed an address I had found when I couldn't sleep the night before.

He stood and headed toward the kitchen. "Need more coffee?"

I set down my phone. "You feel like going for a drive to the south side?"

"Care to tell me why?"

"Something's not sitting right with me, and I'm hoping this will help."

"What did Leland say was rule number one?" he asked.

"Fine. You can drive."

Parks revved the engine and furrowed his brow as he glanced at me. "The Cleveland Avenue Corridor? You sure about that?"

"Did I mention I didn't sleep last night?"

He backed out of his parking spot and used the side exit for my complex. "Okay. What did you find?"

"John Sr. snagged a double plot of land at the intersection of Cleveland and Metropolitan Parkway."

"Interesting. When was this?"

"Back in 1997," I said, tucking a stray hair behind my ear. "Built a warehouse, but I'm not sure if he ever used it. He never rented it, so there's that."

"Did you get a photo of the lot?" Parks asked. He eased onto the highway.

"I couldn't find anything online, but I sent an email to the assessor's office. They might have one."

"What's your intuition telling you?" he asked.

"That it's important to check it out."

"GPS the directions on your phone," he said. "Please."

An hour and forty-five minutes, three accidents, and one stalled van later, the Cleveland Avenue Corridor stretched out before us.

"Look at that," I said with sarcasm. "Made it in record time."

"They need to revitalize this area," Parks said. "It's high crime."

I held up my bag and gave him a wry smile. "Brought my own peacekeeper."

"Carrying it in a purse won't do much good."

"I'll stuff it into my waistband, smartass." I removed it from my bag and did as I said.

He laughed.

He was right. The area needed help. A patchwork of worn-out storefronts, crumbling brick buildings, and rusted-out cars parked haphazardly along cracked sidewalks proved that.

"What's the address again?"

I scanned the buildings. "It's at the intersection of Metropolitan Parkway."

"Also not a great area," he said.

"The corridor isn't a great area in general."

A double lot came into view—a hulking, empty building squatted on it, its broken windows a sign it was the right place. "There," I said. "That's the place."

"It looks abandoned."

"Perfect," I said.

"We're going inside, aren't we?"

"After we check out the outside, yes."

He exhaled. "Nothing we find will be admissible in court, Jenna. You know that."

"Maybe, maybe not, but in my experience with the GBI, there's always a work-around."

"Not with NCIS. The Navy doesn't play that way."

"I don't doubt that, but it's not illegal entry if the windows are open and we don't see any 'no trespassing' or 'private property' signs."

"You're pushing it," he said, "but okay." He parked the car behind the building, stepped out, and slipped his weapon into a holster connected to his belt. "You got extra magazines?"

I climbed out of the car and removed two extra magazines from my bag. I held them up for him to see. "Can you open the trunk so I can toss in my bag?"

He clicked the key fob, and the trunk opened. "Done."

The back of the building had been set up for deliveries, with two garage doors and a door in between them. Shattered glass from the door's window covered the ground, and the door had been partially propped open.

How They Were Taken   167

"This is a high-crime area," I said. "I'm worried someone is inside and in danger."

"Could be a haven for addicts," he said. "And with our drug problem in the city, the chances are high."

"We should check," I said.

Parks used his shirt to push the door open further.

Graffiti covered the walls, the shipping crates, and the floors.

"Looks like every other abandoned warehouse I've seen," I murmured, my voice echoing off the cavernous walls.

"It's sad and pathetic," Parks said, sweeping his flashlight across the concrete floor. His light caught on a circle of charred stones, remnants of a fire, surrounded by empty bottles and a constellation of syringes and spoons. My throat tightened. "I've been around a lot of addicts. Some choose the life, but most don't. That craving kidnaps them, and they just can't fight it."

"Can't imagine that kind of life," he said.

We moved deeper into the building, each step kicking up the scent of chemical decay and mold. Near one corner, I stopped, my flashlight highlighting a crude encampment. Pallets and discarded cardboard formed a makeshift bed, with the bedding moldy and damp. A spool table held the sad detritus of addiction—a lighter, a tarnished spoon, and tangled rubber tubing.

Parks stood in front of a wall and read the graffiti. "Some of this is good," he said, his voice low, his gaze fixed on the desperate messages scrawled across the concrete.

I traced one of the messages with my finger, feeling the rough texture of desperation under my skin. "It's like they're all screaming to be heard," I murmured.

Navigating past towering columns, we came to a section divided by partitions of scavenged wood and metal sheeting. The makeshift rooms formed a labyrinthine network, each turn and alcove holding the potential for shadowed secrets. My heart thumped louder as we approached one particularly dark partition.

Inside, a stained mattress lay surrounded by candles that had burned down to stubs, their wax pooled in the floor's cracks like frozen tears. I paused, my breath catching. "Someone was living here, Parks. Really living."

"And probably suffering," Parks added, nodding solemnly.

My flashlight flickered slightly, causing my pulse to jump before steadying as the beam settled on a peculiar sight on the floor. "Parks, look at this."

He came up beside me, his own light converging with mine on a patch of concrete that appeared markedly different from its surroundings. The rough edges and uneven coloration stood out—a rectangular patch, about six feet by three feet, meticulously cut and then awkwardly resealed.

"Looks like they had a leak or something." He flashed his light to the ceiling. "Don't see anything up there."

I kept my light on the spot. "This thing is at least six feet long, and maybe three feet wide. We'd notice the repairs to a leak that big, especially if it came from the ceiling." I crouched down and ran my fingers over the gritty texture. "This has been dug up and replaced. From the looks of the concrete, it wasn't too long ago."

Parks crouched down and examined the concrete. "It's a grave."

The stillness of the warehouse shattered with the deafening crack of a gunshot. The sound ricocheted off the steel beams and concrete walls, reverberating like an explosion in a metal drum. Each echo bounced and twisted, making it impossible to pinpoint the origin immediately. The sharp scent of gunpowder mingled with the stale air, burning at the edges of my nostrils.

At the whistling scream of the bullet, I yanked my weapon free and gripped it tightly as I ducked and rolled hard. My shoulder collided with the cold concrete, sending a sharp jolt of pain up my arm.

The bullet had punched a jagged hole in a rusted metal support beam before clanging against the far wall, sending a spray of concrete dust cascading like a fine mist. A metallic clink followed as it hit the floor, the faint sound swallowed quickly by the vast emptiness.

I scanned for Parks and spotted him pressed against a concrete pole, his gun ready. "I'm good," I murmured, keeping my voice barely above a whisper. I hurried to another pole near him and flattened myself against it, standing ramrod straight.

How They Were Taken

We locked eyes, and we each nodded a quick confirmation of survival. "You see where it came from?" His voice was low and steady.

"No," I admitted as frustration tightened my chest. My gaze flicked to the jagged hole in the beam above him. "Either it was a warning shot, or the shooter needs glasses."

"Figured that out," he muttered, his jaw clenching as his eyes swept the vast expanse of the warehouse.

"There are two doors over there," he said, his gun lifting to point toward the far wall. "The one on the left wasn't open when we got here. You ready?"

I nodded.

We each maneuvered toward nearby shipping containers, creeping toward the door, but we froze when another door slammed in the distance. Then, faintly, the sound of footsteps—quick and uneven—echoed through the space, the metallic ring of boots on concrete.

"North side," Parks whispered, tilting his head in the direction of the noise.

"I hear it," I said, dropping into a crouch. My eyes locked on the far side of the warehouse, but the maze of concrete columns and abandoned debris blocked the exit. The footsteps grew fainter, fading into the shadows.

"Damn it," Parks growled, frustration bristling in his tone. "There's got to be another entrance. We're losing them!"

I moved fast, trying not to make a sound.

The echoes in the warehouse disoriented me. The runner could have been twenty feet away or a hundred, but their fading footsteps hinted they were close to escaping. My mind raced through possibilities. Why take one shot and then run?

"Did you spot a tail on the way here?" I asked, my eyes still searching.

"No, but it can't be the McAllister kid if they've got eyes on him. You see anything?"

"No, but that doesn't mean it's a McAllister. This could be anyone—a gang member, a junkie, anything."

"Doesn't mean it isn't. We don't know if Titanium has found the aunt." He gestured toward a cluster of stacked pallets near the far wall. "Cover that side. I'll check the other."

"No splitting up," I snapped, my voice low but forceful. "Not with a shooter on the loose."

He hesitated, then gave a curt nod. "Fine. Your call."

We moved together, our weapons drawn, covering each other's blind spots as we advanced. Every nerve in my body buzzed, my muscles taut with tension. The wide concrete floor offered little cover, making every step feel like a gamble.

Another sound—a door creaking open, then slamming shut—pierced the quiet. My heart sank. Whoever it was, they were out.

"East side," Parks said grimly. "That service door by the loading dock."

I bit back a curse and sprinted toward the door. Parks flanked me as I pressed my back against the wall, peering out cautiously. The late morning air rushed in, sharp and biting.

"Clear," I muttered, stepping outside to scan the cracked asphalt and the gas station beside us.

Parks kept his gun drawn, his posture rigid. "It's them," he said, his tone resolute. "They know we're close."

I turned back toward the warehouse, its towering walls casting long shadows. "My gut agrees."

"We need to clear the warehouse," he said, already pivoting back toward the door.

I nodded, my mind racing. "I'll call Leland. He can decide if we bring in the GBI or Atlanta PD."

We reentered the warehouse, weapons at the ready, every sense honed for the slightest movement.

The sweep was slow and methodical. We checked behind every stack of pallets, inside every rusted crate, and through every shadowed corner. The emptiness mocked us, offering no clues.

"Clear," Parks said, emerging from the far side.

"Clear," I echoed, lowering my weapon but keeping it in hand. My pulse still pounded, the adrenaline coursing through my veins. My hands trembled slightly, a sensation I despised. Vulnerability cloaked in tension.

Parks leaned against a column, his face a storm of frustration and determination. "This isn't over," he said. "Not by a long shot."

How They Were Taken

Leland and his team—formerly my team—stood around the rectangle and stared at it like it was some kind of foreign object. "We'll have to get a warrant," he said.

I knew procedure. "I have all the information at my place, but I'd like to be on the call when you ask."

"I would as well," Parks said.

Leland and APD Deputy Chief Jason Miller examined the empty warehouse.

"Who owns this space?" Leland asked.

"John McAllister Sr.," I said.

"Why are you here?" Miller asked.

"We're investigating the Steadman case," Parks said.

"And it led you here?" he asked.

I bit my tongue, knowing if I said something, I'd get a look from Leland that would burn into my soul.

"We have reason to believe at least one of the owners might be involved," I said.

"At least one?" Miller asked.

Leland and I exchanged a look, then I said, "There are four girls we can link to the McAllister HVAC company. We came here to check out the space to see if it had any connection to the missing girls."

Parks added, "We need an excavating team to dig up a spot we think might be a grave."

Miller's eyes widened. "I can't just—"

Leland cut him off. "This is a sensitive investigation, Jason. Jessica Steadman hired these two to find her daughter. I would appreciate it if you would step aside and let the GBI handle this with them."

Miller looked at me. "She hired you?"

I nodded.

He dragged his hand down his face, blew out a breath, then nodded at Leland. "Fine, but if this thing gets bigger, I want in."

"Appreciate that," Leland said.

Miller looked at me and Parks. "What about them?"

"What about us?" I asked, blowing all politeness out the window. "It's our investigation."

"They'll assist." Leland threw me a look that said zip it. Thankfully, I didn't work for him anymore. "I'm confident Jessica Steadman's relationship with the governor will impact who handles the investigation. I'll contact her now."

Miller smirked. "I'll leave you three to battle it out."

After he left, I asked Leland, "What the hell was that? We'll assist? I wasn't kidding about calling Steadman. Everyone knows she's close with the governor."

"Calm down, princess. I didn't want Miller ramming the APD down our throats. I'll call the governor myself and let him know it's your investigation and we're assisting." He called over Agent Buckley. "Get on the phone with Judge Garrett and let him know we're working with Wyatt. Then give her the phone and let her handle the rest."

"Yes, sir," Buckley said.

16

I stood at the edge of the excavation zone, my arms folded over my chest to ward off the chill of the cavernous warehouse—or perhaps the deeper, gnawing cold of anticipation that had settled in my bones. To an onlooker, I might have appeared calm and collected, poised even, with my firm stance and the implacable set of my jaw. But beneath that composed exterior, anxiety churned relentlessly. I had been in grim situations before; some so horrible, multiple agents couldn't handle them—too many to count—but nothing quite like boring into concrete hoping to find the remains of a five-year-old girl. Or several five-year-old girls.

Mark Levine, the head of the forensic excavation team, briefed us on the procedure. He spoke clearly and with a matter-of-fact tone. "We're set to penetrate the layers," he explained. His eyes scanned over the blue X spray-painted on the floor marking where the remains of Emma Steadman or one of the other girls might be found. Though the chance was slim, the thought made my stomach churn.

The roar of the core drill filled the warehouse as it sliced into the concrete, its shrill cry echoing off the walls, jarring me. Dust billowed around us, caught in the beams of light streaming from temporary flood-lights. I watched as the team worked with surgical precision, their movements practiced and efficient, each phase executed with a meticulousness that mirrored the importance of what we hoped to unearth.

"We're about to breach the core," Levine shouted over the din. He nodded at me. I edged closer, the law enforcement professional in me needing to see, to understand every step of the macabre excavation. As they withdrew the core sample, a muted anticipation gripped everyone present. A thickening silence enveloped us when the drill finally halted, and the dust settled.

"Hawkins," Levine barked, "is the camera probe ready?"

He nodded. "Yes, sir, boss."

I held my breath as he lowered the small, illuminated device into the dark cavity. We all crowded around the screen as the monitor flickered to life, our eyes fixed on the grainy images being transmitted back to us. Suddenly, the camera passed over a metallic object. "There." I pointed to a metal box, my heart racing. "It's a container of some sort."

While our demeanor stayed professional, every one of us understood the seriousness of what lay ahead. Using a small crane, the team hoisted the container from its grave. The clang of metal on metal reverberated through the silent warehouse, heightening the tension as the sound of the metal scraping against the sides of the hole sent shivers down my spine.

Once on the surface, the reality of our discovery set in. Mark, with a solemn nod to me, opened the clasp. The creak of the hinge resonated in the hushed atmosphere. It groaned as the lid swung open.

I recognized the girl immediately. Inside, sealed in a clear plastic bag, were the small, painstakingly preserved remains of Emma Steadman.

My vision blurred momentarily, tears unbidden but not unwelcome. "We found you, Emma," I whispered. "You're going home now."

Parks cleared his throat. "It's her."

"Emma Steadman," Leland said.

I could barely speak, partly because we couldn't save her, and partly because it wasn't Molly in that trunk. "I'll call Steadman. She'll want to be here."

"You think that's a good idea?" Leland asked.

"No," I said, "but her money has more influence than my miniscule amount of authority."

How They Were Taken 175

The forensic team sprang into action, documenting and carefully preparing Emma's remains for transport. The little girl who had disappeared a year ago was no longer just a file on a desk or a face on a missing persons poster. She was real, and she had been waiting for us.

The solemn procession of her remains out of the warehouse felt like a silent vigil. As they worked, I stepped back, allowing the professionals to do their job while I processed the whirlwind of emotions. This was a somber victory, shadowed by the weight of a young life lost.

This wasn't the end of the case, far from it. It was the beginning of another chapter, the most important one, where justice needed to be sought and served. An abductor and a killer lurked in the shadows, and we were closer than ever to dragging them into the light. I walked outside. The city hadn't stopped; it never did. But for a moment, I wanted everything to pause, just for Emma Steadman.

Jessica Steadman walked in with a calm I couldn't begin to imagine. She had known that finding Emma alive wasn't likely, but I hadn't expected her stoic demeanor.

"I'm sorry," I said.

"Don't be." She scanned the space. "Just find the bastard that killed my family."

"We're close," I said. "It's just going to take a little more time, but now we have the GBI supporting us, and that will help."

Her straight lips flinched, telling me her lack of emotion wouldn't last. "Where is my daughter?"

I pointed to the metal box. "She's over there. We'll give you a few minutes."

"I won't need that much time," she said. I glimpsed her push her shoulders back and straighten her neck as she walked toward the box.

Parks caught my eye and exhaled. He dropped his head and walked to her. She leaned her head onto his shoulder when he placed his hand on the small of her back.

"That's interesting," Leland said behind me. He stood next to me with his hands on his hips. "I guess working together for a year made them close."

I shrugged. "Or he's disgustingly unprofessional."

He turned and looked me in the eye. "Sounds like someone's jealous."

"Uh," I said as I held back a laugh. "Not even close. It just hinders an investigation. Isn't that why GBI says agents can't get involved with their witnesses or victims?"

He nodded. "Doesn't mean it doesn't happen, Jenna. The world isn't perfect."

I watched Jessica Steadman kneel next to the box and whisper something to her daughter's remains. "Tell me about it."

A few minutes later, she and Parks walked over.

"Tell me what's going on," she said to me. She stepped to the side, creating distance between her and Parks.

I spoke first. "We discovered matching shoe prints on several of the cases, but not all, though we also discovered the same sole and similar, but not identical, wear patterns for another girl."

"A shoe print?" She breathed out her nose.

"No, ma'am," I said. "As I mentioned before, we also have the McAllister Heating and Air connection."

She raised an eyebrow. "And you've confirmed this with the rest of the families, as I asked?"

"Yes, ma'am, but we would have done it without your request. It's part of the job."

"And what exactly did you find?"

"Within a short time frame of each abduction other than my sister's, which can't be confirmed yet, one of the McAllister team serviced the HVAC system at the homes."

"Which means their service guy cased the place ahead of time," Parks said.

"I already determined that," she said.

His jaw tightened. "It also explains why the girls were abducted without being noticed."

"Except in Emma's case," she said. She looked me in the eye. "And Molly's."

How They Were Taken   177

"Which is why we believe your husband was shot," I said. "The abductor didn't expect your husband to be there and felt he had no other choice but to take his life to abduct Emma."

"What about Molly, then? Why are you still alive?"

I had asked that same question for years. "I can't answer that."

"But you think it's the same person?"

"Not exactly," Parks said.

She glared at him. "I was asking her." The disdain dripping from her tone didn't surprise me anymore.

"No. We think it's a family affair. We just aren't sure if it's a father and son, or a grandfather, son, and grandson."

"And when will this be finished?" She cleared her throat.

I thought I saw a flicker of emotion, something other than control or anger, flash across her face, but it was gone in an instant.

"When will you find my daughter's killer?"

"I wouldn't want to guess, but I can promise you we're doing everything we can to find your daughter's killer."

She waved her finger between me and Parks. "And this arrangement, it's working for you?"

"Yes." I caught Parks's eye and smirked. "Contrary to what I expected, Parks has been incredibly helpful."

She rolled her eyes. "Well then, carry on."

"There's one more thing," I said.

She swirled her hand in tight circles, encouraging me to continue.

"Someone's been watching me, and we suspect they've been watching you as well. I'd like to get security on you."

"I already have security," she said.

It would have been nice to know that. "Are they here now?"

She nodded. "They're across the street in a Georgia Power van."

"How many?"

"Four," she said.

I glanced at Buckley standing beside Leland. "Would you mind bringing one of them in?"

He nodded and hurried to the exit.

"Has anything happened with them?" I asked. "Any threats or damage to property?"

"No."

"No strange phone calls? No one trying to run your vehicles off the road?"

"I said no."

A tall, muscular man in a black suit walked in with Buckley. His look bled former Secret Service.

"This is Steven Turner," Steadman said. "He's been the lead of my security team for several years now." She introduced us.

It would have been nice if she had done that before, and I made sure to mention that.

"We ask that she keep our work with her private," Turner said. "The more attention we receive, the bigger the chance of something happening."

"Understood," I said, which I did, but things had changed. "Have you seen anyone in a black SUV around the Steadman home or when Mrs. Steadman is out in public?"

"No, ma'am."

Then he wasn't doing his job. "Mr. Turner, I personally have had a black SUV tailing me multiple times, and this has occurred after leaving the Steadman property."

"Yes, ma'am," he said. "We noted that."

I cocked my head to the side. "You noted it but did nothing about it?"

"We ran a check on the vehicle, but the plates came back as stolen. We reported it to the police."

"But not to me." I crossed my arms. "Why is that?"

"It was clear you already knew about the tail."

I looked at Steadman. "Ma'am, we need your security team to stay in constant contact with us. Our suspect knows we're closing in on him, and it's important we know what your men see or do."

"Steven," she said, "please follow Ms. Wyatt's lead."

"Yes, ma'am."

The coroner walked over. "We're ready to transport the remains."

"Very well," Steadman said. She looked at me. "Please update me as soon as possible."

How They Were Taken 179

Leland scrubbed his hand down his face. "I wish you would have told me about this tail before they blew up Parks's vehicle. I could have prevented all this."

"First off, you can't guarantee that. Second, I don't report to you anymore, Leland."

"Oh, don't give me that crap." He paced a short line back and forth in front of me. "You know we're more than boss and agent. You should have told me the minute you noticed someone on you."

He was right. Our relationship had been more than just work, which was exactly why I didn't tell him from the start. "I didn't want you worried or more involved than you already were."

"What else aren't you telling me?"

"That's it," I lied.

"I know when you're lying, so just cut the bullshit and tell me."

"Fine. Someone shot at us before we called you."

"Here?"

"Yes. They got away."

He mumbled something inaudible under his breath, then added, "Why didn't you tell me?"

"Look at this place. It's a multi-use structure. There are obvious signs of homeless people staying here, addicts, gang members, God knows who else. It could have been any of them. We can't guarantee it was our guy."

Leland tipped his head back, then said, "Can't guarantee it wasn't, either. Did you see the SUV?"

"No," Parks said.

He called an agent over after we filled him in on what had happened. "Get on this," he said, and explained the details.

The agent acted quickly.

He raised an eyebrow while staring at me. "What else?"

"You already know we've got people on Nick and Alyssa. That's it."

He referred to Parks. "Is she telling me the truth?"

"Yes."

"At least Parks is smart enough to do the right thing. From now on, you bring us in when it gets dirty. Neither of you are equipped to handle this alone."

"We're not alone," I said. "We're working as a team."

"Don't push me, Wyatt."

"Fine, Leland, but can we save the lectures for after we catch the McAllister family, please? I'd like to get back to work."

I filled him in on Linda McAllister's indirect threat, ending it with, "Either she found out her niece talked to us, or the niece is involved too."

"And you haven't heard from her?" he asked.

"Not again. Since you're assisting, I thought we could send one of the agents in undercover. They might be hiring."

He opened his mouth slightly, something he did sometimes while thinking. "Okay, we'll send in Fletcher." He made a call and said, "Let's let the team finish up here. Meet me at the department. We'll get Fletcher set up."

"No," I said. "If we go, it'll be obvious. You prep him and call me if you have any questions." I made eye contact with Parks. "We're going to find Lisa McAllister."

17

Parks had dropped me off at home and picked up a rental after donning a fresh outfit, one that didn't scream former NCIS and current PI. He returned to my place and knocked on the door.

I had showered and changed into a short black dress, a pair of stilettos that killed my feet in less than two minutes, slopped on a ton of makeup, curled my long hair, then clipped it away from my face.

He whistled when he saw me. "Damn, Wyatt. You clean up nicely." He handed me a dozen red roses.

I took them and said, "Oh, nice touch." I admired him in his black tux but cringed at the fake hair he'd pulled over his own. "Balding isn't a good look for you."

He laughed. "I'm sure it's coming. Every man in my family had or has a horseshoe."

"Sorry about that." I smirked. "You had a tux?"

"PIs need everything from overalls to formal attire. You'll learn that soon enough."

I laughed because he likely knew I had outfits to look like a hooker and everything else.

"What kind of car did you get?"

"Ferrari."

"From a rental company," I said with a hint of sarcasm. "Bet that wasn't cheap."

He laughed. Jessica Steadman had set him up with one of her luxury cars, then had one of her men drive it to the rental company for him to sneak off in.

"We hung out inside talking about UGA football, and after a few minutes, I took the car, and he got a ride home from another one of Jessica's men."

"That's brilliant," I admitted. "I'm surprised you thought of it."

"Nice, Wyatt," he said.

"Did you get the other car set up too?"

"Are you planning to grade me on this or something?"

"Possibly."

"Then I'll get an A." His eyes sparkled when he smiled. "You ready?"

"One sec," I said. I grabbed my small purse, my overnight bag, and a pair of flats off the table.

He raised an eyebrow at my shoes. "What are the flats for?"

"Put on my stilettos and you'll find out."

We walked to the car arm in arm, him limping slightly, and me wishing I could kick off the stilettos setting the balls of my feet on fire.

He whispered in my ear. "You like the limp?"

I giggled. If we were being watched, we needed to play it out. "It's perfect."

The plan was simple. Create an elaborate distraction, drive to the Waldorf in Atlanta and act like we had a formal event and would be there for the night. Once inside the room Steadman had reserved for us, we would change into our next disguise, then leave through an employee entrance and head to Lisa McAllister's without a tail.

"Traffic sucks, but that'll give us time to find out where Lisa McAllister lives," he said.

Tricks of the trade made getting her address easy. What shocked me was learning she lived with her aunt.

Parks said the obvious. "At least we're prepared."

How They Were Taken 183

Parks smiled as we climbed into the Fulton County Animal Control truck. "You look good with red hair."

"Thanks. Wish I could say the same thing about your mullet."

He feigned shock. "Babe, I'm all business in the front, party in the back."

I cringed. "Ew, and please, never call me babe again."

He laughed. "Green contacts are a nice touch too."

"Good, because they were a bitch putting in."

"You'd get used to it if you really needed them."

Twenty minutes later, we had pulled up to Linda McAllister's home and parked in the driveway behind only one car, a newer-model Honda Civic.

"That's Lisa's," I said. "I had Leland get me the 411 on every vehicle the McAllisters own."

"Nice work, partner, but we're following our plan anyway, correct?"

"Yes."

We climbed out of the truck, grabbed the necessary equipment, and headed to the front door.

Lisa answered. "Yes?"

We had planned for me to talk as little as possible until identifying ourselves. I didn't want her to recognize my voice. She could have recognized Parks's as well, but the chances were less.

"Ma'am, I'm Billy Fuller, and this is my partner, Sue Bain." He flashed her a fake ID. "We're Fulton County Animal Control officers, and we're here to discuss a rabid German shepherd on the loose."

Her eyes widened. "There's a rabid dog on the loose here?"

"Yes, ma'am. If you have a moment, we'd like to step inside and discuss it."

"Inside?" She took a step back.

"Ma'am, there have been multiple sightings and two attacks already. I'm surprised you didn't hear the sirens. A man two streets over was bitten just over an hour ago. It's not safe for you outside."

"Sure," she said hesitantly. "Come on in."

I walked in last and closed the door behind me.

"Is your husband home?" Parks asked.

Lisa chuckled quietly. "I live with my aunt, but she's not home. You're lucky I am. I have the day off."

I set my catch pole and net on the floor. "Lisa, we need to talk."

She looked at me. "How did you know my name?"

"Because it's me, Jenna Wyatt, and my partner, Jack Parks. You haven't returned my calls."

Lisa McAllister's face transformed at the mention of my name. Her eyes widened for a split second before her gaze darted to the floor. I watched as her fingers twisted nervously at her sides. Her knuckles whitened with each twist. When she finally spoke, she stammered, clearly struggling to maintain her composure. "You can't be here."

"Why not?" I asked. "Is it Linda or Jimmy that's been following us?"

She cleared her throat. "I don't know. I don't know anything."

I walked toward the small love seat in the main room, told her to sit, and then I settled into the worn chair opposite her. Parks leaned against the wall near the door, his presence an unspoken barrier between Lisa and any thought of escape.

"Lisa, this is important." I kept my tone deliberately gentle yet firm enough to convey the seriousness of our visit. "Where is your aunt?"

"I don't know."

"We have people looking for her, but we can't find her."

"I don't know where she is. Why are you looking for her?"

"We found Emma Steadman's remains in your family's warehouse."

Her eyes flinched at the mention of the warehouse, and a visible swallow tightened her throat as she absorbed the implications. "I didn't—I don't know what you want me to say. I don't know what you're talking about."

"Yes, you do," I said.

Parks pushed off from the wall and walked over, his footsteps soft on the hardwood floor. "We know your family is involved, Lisa."

I added, "What we don't know is if you're involved."

"I'm not," she said quickly.

"Why didn't you return my calls?" I asked, watching as her fingers clenched into the fabric of her shirt.

She glanced nervously toward the window, as if expecting to see her

How They Were Taken 185

aunt's face pressed against the glass. "You should go. She could come home any minute."

"You just said you don't know where she is," I said. "Listen, if you play nice, we can make sure the police do too. You may not have to go to jail."

Her mouth hung open. "Jail? Why would I—" She dropped her head into her hands and sobbed.

"Tell us what you know. You can start with why you didn't call me back, and why your aunt threatened me."

She looked up and wiped her eyes. "She threatened you?"

"Yes. What did you tell her?"

"Nothing, I swear. She must have seen the email from you."

"She has access to your email?" Parks asked.

"It was the main email for the company."

"Did she say something to you?" I asked.

She nodded. "She told me to stop talking to you, that you were setting a trap to destroy our business."

"Did she mention why we might want to destroy the business?" Parks asked.

She shook her head. "All she said then is that if I didn't stay out of it, something bad would happen." She wiped her nose and added, "I think she knows I've been going through our files."

Parks and I made eye contact. "The aunt's definitely involved," he said.

"Lisa," I said, "what does your aunt do during the day?"

"I don't know. She still comes to work sometimes, but I try not to talk to her much."

"Someone blew up my car," Parks said. "And shot at us in your family's warehouse. Do you think it's her?"

Lisa's gaze flickered to mine, fear stark in her eyes. She nodded. "I think she's protecting my family—she always has."

Parks knelt in front of her, trying to level himself with her sight. "Protect them from abducting more girls?"

"From getting caught. I told you they're not nice. My brother isn't either. He does bad things."

"Bad things like drunk driving, stealing cars?" I asked. "What kind of bad things?"

"I think you're right. I think he killed that man and took her daughter. I checked the records, and he was at their house a few weeks before it all happened."

"Do you still have access to those records?" I asked.

She nodded. "I made copies. I was afraid she would know I took the originals."

"May we see them?" Parks asked.

She stumbled over her words. "I don't have them with me. They're with the others."

"The others?" I asked. "What do you mean?"

"I knew something was going on when you sent that email. Everyone knew about the rich girl disappearing. I looked her up after we met. When I saw what she looked like, I knew. I just knew." She shook her head and dabbed a finger into the corner of her right eye.

"Knew what? What did you see?" Parks asked.

"I can't believe I didn't see it before." She looked him in the eyes. "That my family was involved.'

"Lisa, we can protect you, but you have to tell us what you know," I said. "What about Emma Steadman made you realize that?"

She sucked in a shaky breath as her eyes darted between me and Parks. "It started with my grandfather, then my father took over. Now it's my brother." Tears pooled in her eyes and spilled over as she confessed. "I think one of the girls' fathers killed my dad."

"What didn't you see before?" I asked.

"The girls all look like my dead aunt."

I glanced at Parks, hoping he would feign surprise with me. "Dead aunt?"

"She was raped and murdered when she was five. Three months later, my grandpa found her remains by the creek near our old property."

"Was she buried in anything?" I asked.

"A metal box. According to my aunt Linda, the autopsy showed she had been strangled, but I don't know if that's true. She said the police barely did anything, and they never found the person who did it. My dad always said it was because we weren't rich, and people only cared what happened to their rich friends' kids."

How They Were Taken 187

"What year was this?"

"I think it was 1967. Mary was my aunt's twin."

"Do you have a photo of her?" Parks asked.

She pointed to a photo on the bookshelf.

Mary and Molly could have been sisters. Lisa hadn't known the truth before. She might have suspected it, but something had confirmed it for her. "You checked the other names and dates, didn't you?"

She nodded. "It wasn't as hard as I thought. My aunt is very meticulous and organized. My grandfather serviced the Simpsons and the Rylands. My dad went to the Bryant and Hansen houses, and my brother to the Steadmans' house."

Her gaze settled on the faded carpet. "My mom told me my grandparents never got over it. She said it hardened the entire family. I overheard conversations as a kid, and I saw some things I probably shouldn't have."

"Things having to do with the girls?"

"Maybe? I'm not sure. Things got better when my grandpa died." She breathed in a sob. "Until they weren't."

"How so?" Parks asked.

"My father started staying out late, and sometimes he didn't bother coming home. My parents argued all the time."

"Was he having an affair?"

"I don't know, but she used to bring up his sister and other girls like her, but I didn't put it together." She paused, then added, "They divorced a year before he died."

"Go on," I said.

"Like I told you before, my brother took over the business. My aunt kept up everything until she went part-time." She stuffed her hands under her thighs. "I knew something was going on with the dates when I saw the more recent ones."

"You lied to me about not being close to your dad's family," I said. "You're living with your aunt."

"I'm not close to them. I'm having a house built, and I couldn't find a place for a few months that I can afford."

I asked a question I already knew the answer to. "Lisa, do your servicemen wear uniforms?"

"Of course. We order their first outfit when they sign on, but the rest are at their expense."

"And the shoes?"

She dropped her head and stared at the floor again. "I lied about those. I didn't want to think my family was involved."

Parks stood and paced a small circle before stopping in front of her again. "Is that all?"

"Yes."

"Where are the copies of the files?" I asked.

"In the attic of the house I'm having built."

"Is the home in a community like this?"

"Yes. Why?"

"So other people live there already?"

"Oh, it's a new community. My house is the third one being built. Does that matter?"

I walked over to the window and glanced outside but couldn't see Hallowell's men. "Parks, we can't have security follow us. Too many cars could be a dead giveaway."

"I agree," he said.

I called Hallowell and asked for his men to stand down.

"Are you sure you want to do that? We still haven't located the aunt," he said.

"I'm sure."

We left Linda McAllister's home and drove to the community's entrance, then pulled over and waited for Lisa to pass. It had been a risk leaving her to drive alone, but it would have been an even bigger one to take her with us.

We parked a few lots away from Lisa's new place, a modest two-story that matched the design of the model home. Parks killed the engine, and then we hurried to the back of the house, carrying our animal control equipment to keep up our act.

She met us at the back door. Her nose and eyes were even more swollen

How They Were Taken

from crying. "Do you think we were followed?" she murmured. Her voice was shaky as she led us inside.

"No," I said. "We made sure that wouldn't happen." At least I hoped we had.

"The attic door is in the master. The only room on the left."

The house still echoed with the emptiness of a place almost finished but not yet lived in as we climbed the stairs.

"There," she said. "There's a light just on the right side. It's a metal box underneath the insulation near the window."

"I'll get it," Parks said. He climbed the ladder and disappeared into the attic. He returned moments later with a metal safe in his hands. He set it on the floor. "Where's the key?"

Lisa's hands trembled as she handed it to him. "What's going to happen to me?"

"We'll keep you safe," I said. "I've contacted the Georgia Bureau of Investigation, and they've already got a place for you to stay."

"Okay. Everything is in there," she said as her voice broke.

I placed a reassuring hand on her shoulder. "You did the right thing. Those girls' families need closure."

She nodded and wiped away tears that had spilled from her eyes. "I just want all this to end."

Most murder investigations were seventy-five percent grunt work by the investigators, twenty percent witness statements, and five percent luck.

That lockbox held the million-dollar five percent we needed. The final nail in the McAllisters' killing coffin.

"What's this?" Parks asked. He held up a black leather-bound journal.

"That's everything," she said.

Parks's eyes widened after skimming through the first pages. "I don't even know what to say." He handed it to me.

I flipped through the first pages and asked, "Why didn't you tell us about this?"

She shook her head, and through sobs said, "I don't know."

Taped photos of Lisa McAllister's aunt Mary filled the first few pages of the journal. On the sides of each picture, someone had noted where they had been when the photo was taken. From the descriptions, it was clear the journal belonged to the first John McAllister, Lisa's grandfather.

Further into the journal, after several blank pages, were pages of taped photos of Lizzie Ryland and my sister. My breath caught in my throat when I glimpsed a photo of Molly and me at the park near our house. I remembered the day like it had just happened. I had complained about taking her, but my mother had had a date, and she needed to get ready. Next to the photos he had written the details of his abduction and what he had done to her. Parks tried to take the book from me, but I gripped it so tight, he couldn't.

"You shouldn't read that," he said.

"Are you kidding me? I need to." But just a few sentences in, I handed it back to him. "I can't. Not now."

He flipped through the next few pages with photos and details about Lizzie Ryland. When he got to Lily Hansen, he stopped. "The writing's changed."

"That's my father's," Lisa said.

He scanned the pages, then backtracked to the previous ones, then continued to Zoe Bryant and Emma Steadman. "It changes again with Emma's photos."

Lisa whispered, "My brother."

A sharp creak shattered the brief silence and snapped my attention toward it. My pulse quickened as I instinctively reached for the weapon tucked at the small of my back. But before I could draw, a hand holding a gun pointed at me, firm and unyielding, and stopped me cold. My gaze darted to the woman, her eyes locked on mine with an intensity that froze me in place. Her sharp voice sliced through the tension. She kept her gun aimed at me.

"Don't even think about it." Her eyes darkened with a dangerous intensity. She flicked her gun to Parks. "And you, don't move. Man, I've wanted to take you out forever."

The way she tilted the gun, cocked slightly to the side, told me she

How They Were Taken 191

wasn't bluffing. From this distance, she didn't need to be accurate—just close enough. And she was. Dangerously so.

"Aunt Linda," Lisa cried. "Please!"

"Put the gun down, Linda," I said. "Two against one won't end well for you."

"I'm the one holding the gun!" she hissed, waving it between me and Parks. Her lips twisted into a cruel smile. "That gives me all the power. Now shut up and hand me the journal."

Lisa cowered behind me, her breath so heavy I felt it against my neck. "Please," she said. "They can help us. We can end this."

"You shut up, little girl. I knew bringing you on was a bad move. You're just like your mother. Should have killed her when we had the chance."

We?

"Linda, listen to me," I tried again with a calm but firm voice. "This isn't the way to protect anyone—not even yourself."

"Protect?" Linda scoffed, a bitter laugh escaping her. "You think we need protection from the likes of you? I've kept our family's secrets safe from prying eyes all these years, and I won't stop now, especially not because of her." She spit her words toward Lisa with a look of pure contempt.

Parks adjusted his stance, readying himself to intervene at any second. He tried to calm her. "There are other ways to handle this, Linda. Ways that don't end in more tragedy. Think this through."

"Think this through?" Her voice rose, sharp as the edge of a knife. "I have thought this through. Every night, every day, for years! You don't understand the necessity of our actions! I can't let anything happen to Jimmy. It's not his fault. He was doing what he had to."

"He didn't have to," Lisa said. "He could have been a better person, but you and my father had to ruin him!"

Linda's face twisted with rage. Her voice dropped, ice-cold. "I've had enough of you."

Her arm extended. The gun shifted.

Time slowed.

And then she pulled the trigger.

Instinct kicked in. I pulled my weapon from my waist before she could take another shot.

Linda's head snapped back as the bullet struck her square between the eyes. She staggered, the gun slipped from her grasp, and she tumbled backward. Her body slammed against the stairs before crumpling in a heap at the bottom.

Parks dropped to check on Lisa. "She's breathing, but barely. The bullet hit her in the right side of the abdomen. She shouldn't be unconscious."

"That's not what did it," I said as I watched the insulation under her head redden. "She hit her head on something when she collapsed." I called 911, reported where we were and what had happened, told them to put out a BOLO for Jimmy McAllister, and then asked them to contact Leland.

"She's not breathing," Parks yelled. "I'm starting compressions." He climbed around her, spread his legs to keep weight off her, and counted. After thirty compressions, he checked her breath. "Still nothing!" He pinched her nose and blew two breaths into her mouth.

I watched her chest rise and fall. "She's breathing," I said. "Stay with her. I need to check on Linda." I raced down the attic stairs knowing she was dead because I never missed a target.

I stood outside with the Alpharetta PD officer watching the ambulance drive away with Lisa McAllister hanging by a thread. "Get the reporters out of here. No one announces the victims' names until we find the brother. Do you understand?"

He looked at me with confusion plastered on his face. "Who are you?"

Leland flashed his badge as he walked over. "She's with me."

"Yes, sir," the officer said.

He saw the blood on my clothing and asked, "You okay?"

I glanced down. "It's Lisa's."

"Is she alive?"

"Barely. Her aunt shot her in the gut. She fell backward and hit her head on a brick under the insulation. She stopped breathing, but Parks got her going again."

"Was he injured?"

"No."

How They Were Taken 193

"Who killed the woman?"

"Me. It's Linda McAllister."

"Jenna, tell me what happened."

I explained how we had been right, but that the three men had killed the girls, starting with Lizzie Ryland. I left out a few details.

He pinched the bridge of his nose. "Did you read the journal?"

"Only part of it. Parks skimmed the rest."

"You know you can't work this case anymore," he said.

"Hell yes, I can. I'm not on the state's payroll anymore, and I don't give a damn about procedure."

"That weakens Jessica Steadman's case."

"Leland, they noted where they buried the girls. Nothing's going to weaken Steadman's case, but we need to find Jimmy McAllister. We don't know what he'll do if he finds out his aunt is dead."

18

Tension crackled through the air outside the Waldorf Astoria.

"Do you see the SUV?" Leland asked.

"No." We had walked the perimeter and checked the parking garages but couldn't find the SUV. Despite the thorough sweep conducted by GBI agents and Hallowell's men, McAllister was still nowhere to be found.

"My agents swept the main areas inside the hotel," Leland said. "No signs of him. If he's here, he's cloaked himself well."

"Where's Hallowell?" I asked. "His men were supposed to keep tabs on him." My temper rose. "I trusted him to do the job."

Hallowell walked out the front entrance of the Waldorf with his arms crossed over his chest. The set of his jaw and the tension in his shoulders told me everything before he even spoke.

"We lost him." His voice was clipped, each word sharper than the last.

"How?" Parks asked. "You don't lose people."

"It's rare, but it happens. He got a call and ran."

"When was the call?" I asked.

"Three hours ago."

Parks said, "Linda McAllister."

"You never got eyes on her, did you?" I asked Hallowell.

How They Were Taken   195

He shook his head. "We did our due diligence. She must have been hiding somewhere we weren't aware of."

"Did you know about the warehouse?" I asked.

"Yes, but you had already been there."

I glanced at Parks. "Lisa said her aunt protected the family. She's the one that shot at us at the warehouse. She knew we found Emma Steadman and called Jimmy. Then she shot Lisa."

"Because she was watching us, not Jimmy," he said.

Damn it. I should have pushed my ego aside and let Hallowell's men help. "I took the surveillance off Lisa. She might not have been shot if I hadn't."

Leland walked inside as a woman's alarmed voice caught my attention. "I think there's a man up there," she said to her friend. Her finger, shaking visibly, pointed toward the top of the building across the street.

I placed my hand on my weapon. "Parks, can you see anything?" I shifted my eyes upward to trace the woman's line of sight.

"There," he said as a sharp crack fractured the momentary calm.

The bullet shattered a window behind us. Some people dropped behind cars while others ran into the street in panic or into the building.

"I can't get a clear view," I screamed. "We're at the wrong angle."

Another bullet struck the pavement nearby, sending sparks flying.

"Shit!" Parks yelled. "Stay down!"

Leland's voice cut through the chaos, crisp and commanding as he spoke into the radio. GBI agents rushed out of the hotel and from inside surrounding buildings. "Anyone have eyes on the shooter?"

"We're too close to the building," I replied.

"Our team is en route to the roof," he said.

"Not without me." I made eye contact with Parks. "On three."

He nodded.

"One. Two. Three!"

We sprinted across the street, weaving through the clutter of honking horns and screeching tires—everything a frantic blur of motion. The world fractured into a kaleidoscope of noise and motion—flashing headlights, shouting voices, and the gut-punch thud of my heartbeat in my ears.

A car surged toward us. I yanked my arm out instinctively, my breath catching as its tires shrieked to a halt, stopping just shy of my hip. The heat of the engine pressed against my skin.

"Slow down!" I shouted, my voice breaking with adrenaline, the words almost swallowed by the cacophony.

The driver threw up his hands in anger, but I didn't wait to see if he had more to say. My pulse surged, legs burning as I pushed forward, my focus locked on the shadowy alley ahead—the only refuge from the chaos closing in behind us.

A man saw us coming and held the door open. "Use the staff elevator. It's faster to the roof," he instructed. "Follow me."

He ran to a small hallway off to the right and quickly swiped his card to open the doors. "It's floor forty-five. Forty-six is storage with no external access."

"Thanks," Parks said.

"You'll need the code to get back in. Five six four seven."

"Thanks," I said as the door closed. I looked at Parks. Sweat pooled at his hairline, but he wasn't panting. "You ready for this?"

"I live for this shit."

We pressed our backs against the side walls, our guns drawn, and waited for the doors to open. Seconds later they opened with a metallic grind. We exploded onto the rooftop. Wind lashed against us, clawing at my face as I sprinted into the open. The rooftop stretched wide, the noise of the city below us drowned out by adrenaline and the gravel crunching beneath my boots. The Atlanta skyline loomed in jagged, glowing silhouettes against the deepening night.

"Go right," I whispered to Parks.

He blocked me with his arm. "Wait." He spoke with a tight coil of readiness as he pointed toward a shadowy figure sprinting toward the roof's edge. "There!"

We gave chase without a second thought, our bodies fueled by a new rush of adrenaline.

The rooftop terrain turned into a treacherous gauntlet covered in loose

How They Were Taken   197

gravel shifting underfoot, antennas jutting like spears, and hulking HVAC units. A misstep sent me staggering, but Parks's steadying grip pulled me up.

I yelled to Parks, "He's heading for the other building!" My eyes tracked McAllister as he closed in on the fencing surrounding the rooftop's edge—a mesh of metal meant to keep sane people from doing exactly what he was about to attempt.

He stopped, looked toward the building's ledge, then flipped around toward us. His long, black coat snapped in the wind as he locked eyes with me. For a heartbeat, everything froze. The city's noise dulled to a distant hum, leaving me with the sounds of Parks's breath and my own heartbeat. McAllister's lips curled into a smug grin, one that ignited a fire deep in my gut.

I aimed my gun at him and yelled, "Freeze!"

Then he moved.

His feet hammered against the gravel. His twisted as he ran toward an opening in the fencing.

"McAllister, stop!" I shouted, but my voice barely carried over the roar of the wind. I moved my shoulder too quickly, and a knife-like pain shot through it. I clenched my jaw and swore, but forced myself to ignore the pain.

He didn't falter. He ducked low and angled his body, slipping through a narrow opening in the fence as if he'd mapped it out beforehand. My breath hitched as he reached the ledge, his silhouette outlined against the growing glow of the city below. He glanced back one last time, his grin widened, and then he launched himself into the air.

Parks was only a few feet from him. "Damn it!"

I skidded to a halt at the edge as my boots scraped against the concrete lip. My gaze darted to the dizzying drop below—a kaleidoscope of blurred headlights, glowing windows, and twisting steel. Vertigo tugged at my stomach, but I shoved it aside, snapping my focus back to McAllister. He hit a rooftop below us, hard. His legs had buckled as he rolled into a rough landing. Gravel sprayed out from under him, but he scrambled up, adrenaline keeping him moving. He darted behind a vent. His shadow twisted against the golden haze of the city lights.

Parks aimed his gun, but McAllister had disappeared from view. "We've got to cut him off."

I didn't reply, my gaze locked on that vent. My jaw clenched. He wouldn't keep that lead for long—not with agents blanketing the area.

"Over there," Parks said. He pointed to a metal ladder on what must have been the storage room the man had mentioned. We hurried toward it and climbed it to see if we could get a look at McAllister. There he was, trapped against a backdrop of a massive billboard. He whirled toward us and fired.

The bullet ricocheted off an air duct with a deafening clang.

We returned fire, but McAllister disappeared again.

I flew down the ladder and ran toward the edge where McAllister had jumped. I stared down at the rooftop of the building where McAllister hid, closed my eyes, and jumped. Just before landing, I curled into a ball and dropped into a roll on the roof. My shoulder screamed. I winced and cradled it with my other hand, hoping to somehow protect it from any more damage. Each shard of gravel bit into me like tiny blades. I sucked in a breath and rolled to my left as Parks landed beside me.

He breathed heavily and said, "Damn it, woman, give me a little notice next time you jump off a building, will you?"

I clutched my shoulder again.

"Shit, your shoulder. Let me handle this," he said.

But it was too late. McAllister fired multiple bursts in quick succession.

"That's what? Five?" Parks asked.

I nodded. "He's got anywhere from four to twelve rounds left until he has to reload."

"Too many to waste our time," he said. He eyed my shoulder. "Can you do this?"

I nodded. "I'll take the right."

We split, using the billboard and the labyrinth of air ducts for cover. My heart thundered against my ribs as each silent step tightened the noose around McAllister.

McAllister bolted toward another area, his movements reckless and desperate. He sprinted to the edge of the building and looked down, then pivoted and stared at me.

How They Were Taken 199

"It's too far," I shouted. "You won't make it!"

He ignored me and moved to jump but tripped and rolled over the ledge.

"Shit!" I yelled.

Parks and I hurried over and found him hanging onto the building's edge with the tips of his fingers. His body dangled perilously toward the ground below.

I dropped to my knees. "You should have listened to me."

"Help me," he yelled.

Parks dropped on his other side.

"Jimmy," I said in a softer tone. "We're going to grab your arms and pull you up, but I need you to stay calm. Do you understand?"

"Yeah, just help me, damn it!"

"I need you to look down and tell me if there is anything under your body you can use to leverage your feet."

"I can't look down! I don't want to die!"

"You're not going to die," I said. "Not on my time, but I need you to listen to me. We need your help to get you up. Engage your core and push against the wall with your legs. Do you understand?"

He nodded. "Just hurry the hell up."

"On the count of three," I said. "One, two, three!" My shoulder erupted into even more agony.

We yanked him up with so much force we fell backward. McAllister landed on top of us.

I rolled him off my side and said, "Stay down," but it was too late. He had already pulled a knife and slashed my calf opposite my shoulder injury.

"Are you serious right now?"

Instinct took over; I grabbed my gun and fired at his leg. His scream ripped through the noise as the bullet burst through his shin.

"Damn," Parks said. He stood above McAllister with his gun aimed at him. "Shin shots are a bitch."

McAllister screamed in pain. I had no sympathy. "Parks, give me your shirt."

He glanced at my leg and carefully removed his top shirt without taking his eyes or weapon off McAllister.

I wrapped the shirt around my wound and tied it into a knot.

I caught my breath and crouched down, my leg taking over the top spot on the pain chart. I swallowed back the nausea building up inside my stomach and lifted McAllister's arm to remove it from his coat. "Learn a damn lesson, will you?"

I smirked at his f-bomb reply.

I reached over and yanked out the other arm, maybe a little harder than I should, then wrapped the coat tight around his leg.

"That hurts!"

"I need to stop the bleeding," I said. "I think I missed the anterior tibial artery," I said to Parks. "It's bleeding bad, but not enough for that." I pulled the coat tight just as several agents burst through the building's rooftop door.

19

Lisa McAllister had been transferred to Grady Hospital in Atlanta, the same hospital treating her brother. She had survived surgery, but the doctors put her in a medically induced coma to allow the swelling around her brain to lessen.

Her brother's surgery lasted over four hours. I waited in the surgery waiting area after another doctor stitched up my leg. I'd have a wicked scar, but I didn't care. Catching that bastard was worth it. Leland had brought coffee and sandwiches from a RaceTrac nearby.

"It's the best I could do," he said.

"It's perfect," I replied.

Parks said the same.

"Any word?"

"He's in recovery," I said. "He'll be fine."

"Damage?"

Tense events always increased my appetite. I attacked my club sandwich like I hadn't eaten in days. It tasted like heaven. "You tell him," I said to Parks. "I'm eating." My empathy for McAllister sat somewhere below zero.

"The bullet shattered his tibia, tore through his calf muscle, and ripped his patellar and tibialis anterior tendons."

"Parks is a go-big-or-go-home kind of guy," I said between bites.

"You shot him?" Leland asked Parks.

He flicked his thumb at me. "No. She did. Is she always so sarcastic?"

"Usually more so," he said.

I finished chewing. I had given Leland the journal earlier for safekeeping. "I need the journal."

Leland removed it from inside his jacket and handed it to me. "I've already got excavators there, Jenna. I think you should stand down." He was talking about Molly.

"I'm going."

"I'll contact the families," Parks said.

"Already handled before we got to the hotel," Leland said.

He liked to sneak around behind my back and get things done. I knew Parks wanted to be the one to tell the families. "Parks should have done that. It's our investigation."

"Ours?" Parks said with a smile. "I thought I was assisting you."

I shrugged. "Easier to say it the other way, which, had you been paying attention, I made clear to Steadman already."

He laughed. "I caught it." To Leland, he said, "It's okay. I'll see them after." He patted my leg. "You ready?"

I raised an eyebrow. "For?"

"To bring your sister home."

John McAllister Sr. had buried my sister and Lizzie Ryland on a piece of land about sixty miles north of Atlanta. Parks had called the Rylands on our way. Even at the late hour, they had answered immediately. They had already arrived on scene, but the excavation team would not let them near the area.

"Hold on," Parks said through the car's Bluetooth. "Let me make a call. We'll be there soon."

He asked Siri to call Jessica Steadman.

Brave man.

How They Were Taken

She answered as if it was normal for her to be awake so late. "I understand you and Ms. Wyatt caught the man that murdered my husband and daughter. Thank you."

"I'm not calling for thanks," he said. "I'm calling with a favor." He didn't bother to wait for a reply. "The excavation team won't let the Ryland parents near the burial site. I doubt they're letting the other parents near their daughters' remains either."

He didn't need to continue.

"I'll call the governor now," Jessica replied. "Where is Jenna?"

"I'm here, Mrs. Steadman."

"How are you?"

I had been fine, detached even, until she asked. I swallowed back the lump in my throat. "I'm fine. Thank you."

"I'd like to see you two tomorrow morning. Nine o'clock at my home." She disconnected the call.

"Does she ever lighten up?" I asked Parks. "Wait, don't answer that."

He smiled.

We arrived at the property thirty minutes later and found Lizzie's parents waiting beside their car.

Mr. Ryland asked, "Can we get in?"

"Yes," Parks said.

The supervisor met us at the crime scene tape. "Ms. Wyatt," he said. "Randy Melrose. The governor has requested we allow you in, but I would like to warn you, after all this time, there isn't much to see."

I looked at Mr. Ryland. He nodded. "We're okay with that," I said to Melrose.

"Okay then. Based on information in the files, we believe, though we can't be certain, Molly Simpson is on the left, and Elizabeth Ryland, the right." He turned to his team. "Let's give the families some breathing room."

"I'll wait here," Parks said.

I forced myself to stay strong. "Come with me."

He blinked. "Of course."

The smell enveloped my senses—damp earth mixed with rust and something faintly metallic that twisted my stomach. The ground near the hole felt soft, unstable. I took a breath as we walked closer.

"You want me to look first?" Parks asked.

I shook my head, unable to speak.

We moved close enough to see the metal box visible at the bottom of the makeshift grave with its lid tilted awkwardly to the side. I closed my eyes for a moment and exhaled, willing myself to look, to make it real. To see the loss that had ruled my life for years. I needed closure, and the only way to get it was to look at what lay inside that box.

At first, I couldn't bring myself to step closer. My boots stayed planted on the ground. The cool air cut through my jacket as I gathered the strength to take another step. Finally, I said, "I'm ready," and Parks pressed his hand against my back as we walked to the edge of Molly's grave.

Floodlights illuminated the grave. I crouched down, Parks following my lead, and looked at the skeletal remains of a young girl curled within the corroded metal confines. The sight of those bones—what was left of her—robbed the breath straight from my lungs.

Molly.

The name thundered through my head, louder than the rush of blood in my ears. My hands clenched into fists at my sides, nails biting into my palms as I fought back the rising wave of nausea. I had imagined this moment for years, running through every possible scenario, ones that had never come. Finding her alive. Finding nothing. But not this. Nothing prepared me for the hollow ache of seeing her there, discarded like trash.

Parks stepped back and whispered something to someone behind us. When he finished, he quietly stepped back beside me. I pushed myself into a standing position to be closer to him. I couldn't admit it, but I needed him there. His presence grounded me like an anchor in a storm. He didn't say anything, and I was grateful. Words would've shattered whatever fragile control I had left.

My gaze drifted back to the box, scanning the remains with a methodical detachment I didn't feel. The brittle, stained bones. The scraps of decaying fabric barely clinging to the bones. And then I saw it—something

How They Were Taken 205

faintly shiny amid the ruin. My breath hitched, my chest constricting as I squinted, unable to believe it.

The belt buckle.

My knees ached. I forced myself to stay upright, the image of that buckle searing itself into my brain. A bratty cartoon girl with oversized lips and glittery hair, forever frozen in a mischievous grin. The year before she disappeared, Molly had begged for it. Pleaded, really, circling it in every catalog that came through the mail. Mom had caved and bought it for Christmas that year. I'd teased her about wearing it with every pair of jeans she owned, but she had rolled her eyes, grinning at me as if to say, *It's perfect, Jenna. Don't you get it?*

I finally got it.

"It's her," I said, my voice barely above a whisper. It scraped out of me like gravel, raw and uneven.

Parks shifted beside me. "You sure?"

I swallowed hard, the motion feeling sharp and deliberate. My throat burned, but I refused to let the tears come. Not yet. Not here. "That belt buckle," I said, pointing toward the faint glint. "My mother got it for her. Christmas. She never stopped wearing it. She wore her clothes to bed the night he took her because she loved that buckle so much."

Parks followed my gaze, his expression unreadable. For a moment, he didn't move, didn't speak. Then, slowly, he wrapped an arm around my shoulders, pulling me closer. The gesture was solid and comforting, something I hadn't known I would need.

I wanted to scream. To rip the entire world apart until it made sense again. But instead, I just stood there, staring at the buckle and the bones and the box, my jaw clenched so tight it ached.

"I never stopped looking," I murmured, more to myself than to him. "Not for a single day. I thought if I just kept searching, I'd find her somewhere. But I never considered what it would feel like to see her like this."

Parks didn't say anything. He just held on to me, his arm a steady weight across my shoulders. I didn't look at him; I couldn't. If I saw sympathy in his eyes, I'd lose it. And I couldn't lose it.

Elizabeth Ryland wailed and collapsed into her husband's arms. As a mother, I understood how that had felt, and hearing her made me want to run to Alyssa and never let go.

I took a slow, measured breath and tried to force the tremor out of my hands. "I need a minute," I said to Parks. "I'll be back."

He cocked his head to the side. "You sure?"

I nodded. "Go to the Rylands. They need you." My fingers brushed against the phone in my jacket pocket.

Parks's arm dropped, though his hand lingered briefly on my back, like he wasn't sure I should be left alone. "Take your time," he said, his tone low and even.

I nodded, but my gaze stayed fixed on the box for another heartbeat, my mind spinning with every moment Molly and I had shared—every laugh, every argument, every stupid little thing I had never cherished until she was gone. And then I forced myself to turn away.

Each step away from that grave dragged like a chain behind me, heavy and relentless. I forced my legs to move, each one weighted with a sorrow that threatened to pull me back and sob just like Mrs. Ryland. I stopped a few feet away, pulling out my phone with hands that still shook. I stared at the screen, the light glaring in the darkness, and hesitated.

I inhaled sharply, locking my jaw against the sob that threatened to break loose. The tears could wait. I dialed Nick's number.

He answered on the second ring. "We heard. Are you okay?"

The compassion in his voice didn't surprise me. "Yes."

"Where are you?"

"Where the bastard buried her." I bit back the bile rising in my throat.

"Give me the address," he said. "I'll meet you there."

"It's okay," I said. I wasn't sure I could hold myself together with him there. "Is Tiffani still with you?"

"We're home. They said it was safe."

"It is," I said. "How's Alyssa?"

"She's fine. She's sleeping. She swam in the hotel pool for hours. She was exhausted."

I laughed. Alyssa loved swimming.

"Where are you going next?"

"They'll take her to the coroner's office in Fulton. I won't let them take her to Dawson."

"Okay. Call me when you find out more, but I'll call you the minute Alyssa wakes up."

"Thank you."

"Jen," he said.

"Yeah?"

"You did it."

20

Parks and I stood outside the morgue as the Rylands finished talking with the coroner. It had taken several hours for each girl to arrive, and the coroner, Dr. Mike Barron, took his time with their families. We had been there for hours. Though it was sullen and windowless in the morgue, a check of my watch told me the sun had already begun rising. I was exhausted and energized. When it all finally ended, I would sleep for days.

Footsteps down the hall distracted me. I turned to see Nick heading toward me and cleared my throat.

"Hey," he said. "I hadn't heard from you, and Alyssa's down for the night, so I thought I'd come check on you." He pulled me into a hug.

I wanted to resist, to step back and tell him I was fine, but my body betrayed me. I melted into his arms, leaning into the security he had provided before our marriage fell apart. I held my breath knowing I needed to control myself or collapse in tears.

"I'm sorry," Nick said.

I separated myself from him. "It's okay. I never expected to find her alive." Tears pooled in my eyes. I couldn't stop them from streaming down my cheeks.

"No," he said as he wiped a tear away. "I'm sorry I didn't understand. That I didn't support you."

How They Were Taken 209

Parks cleared his throat, said, "I'll give you two a minute," and walked away.

"Alyssa's safe now," I said. "At least from the skeletons in my closet." The expression hit me hard.

"I know," he said. "And I might not like it, but I know you'll continue keeping her safe, Jen. It's what you do."

I watched Parks wait for the elevator down the hall, then looked at Nick. "I have to meet with Jessica Steadman in a few hours, but I'd like to see Alyssa after. Can she stay home from school?"

"Sure," he said. "I'll take the day off and figure out how to get Heather out of the house."

"It's okay. She and I need to talk anyway."

He raised an eyebrow.

"I'll behave."

The elevator door opened. I turned and said to Parks, "Wait. I need to talk to you." I looked at Nick. "Thank you for coming. I'm fine, but I need to do this on my terms, okay? Go take care of your family."

His lips straightened. "It's—"

I smiled. "I'm okay."

He nodded, then smiled, and walked to the elevator where Parks held the door open with his back.

Nick mumbled something to him, but not loud enough for me to hear. When the door closed, Parks looked at me and cocked his head to the side.

Dr. Barron stepped out of the morgue. "Jenna?"

I blinked. "Where are the Rylands?"

"They're still in my office. I thought you might want to—"

I cut him off. "Yes, I do." I turned back to Parks, who had stopped in the middle of the hallway. "You coming?"

He picked up his pace.

Parks knocked on my door a few hours after I got home, holding an open box of donuts and a carrier with two coffees. "I brought donuts and coffee." He smiled.

I shook my head. "I didn't give you free entry with my code, but you brought donuts, so I forgive you."

He laughed. "Thought I'd drive you to our meeting this morning."

"I'm going to see Alyssa after." I broke a chocolate donut in half and stuffed a piece into my mouth, thinking it was smaller than it looked. With a mouthful of donut, I said, "Oh, that's bigger than I thought."

Parks cleared his throat.

I narrowed my eyes. "You're gross."

He set the donut box on the table and began stuffing the case files into the empty boxes.

"What are you doing?"

"We'll take these back," he said. "I've already got mine."

"I'm keeping them."

"What?" he asked. "Why?"

"Because that's what private investigators do."

"Private investigators with offices might, but this place doesn't have enough room."

Bob strutted in and rubbed his head against Parks's leg. He crouched down and pet him. "Tell your mom I'm right."

Bob meowed.

"Even your cat agrees."

"I'm thinking about getting an office. You can help me move them there."

"Hey, we could share office space," he said.

"Absolutely not," I said. "Men are messy."

"I'm former military. My place is spotless."

He was probably right, but I didn't care. I wasn't sharing office space with anyone. "Come on," I said. "I'll drive."

"But Leland said never drive with you."

"On the highway. I'll take back roads."

"How about I meet you there instead?"

"You really need to grow a pair, Parks." I turned toward the counter and grabbed my bag so he wouldn't see my smile.

"That's not what—"

I cut him off. "Don't make that donut come back up, Parks."

How They Were Taken   211

"I'll meet you there," he said. He grabbed a donut, paused, then grabbed another one, smiled, and walked out my door.

I crouched down and pet Bob. "Hey, don't blame me. You came without a pair. It wasn't my fault." I grabbed another donut and headed out.

Jessica Steadman sat on a leather sectional in her living room. She had dressed in a pair of dark, slim-fit jeans and a white sweater with her hair pulled back in a ponytail. A more casual look than I had seen on her. "Jenna," she said. "Please sit."

I sat beside Parks, who had arrived a few minutes before me.

"My staff has prepared an assortment of breakfast items for us." She clicked a button on a fob in her hand. "We'll sit in the garden room." She stood. "Follow me."

Parks stared at my mouth. I swiped my finger across my mouth, thinking I had donut remnants stuck to my lips. "Do I have something on my face?"

The corner of his mouth twitched. "I'll never tell."

I squeezed his upper arm, surprised at the rock of muscle I felt.

An assortment of breakfast items? Every breakfast item imaginable sat on a buffet in the garden room. I instantly regretted eating those two donuts. "This is too much," I said. "We're only two people."

"It's the least I can do."

She sat at the head of the table. "Please, pick whatever you would like."

A maid prepared a fruit and muffin plate and set it in front of Mrs. Steadman.

"Thank you, Olga," she said.

The woman smiled and left the room.

Parks stood in front of the buffet, then proceeded to fill his plate with some of everything.

I furrowed my brow as he turned back to the table.

He stopped. "What? I'm hungry."

Mrs. Steadman laughed. "It's not the first time Mr. Parks has filled his plate with food."

I had no idea how to respond to that. I plopped some fruit and a blackberry muffin onto my plate and returned to my seat.

"Aren't you hungry?" she asked.

"I'm not a breakfast person."

"Please don't force yourself. I won't be offended."

"Thank you," I said.

"You should know I have contacted the parents of the other girls." She smiled at me. "Except for yours, unfortunately, which is part of the reason you're here." She cleared her throat. "I have informed them that I will be paying for each funeral, and the governor has approved memorials for each of them at their initial burial site. Of course, I am paying for those as well. We can't bring their babies back, but we can give them the funerals they deserve."

She had rendered me speechless. I had never thought what I would do if I found Molly's remains. I had only focused on finding her and bringing down the person who took her. "I don't know what to say."

"I'll consider that a thank-you," she said. "It's the least I can do for you."

"Are the families setting up the funerals?" Parks asked.

She nodded. "I discussed dates with them all, and my legal team is in the process of organizing them. They are to begin in a few days." She nodded to me. "You'll receive a call as well."

Olga had also brought two envelopes and set them beside Mrs. Steadman. I suspected they were our final payments.

She handed one to Parks and the other to me. "I have no words to express my thanks." She smiled. "I hope you will accept my gift as my attempt."

"Jessica," Parks said, "I don't want your money."

She rolled her eyes. "Jack, just take the damn check."

I wanted to duck under the table in case fists started flying.

She smiled at me. "I'm sure you're aware that your partner and I have a history."

"It's none of my business," I said.

"But it is. I would like to keep you two on retainer, and to do that, I need to be honest with you. There are two checks in each envelope. You will

How They Were Taken   213

know which is for which. My attorney will have your contracts to sign later today. Stop by whenever you have time."

I couldn't imagine why she might need two private investigators, but I wasn't about to argue. "Thank you. I would be happy to work with you again."

Parks said, "I'm in."

"Very well," she said.

My cell phone dinged with a message I had been waiting for from Leland.

McAllister is ready to talk. Come to the hospital. Bring Parks.

"Um, I hate to do this, but Parks and I have somewhere we need to be."

"What's going on?" Parks asked.

"Jimmy McAllister is ready to talk."

Jessica Steadman stood. "Go. Keep me updated."

"Thank you," I said while pushing my chair back to stand.

She drew me into a hug as I walked past her. "Thank you for bringing my daughter home to me. Please call me Jessica. I'm not as formal as I seem." She squeezed tight and whispered, "Watch yourself with that one. He's a charmer."

I smiled and returned the squeeze, trying hard to keep from laughing at that.

Parks lightened up the heaviness in the room. "Is this a group-hug thing?"

Jessica laughed. "Not a chance."

"Fair enough," he said.

Parks and I drove to the hospital separately but parked near each other in the far recesses of the parking garage across the street.

I climbed out of my car, complaining. "They really need to do something with the parking problem in the city."

"Did you open the envelope?"

I shook my head. "Not yet, but clearly you did."

"Open it."

"I'll do it when we're done here. I want to hear what this piece of shit has to say."

"Jenna, open it. Trust me."

"Fine. I'm sure she gave us the same amount, if that's your concern. She seems to be less mad at you now." I grabbed the envelope from my passenger seat.

"Just open it."

"I am, geez." I slid my fingernail through the flap. I read the numbers on the checks and froze.

"How many zeros?" he asked.

"Too many." I read the numbers again. "What about you?"

He removed the checks from his back pocket and handed them to me. Normally, I wouldn't share that kind of information with someone, but he would give me a lot of flak if I hadn't.

He looked at me. "It's the same?"

"This is too much money."

"As my mother used to say, don't bite the hand that feeds you."

"I can't keep this."

"Well, I can, so don't ruin it for me."

I shook my head. "Let's get inside."

Leland met us at the elevator leading up to McAllister's floor. "I checked on the sister. If all goes well, they'll take her out of her coma in a few days."

"That's good news," I said. Inside the elevator, I asked, "Has he said anything yet?"

"Only that he wants to sue you two, the GBI, and the state."

I chuckled. "For what?"

"Damages, defamation of character, infliction of emotional distress."

"You lost me at defamation of character," I said.

"I doubt a public defender is qualified to take on that case," Parks said. "But good luck to him."

"But some pro bono lawyer might." To Leland, I asked, "Has the district attorney arrived?"

How They Were Taken

"Assistant DA Zach Christopher is on his way." He glanced at his watch. "Should be here any minute."

Leland walked out of the elevator and pointed to the room with two GBI agents standing on both sides of the door. "It's room 224."

"I figured that," I said with a smile.

Two additional agents stood inside the room. They moved and sat in chairs near the window when we arrived. I acknowledged them both with a nod. I turned on my recording app and set my phone on the windowsill and checked to make sure McAllister had been cuffed to his bed. Not that he could go anywhere with his leg elevated and wrapped like a baby, but old habits die hard.

"I'm not saying a thing until my attorney gets here," McAllister said.

I shrugged. Even as lead on the investigation, if I showed my anger, Leland would kick me out and take over. He had done me a favor by letting it stay under my control, but Carl Mosley, the GBI director, would kill that soon enough. I didn't need to make it happen any earlier.

"You can't pin those girls' deaths on me," McAllister said.

So much for waiting on his representation.

"Shooting at us from the top of a building and running speaks for itself, McAllister," Parks said.

"You forgot about my calf," I said.

McAllister narrowed his eyes at me. "That wasn't me. I've got unpaid parking tickets. I heard you were coming at me for them."

"Oh, cut the BS. You're wasting our time."

"I'm innocent."

"Innocent people don't follow women around."

His public defender walked in. "Scott Nixon," he said. "Nothing my client has said without my counsel will stand up in court."

He wasn't exactly right, but I wasn't going to argue. "Your client claims he has outstanding parking tickets which caused him to shoot at two private investigators and run when in pursuit."

Nixon rolled his eyes. "He's ready to talk, but he wants a deal."

"You can't prove nothing," McAllister said.

Zach Christopher walked into the room. "I beg to differ," he said. He smiled at me. "I guess I can't call you Agent Wyatt anymore?"

"Nope, but Jenna is fine."

"So," he said to Nixon. "You want a deal?" He shook his head. "Five girls are dead. Your client doesn't deserve a deal."

"I didn't kill them all," McAllister said. He groaned in pain.

"Mr. McAllister," his attorney said, "please refrain from speaking until you clear it through me first."

"Let's begin questioning," Christopher said. "We'll go from there." He looked to Parks and me. "Go ahead."

I spoke first, asking him, "Why don't you start with what happened to Emma Steadman?"

"Newspeople said someone took her. That's all I know. Tell me why you killed my aunt."

I ignored that question and continued. "Where were you on the night of April 18th, 2023?"

He grimaced, though I suspected it was from the pain. "It's been a year. I can't remember that far back."

"You serviced the Steadmans' HVAC prior to Emma's disappearance. Your company serviced the homes of several of the victims prior to their deaths. Is that a coincidence?"

His attorney whispered in his ear, but from the frustration on Nixon's face, McAllister refused to comply.

"I don't know, lady. I don't know about any of this."

My patience waned. Parks caught it and took over. "On the night of April 18th, 2023, while putting his daughter to bed, Richard Steadman was shot and killed in his home," Parks said. "Emma Steadman was taken then. We found her remains in the warehouse, McAllister."

"The one you tried to kill us in," I said.

He played our first ace sooner than I had wanted, but I understood his game.

That stomped McAllister's confidence into the ground, but he recouped well. "I don't know what you're talking about."

"Got it," I said. "How about this? Your aunt disappeared in 1967. Your grandfather found her near the creek on his property buried in a metal box."

"The aunt you killed? How's that possible?"

How They Were Taken

"Her twin."

He looked at his attorney. "My aunt didn't have a twin."

"We have the journal with the news articles," I said. To his attorney, I said, "Your client's a lying piece of—"

Parks placed his hand on the middle of my back. "Wyatt."

I took a breath and named each of the five girls. "All redheads. All five years old. All buried in metal boxes. All died on the 18th of a month."

"Doesn't mean we did it."

"Your grandpa was a vengeful man. He couldn't handle the police dragging their feet to find his daughter. Even after he discovered her body by that creek on his property, the police did nothing, nothing to give the family closure or justice. So, he decided to take matters into his own hands. What I don't understand is why you and your dad continued his work. Wasn't two dead girls enough?"

He motioned for his attorney to come closer and whispered in his ear.

Nixon's face turned white. "Mr. Christopher," he said, "may I speak to my client privately?"

I grabbed my phone and left the room.

When the door opened a few minutes later, Nixon asked to speak with just Christopher.

When the assistant DA walked out, Parks pointed at McAllister and said, "You're going down for this, McAllister. You'll die behind bars."

McAllister tried to laugh but groaned in pain instead. "I need more pain meds."

I smiled at Leland, waited for the eye roll, and said, "Kids today. Always trying to mask their pain."

A few minutes later, Christopher returned. "I need you outside."

Nixon walked back into the room.

As we headed to the door, McAllister said, "You're welcome."

Christopher ran his hand through his short hair. "There's another girl."

21

"What?" I asked. "There's no other girl in the journal. He's lying. He's just trying to get a deal."

"He gave his attorney the location. He wants a deal. I'll need to contact the DAs in the other counties and talk to them, but Nixon believes him."

"So, he can prove it?" Parks asked.

Christopher nodded. "I think we can get the other murders moved to Fulton County, but since this thing is exploding nationally, I need to move fast."

"You want the deal?" Leland asked.

"I'm prepared to take the death penalty off the table, but that's it."

"Did you already tell Nixon that?"

"I told him I wouldn't consider anything until we found the girl's remains. He's talking to McAllister now."

"Did you get a name?" Leland asked.

"Not yet, but we're working on it."

Leland nodded. "I'll get someone looking for a missing girl with similar descriptions of our victims."

"It's possible no one's reported her missing," Christoper said.

"What the hell? Why not?"

"She could have been in the foster system. You know how it works.

How They Were Taken

They don't always report when a kid runs. Hell, the system is so screwed up, and they're so understaffed, I'm not sure they really know who's part of it."

"She was five years old," I said through gritted teeth. "They should know when a five-year-old goes missing."

"I don't disagree with you," Christopher said. "But you know how things work. Let's get her location. See if this guy is telling the truth. If he is, we'll try to match her with someone in the system."

"You two stay out here," Leland said. "GBI will handle this now."

"Like hell you will," I said. "This is our investigation, Leland. You can't just push us aside."

"I can, and I have. You solved your case. You found Emma Steadman's killer. Let us handle the rest."

Heat rose from my chest and into my face. My blood pressure soared as anger built up inside me. Legally speaking, Leland was right. But it pissed me off.

"We're assisting," Parks said. "You owe us that."

"Just not in the room now," Leland said.

"This needs to be handled by the book," Christopher said. "And private investigators aren't allowed in criminal negotiations."

"He's right," Parks said. "Let's go get a coffee."

Parks called in a favor and received the two-page report on Mary McAllister's case.

I reviewed it on the way to their former property. "Her grandfather had a right to be upset. The officer who responded suggested Mary ran away or was lost in the woods around their home, but the family looked for her and couldn't find her. John McAllister followed up every day for three weeks, but they did nothing." I reread the second page. "He found her when he went to fish in the creek."

"God, that's horrible," Parks said.

"Not horrible enough for what the McAllisters did to all those girls."

"I'm not saying that. I'm just—"

"I get it." I had called Nick to let him know I would be there as soon as possible. He had kept her home from school at my request, and I had yet to get there. We hadn't caught Molly's killer, but I had answers, and yet I still tossed my daughter to the side for an investigation. Nick was right. I wouldn't change.

Parks's cell phone rang. He answered on Bluetooth through his car. "Parks."

"Hey, man, it's Charlie again. Did a little digging like you asked."

"Tell me you got a name."

"There are over four thousand kids in the foster system just from the past few years. It'll take a while to go through them, and with just a description, I can't promise we'll find her."

"Thanks, Charlie. Appreciate the help," Parks said.

"You want me to go through it?" Charlie asked. "I'm willing to give it a shot."

I shook my head and whispered, "Not yet."

"We're good for now. Might need to look at it later, though."

"Sure thing. Talk later."

I groaned. "Four thousand missing kids from the foster care system. God, I hope that's a national number and not just Georgia. People are evil."

"You sure you don't want him sorting through them? He's good. He might be able to connect a girl to the one McAllister claims is dead."

"There could be a thousand girls who look like the victims. We don't have time to go through them all."

"Anything's possible," he said.

"If McAllister's lying, and we're doing all this work for nothing, I'm going to shoot him in the other leg."

Parks laughed, then said, "Not if I get to him first."

We arrived at the McAllisters' previous home and approached Mark Levine again. "Leland approved us going in."

"Hopefully this is the last time," he said. "I'm tired of digging up little girls."

We walked to the area where McAllister had claimed to have buried another girl on June 18, 2021. I spotted the cross marking where John McAllister had found his daughter's remains a short distance away.

My life had changed after Molly's disappearance. Watching my

How They Were Taken   221

mother collapse into her grief, and having to raise myself, I was determined to succeed. I refused to let the tragedy destroy me like it had her. I wanted to find Molly from day one. The police worked the investigation until they couldn't because there was nothing to find. I had, at one point, believed I would kill the person who took her if I ever found him, but as time passed, I realized death wasn't a punishment, but a relief. I wanted him to suffer like Molly had, as I had, and spending a lifetime in jail sounded perfect. John McAllister preferred to avenge his daughter's death by inflicting pain on others and somehow passed the choice to his son and grandson.

I would never understand that.

Leland stood to the side of the team. "They're close."

"Can you tell us the rest of what he said?" I asked.

He nodded and motioned for us to step away.

"You should know he was the one following you, but he didn't put the nails in your tire."

"How is that possible? I'd just taken the job."

"I had the same question," he said. "I asked Jessica Steadman if she had told anyone she was considering hiring you before she did, but she hadn't."

"And?"

He held up a small listening device. One the size of a watch battery. "We found it underneath the table in her office."

"Any idea who put it there?"

He nodded. "The aunt took a job with the cleaning service Jessica used after a party a few weeks before she called you."

"They were listening to all our conversations, then," I said. "Holy shit." I shook my head. "I can't believe I didn't check for that."

"There wasn't a reason to, Jenna. Don't beat yourself up over it."

"If anything," Parks said, "it's on me. I was still on the case then."

"We both should have known. I wrote it off at first, the tail, thinking it could be someone from my GBI days."

Leland added, "They didn't put the nails in your tire, but Jimmy did hire a kid in Cumming to do it."

"A kid? Seriously?"

"Kid was bored. He paid him a hundred bucks."

I closed my eyes and then shook my head. "I don't care about any of that. What did he tell you about this girl?"

"He called her a practice kill. He wanted to make sure he could do it."

Parks cussed.

"He picked her up on Buford Highway in Doraville," Leland said. "She told him she was a runaway but never said her name. He thinks she was about fifteen, but he's not sure."

"A kid that young wouldn't think to say she was a runaway," I said. "She'd want help."

"I agree," he said. "But I'm not sure I trust anything coming from a serial killer."

"What did he do to her?" Parks asked.

"Strangled her like the other girls in the journal."

"Does his attorney know about that yet?"

Leland shook his head. "Christopher will have to show it in discovery if McAllister doesn't take the deal."

"So, he killed her for practice." I rubbed my eyes. "Are you sure she's the last one?"

"As sure as we can be, but you know how it goes. He's got to answer a lot of questions before we'll offer that deal."

"We never found out how he got into the houses," I said. "Or how he got the girls out."

"So far, he's not talking," Leland said.

"Christopher needs to push his attorney," Parks said.

"He's working on it."

My stomach rumbled, and I worried I would throw up. It was all so much. The murders, the burials, the evil inside the McAllister family. Of all my cases, the girls were the first one that hit me with such intensity.

The team stopped. Someone hollered, "We got it."

Leland said, "You look like you haven't slept in days. Go home. I'll make sure you're around for the important stuff." He smiled at Parks. "You two work well together. Make sure she gets home safely."

Parks nodded. "When she's ready."

"I need to see Alyssa first," I said. "She stayed home so I could spend time with her. Of course, I screwed that up."

How They Were Taken   223

Parks checked his watch. "If we're lucky, we won't hit an accident on the highway."

I hadn't felt lucky in years, but Parks had been right. We made it to Nick's place in a little over an hour.

"I'll go grab some McDonald's. Text when you're ready."

I turned in the seat and said, "Thank you."

"Nothing to thank me for."

I smiled, climbed out of the car, and hurried to see my kid.

Nick and Heather answered the door. For the first time in ages, Nick smiled, and Heather didn't look like she thought I wanted to kill her.

Kill her was a bit of an exaggeration.

Alyssa pushed between them and hugged my legs. "Mama, we went on a staycation at a big hotel with a pool!" She wore the *Frozen* movie pajamas I'd bought her for Christmas.

"I heard!" I picked her up and hugged her so tight I thought she might break. "Daddy said you swam for a long time."

"Mama, you're hugging me too hard. I can't breathe."

I loosened my grip and apologized. "Did you have fun staying home from school today?"

"Yeah. I like our house. I didn't like that fancy place we stayed."

"Come on in," Nick said. "We'll give you some time."

"Mommy, I got a new book from Tee Tee. It's about bears. Will you read it to me?"

"Tee Tee?" I glanced back at Nick as we walked up the stairs.

"Tiffani," he said.

I smiled. "Thanks." To Alyssa, I said, "I love stories about bears."

She snuggled into her bed but left me enough room to lie next to her. I wanted to stay there forever, but she fell asleep halfway into the book. I carefully slid off the bed, tiptoed out of the room, and pulled the door to almost closed, as she liked it.

Nick offered me a bottled water.

"I'm good, but thanks."

"You look exhausted."

"That's better than I feel."

"I heard on the news Jessica Steadman is paying for the funerals of all the girls?" he asked.

"And putting memorials where their bodies were found," I said. "She's a good person when you look past her money."

"You think Leland's going to want you back because of this?"

"I doubt it, but I wouldn't go anyway."

He cocked his head to the side. "Really?"

"It's time to move on." I smiled. "In several areas of my life. I'll get the divorce papers to you tomorrow."

"Thank you."

I nodded.

Heather walked out from the kitchen. "Jenna?"

I wasn't in the mood for her, so I looked at her without saying a word.

"I need to apologize," she said.

I resisted the urge to say something mean. I forced a smile. "Consider it done." I opened the door to Parks walking up the steps.

He held up my phone. "You left this in the car."

"Oh, I didn't realize—"

He interrupted me. "Jimmy McAllister is dead."

22

"Leland tried calling you a few times, so I finally answered."

"What happened and when? We've only been gone a few hours," I asked in the car. "He was fine. I mean, aside from the leg."

"It was about an hour after we left. Nurse said his blood pressure spiked. By the time she got to him, he was gone."

"That's crazy."

"It gets crazier. The agent in the room said a nurse came in and said she was going to adjust his position on the bed and asked him to step out for a minute. Ten minutes later, he was dead."

"Heart attack?"

"The doctor wanted a blood test to rule out any medication issues."

"And a possible lawsuit," I said.

"Jenna, someone loaded him up with insulin. Enough to kill him in minutes."

"The nurse," I said. "But why?"

"I can't believe I didn't prepare for this," he said.

"Prepare for what?" I asked.

"Did you know Richard Steadman was type I diabetic?"

My eyes widened. "Holy shit, Parks. Jessica said she wouldn't let the killers be remembered."

"I know."

"We need to talk to her."

"You think she's going to admit to having someone murder her daughter's and husband's killer?"

"No, but she needs to know we're onto her. And I'm giving her back the retainer check. If it's true, I can't work for her."

"Damn it," he said. "I hate that kind of logic." He swerved to the right to turn in the direction of her home.

Thirty minutes later, we arrived at Steadman's place and several black sedans crowding her driveway.

"GBI?" Parks asked.

"Not unless they got luxury company cars."

He parked at the end of the driveway, and we walked to the door. I peeked into the cars and saw nothing through the slightly tinted windows. "These are government cars," I said. "Look at the tags."

"She's doing something," Parks said.

I noticed Leland's car. "Leland's here? They're going to arrest her."

"I don't think so," he said. "I think the governor is here."

"Shit."

Parks pounded on the door. Olga answered, first with a scowl but smiled when she realized it was us. "Hello. Please come in. They are in the living room."

The governor paced back and forth behind the leather sectional. I had met him a few times before, but I doubted he would remember.

Jessica Steadman sat on the couch, sipping a martini.

"Jenna, Jack, what a nice surprise. Please, what can we get you to drink?" She winked at Parks like he knew she knew about his recovery.

"I'm good," I said.

"Thanks, but no thanks," Parks said.

Leland walked over. "Not surprised to see you here," he whispered. "Follow me." He called to the governor. "I was expecting them. Give me a few minutes."

He led us outside and to his car. "Get in."

I glanced at Parks and mouthed, "She did it."

How They Were Taken

In the car, Leland said, "Jenna, hand me your phone. I don't want this recorded."

"She had him killed, didn't she?"

He held his hand toward the back seat. "Phone. Parks, you too, please."

We handed him our phones.

"Yes," Leland said. "I believe she had Jimmy McAllister killed. The taxpayer in me is glad we don't have to support him for life, but as GBI, I know she should be held accountable for her actions."

Parks shook his head. "The governor's blocked any investigation into McAllister's death, hasn't he?"

"Yes."

"Does he know Richard Steadman was a type I diabetic?"

"Yes." Leland responded with shorter answers when trying not to explode. "Mr. Steadman and the governor were childhood friends."

"Shit," Parks said.

"She admitted it, didn't she?" I asked.

"I have no knowledge of that, and as I said, I am not to move forward with any investigation."

"He's an accessory to a crime," I said. "Charge his ass too."

Leland gave me a blank stare.

I exhaled. "Parks and I aren't government employees. He can't stop us from going public with this."

"Maybe not, but he can ruin you."

I closed my eyes and leaned my head onto the headrest. "This isn't right, Leland. You know that."

"I do, but it's out of my hands."

I looked at Parks. "I'm not sure I can let this lie," I said.

"We have to. You saw the number of zeros on our checks. She has enough money to destroy us in no time."

I climbed out of the car, saying, "Fine, but I'm ripping that check right in front of her medically altered face."

I reached back in and grabbed my phone from the dashboard. Leland and I locked eyes. "I can't believe you're doing this." I stormed inside the house and pushed through the men in black to Jessica Steadman still sipping her martini.

"Jenna, please stay awhile," she said. "The governor is a friend, and he would like you and Jack to stay for dinner."

Parks and Leland walked in. Leland moved to the side of the room, but Parks stood next to me. "We'll pass," he said.

"We know you had McAllister killed," I said.

She finished another sip of her martini. "I don't know what you're talking about."

Parks burst out laughing. "You're so full of shit, Jessica."

She threw her drink in his face, but it didn't faze him. Two men in black suits walked over and grabbed his arms.

"It's okay," Steadman said. "He's upset things didn't work out with us."

I ripped the retainer check into pieces and dropped them in her lap. "I don't work with killers."

She looked up at Parks. "And you?"

He tossed his check at her without breaking eye contact.

"Gentlemen, please see them out," she said. "Respectfully."

I turned to leave, but pivoted back and said, "Governor?"

He exhaled. "Yes?"

"How many zeros does it take to buy a blindfold these days?"

I watched Alyssa climb into the school bus the next morning, still reeling from what had transpired and frustrated I couldn't do anything. Alyssa didn't sense a thing, but Nick had.

"You okay?"

"I'm fine. Just processing." I handed him the envelope holding our signed divorce papers.

"You always do that after a big investigation. Are you having Molly buried next to your mom?"

"Yes, but not for a few weeks."

"You're not letting Jessica Steadman pay for it, are you?"

I shook my head.

"Care to tell me why?"

"I can't."

He nodded and held up the envelope with our divorce papers inside. "I wish things could have been different."

He said that to be nice, but I knew he didn't mean it. I swallowed the lump in my throat. "They're different, but that's okay." I rubbed his shoulder. "I need to go." I turned and walked to my car, but Heather stopped me on the way.

"Jenna?"

"Not now, Heather."

"Please, I need to say this."

I leaned against my car. "Okay."

She placed her hand on her belly. "It kills me to say this, but I admire you. You do things I can only imagine."

"It's my job."

"I've been awful to you because I'm jealous. I could never be as strong and confident as you."

Yet she still stole my family.

"Are you blaming that on me?"

She blinked. "No, of course not. I'm trying to apologize."

"Thank you.' I opened my car door.

"Listen. What we did to you was wrong, and I am sorry. I don't think I understood what it all meant."

"Got it," I said.

"I'd like us to try to get along. For Alyssa's sake."

"Then you shouldn't have screwed my husband."

Her jaw tightened, but she didn't say anything. I climbed into my car and backed out of the driveway before I could stop and say what I really wanted. Carrying that hate would only hurt Alyssa, and I had hurt her enough, but I wasn't quite ready to forgive the woman for taking my life. Even if it was mostly my fault.

I drove to my bank. Jessica Steadman and I both banked at Bank of America, and I wanted to deposit my paycheck from her before she canceled it. Afterward, I ran a few errands. A few hours later, I called Parks and asked him to meet me for coffee, then waited in the parking lot for him to arrive.

"Hey," I said as he clicked his key fob to lock his car. "Wait for me."

He pursed his lips. "Why are you hiding behind cars?"

"I'm not hiding behind cars," I said. I clicked my key fob, and the lights on my brand-new-to-me Ford Bronco flashed.

He smiled. "It's about time you got a new ride." He opened the passenger door and stepped inside. "Oh, wow. You've even got an infotainment display. You must have cashed the other check."

I raised a brow. "Infotainment display?"

"Car talk."

I nodded. "Ah, got it, and yes, I cashed that check. Did you? We both earned them."

"Hell yeah, I did."

We walked inside and ordered our coffees, then sat at a table in the corner.

"Guess it's back to cheating husbands and insurance fraud," he said. "You know, I was thinking about that sharing-office-space idea you mentioned a while back, and—"

"You mentioned it, and it's still a no."

He held up his hands. "Okay. Okay. I won't tell you about the great space I found in Roswell, then."

"Good."

EPILOGUE

Lisa McAllister had been released from the Marcus Stroke and Neuroscience Center of Grady three months after her aunt tried to kill her. She sold the business and moved to Florida. I couldn't blame her.

The day she called to tell me she had moved, I sat on the grass beside my mother's small gravestone to place Molly where she belonged. I had opted out of a funeral, deciding instead to have Molly's remains cremated. I chose not to bury her. She had been in a metal box in the ground long enough.

But I believed she would want to be with my mother and my mother would want the same. I had kept her with me for those three months because I needed the time with her, but it was time to let her go, to let her rest.

I spread her remains into the grass of my mother's grave. "Rest easy now, Molly."

I sat in my car for a few minutes before heading to meet my next potential client, a woman who believed her husband was having an affair. My cell phone rang with Parks's ringtone.

"Hey," I said. "What's up?"

"Who's this Riley Chatsworth?"

"Someone I knew from Harvard. Why?"

"She called me."

"She called you? Why?"

"You wouldn't answer her calls."

"I don't answer out-of-state calls. I let them go to voicemail."

"Well, I answered."

"This is why I don't want a partner."

Never Speak of It
Jenna Wyatt Book 2

When a high-powered executive is charged with murder, PI Jenna Wyatt must decide whether to trust the one person she's never forgiven—or risk letting a killer go free.

Jenna Wyatt never expected to see Riley Chatsworth again—not after the betrayal that shattered their friendship at Harvard. But when Riley, now a top executive at a powerful insurance company, is charged with murdering her agency's biggest client, she pleads with Jenna to clear her name. Torn between distrust and duty, Jenna reluctantly agrees to investigate, wary of the woman who nearly destroyed her life years ago.

As Jenna probes into Riley's company and the victim's health system, she begins uncovering a dark web of insurance fraud, medical malpractice, and whistleblowers who were silenced for knowing too much. Strange break-ins and cryptic threats soon reveal that this case is far more dangerous than Jenna imagined. And the closer she gets to the truth, the more she begins to question Riley's innocence—wondering if her former friend is still lying, or worse, manipulating her all over again.

Teaming up with seasoned PI Jack Parks, Jenna races against time to expose the deadly conspiracy. But in a world where everyone has secrets, trust could be her deadliest mistake.

In this gripping thriller, USA Today bestselling author Carolyn Ridder Aspenson weaves a tale of betrayal, justice, and the high stakes of corporate corruption. *Never Speak of It* will keep readers guessing until the very last page.

Get your copy today at
severnriverbooks.com

ACKNOWLEDGMENTS

Books don't write themselves—it truly takes a village. This book is no exception, and I'm incredibly grateful to the people who helped make it possible.

First, I want to extend my heartfelt thanks to Georgia Bureau of Investigation Assistant Special Agent in Charge Amanda Carter for sharing her invaluable insight into life as an agent. Your expertise added authenticity and depth that I couldn't have achieved without you.

To Laina Molaski, thank you for your input, encouragement, and, most importantly, your honesty. Friends like you, who tell it like it is, are priceless.

A huge thank-you to my team at Severn River Publishing for believing in me and giving me this opportunity. Your faith in my work means the world to me.

Finally, I owe everything to my husband, Jack Aspenson. Writing books has always been my dream, but without your unwavering support and encouragement, that dream would still be just that. Thank you for always standing by me.

ABOUT CAROLYN RIDDER ASPENSON

USA Today Bestselling author Carolyn Ridder Aspenson writes cozy mysteries, thrillers, and paranormal women's fiction featuring strong female leads. Her stories shine through her dialogue, which readers have praised for being realistic and compelling.

Her first novel, *Unfinished Business,* was a Reader's Favorite and reached the top 100 books sold on Amazon.

In 2021 she introduced readers to detective Rachel Ryder in *Damaging Secrets*. *Overkill,* the third book in the Rachel Ryder series was one of Thrillerfix's best thrillers of 2021.

Prior to publishing, she worked as a journalist in the suburbs of Atlanta where her work appeared in multiple newspapers and magazines.

Writing is only one of Carolyn's passions. She is an avid dog lover and currently babies two pit bull boxer mixes. She lives in the mountains of North Georgia as an empty nester with her husband, a cantankerous cat, and those two spoiled dogs.

You can chat with Carolyn on Facebook at Carolyn Ridder Aspenson Books.

Sign up for Carolyn's reader list at
severnriverbooks.com

Printed in the United States
by Baker & Taylor Publisher Services